The Spy Who Loved Him...

General Stoddard looked appraisingly at the beautiful woman before him. "You and Lieutenant Bell were . . . together in Pusan, weren't you, Adrian?"

"I don't think that's your concern, General," she replied brusquely.

"Well, I know it for a fact. I've been having Bell watched."

"Watched? Why? What's he done?"

"I'm not sure he's done anything. That's why I have to know if he revealed confidential information while you were together."

"One doesn't talk much about war while—I mean, when they're like that, General Stoddard."

The General was obviously embarrassed. "Okay," he said, "I believe you. He told you nothing. Only he knows. Which means you have a choice. You can either go back home, or you can follow him. I can't use my own men for surveillance—it would be too obvious. But I can use you. Gilbert Bell knows you, and he'll let you get close. You can find out if he's revealed anything to anyone, or, if he's captured—"

"Damn it, General! *What* could he reveal to anyone?"

"I can only tell you that Lieutenant Bell possesses information that could make this war explode in our faces. It could mean millions of lives. If the Chinese Communists ever got hold of him . . . but thank God they're not in this thing."

Adrian McAllister was confused, angry, apprehensive. Suddenly the man she loved was a walking bomb—and she'd been assigned to monitor it!

Far Shores of Danger

Jonathan Scofield

A DELL/BRYANS BOOK

Published by
Dell Publishing Co., Inc.
1 Dag Hammarskjold Plaza
New York, New York 10017

Dell ® TM 681510, Dell Publishing Co., Inc.

ISBN: 0-440-02618-0

Printed in the United States of America

First printing—April 1982

Far Shores of Danger

1

1

LIEUTENANT GILBERT BELL stepped out of the official military vehicle which had brought him from the airport and adjusted the jacket of his dress uniform. Dead ahead of him was the Pentagon, the last place he would have expected a U.S. Marine officer to be on June 27, 1950, two days after the North Korean Peoples Army had invaded South Korea.

He had no idea why he was here. While his fellow officers at Camp Pendleton were preparing to be called into action to defend the South Koreans from the invading Communists, he had been yanked away to Washington, on "a matter of national importance," whatever that might be.

He took a deep breath and strode confidently up the cement walk toward the huge white building. Gilbert—"Gilly," his friends had called him since his youth—was a tight, well-knit man of twenty-seven, with thick but close-cropped dark brown hair, a firm, square jaw, and the deep blue eyes of the Bell family. Though he wasn't brilliant, he was clear-headed, strong-willed, and sometimes, when he had to be, forceful.

Inside the Pentagon, he was greeted by Marine Captain Gerald Hollingsworth, who pronounced his name with a mellow Southern drawl and led him slowly down the hall. Bell noted that the other man was a few years younger than he was, but the fact that Hollingsworth had already reached the rank of captain didn't bother him. Gilbert had joined the corps late, ignoring his father's military connections and three invitations to officers' candidate schools in order to work his way up from the bottom. In his rise to lieutenant, he had won the respect of every marine he had met.

"What's this all about, Captain?" he asked the wiry young man walking beside him. "Why would I be called here when we may be in a war at any second?"

"I have no idea," Hollingsworth answered. "But you can be sure it's important. General Stoddard is a great officer. He doesn't call people in just to chat about the weather."

The captain buttoned his lips after that pronouncement and led Gilbert in silence down the long corridor to Stoddard's office. When they finally reached it, Hollingsworth didn't bother to go in. He pushed the door open and motioned for Bell to enter. "You can wait here until the general comes, Lieutenant," he said. "He won't be long."

Still feeling anxious that his outfit could be headed

for Korea without him, Gilbert walked in and looked
around. Stoddard's office was panelled in a rich wal-
nut, carpeted in a dull beige, with a Marine Corps
banner and a United States flag displayed promi-
nently at the window. The glassed-in bookcase housed
thirty or forty books: USMC manuals and histories
of both world wars, H.G. Wells's *The Outline of
History,* and a well-worn copy of Dwight David Eisenhower's best-seller, *Crusade in Europe.*

Gilbert looked at his watch, sighed, and eased down
in the leather chair next to the bookcase and waited.
After ten minutes of sitting and thinking about the
invasion of South Korea two days before, he was
ready to explode. An excruciating hour later he felt
as if the walls were closing in on him. Like most of
his family, Gilbert Bell wasn't an adventurer, but he
was a man of action. Sitting and waiting disturbed
him. He wanted to go back to Pendleton in case the
marines were needed in Asia.

He stayed coiled like a spring for ten minutes more,
then bounced up to his feet, opened the door and
stepped out into the hall. The gleaming white walls
of the corridor were antiseptic and the air was deadly
quiet, like a tomb, as he ambled down the hall, trying to work off his nervous energy.

As soon as he turned a corner, though, he heard
a melange of loud, arguing voices rumbling out of
a room in the middle of the corridor. Trying not to
listen to them, he trod quietly past the conference
room; but the flying words of an argument inside
made him pause in front of the door. Instinctively,
he looked through the ten-inch part in the door.

Gathered tightly around a mahogany table were
a dozen important people he recognized: the Joint

Chiefs of Staff; former Secretary of State George C. Marshall, the World War II strategist; Omar Bradley, the Chairman of the JCS—even the great general Dwight D. Eisenhower, recently appointed President of Columbia University.

A sense of excitement surged through his veins as he stood transfixed, watching and listening closely as General Stoddard paced back and forth in front of the table, punching a white-tipped pointer at a large three-color map covering most of the back wall. Even though he felt he should leave, Bell was too fascinated by what he was seeing and hearing to move.

Suddenly, Stoddard's eyes locked onto his. The general's smooth face turned rigid as he laid the pointer across the table. "Excuse me, gentlemen," he said to the other men in the room, and moved quickly around the table and into the hall.

Closing the door behind him, he looked directly at Bell, clenched both his fists. "Damn it, Lieutenant," he growled, "what do you think you're doing out here?"

"Sir—" Gilbert began.

"Don't 'sir' me, Lieutenant," he said flatly. "I want to know what you're doing out here, listening at keyholes."

"I wasn't meaning to listen, sir," Gilbert explained.

Stoddard stared at him for a moment, then asked, "Why aren't you in my office where you're supposed to be?"

"I should have waited, General," Bell admitted.

"You're damn right you should have," he said firmly. "But the damage is done now. Go back to my office and wait for me. And don't say a word to a living soul until I get there. Do you understand me?"

Gilbert nodded. "Yes, sir. I understand."

"Then go."

"Yes, sir." Bell saluted, then marched back up the hall. Behind him, as Stoddard opened the door to go back in he heard a voice blurt out, "What if Truman hears—" Then there was silence again. He walked back to the general's office with halting breath and a throbbing pulse. All the while he wondered if what he had heard had anything to do with the North Korean invasion; but since the meeting was a secret one, he tried to put it out of his mind.

"Lieutenant," Stoddard said abruptly as he entered his office thirty minutes later, "I've got two problems here." He went to his desk, pursed his lips as he glanced at the file folder in his hand. Looking at the bold letters "USMC—Top Secret," he shook his head and flung the file on the desk.

Lucius Stoddard was a man of iron, proud of his physical condition, his ability to hold his own in three sets of tennis with men twenty years younger than himself. Standing over six feet, he was muscular, well-proportioned, with a clear face and thick, short gray hair.

He was also proud of his quick, comprehensive mind. Great men like Douglas MacArthur, Dwight Eisenhower and Harry Truman often used his brain when it came to matters of national security. "Old Blood and Guts" Patton himself took his advice before his Morocco and Sicily campaigns in World War II. Stoddard had even been asked (unofficially) by Senator Millard Tydings to look into Senator Joseph

McCarthy's searing accusation that the military services were riddled with Soviet-controlled Communists.

But this particular double-barreled problem was a sticky one, even for him.

"Gilbert," he said, trying a calm, familiar approach. "I've known your family a long time. I knew your mother as a girl, and your father and I cracked our heads together a couple of times in World War II. Why don't we forget our brass buttons and be straight with each other? What do you say?"

"Yes, sir," Gilbert responded. "We can do that."

"Good," said Stoddard. "Now maybe I can tell you —off the record, of course—that I wish to God you hadn't walked by that door when you did a while ago."

"It was wrong, General," Gilbert said, "I know that. I was thinking about the Korean invasion so much—"

Stoddard clenched his fist. "If it's not one thing, it's another," he said.

Gilbert was still impatient. "General," he ventured, "maybe if you told me why you had me brought here. . . ."

Stoddard looked at him a moment, then nodded. "All right, let's deal with that first," he said. He reached into the top drawer of his desk and eased out another manila file folder. "I'll ask you pointblank," he said, opening the folder. "Do you know a Chinese woman by the name of Lin Su?"

At the sound of her name an image came into focus in his mind—the dark, beautiful, naked Lin Su, reaching up to him from her bed, whispering softly to him, "Gilly, darling, just this once, please? Before

I have to leave, please make love to me. Just this once. . ."

"Lieutenant?" Stoddard said impatiently, dog-earing the paper in the folder.

"Yes, sir," Bell replied. "I know her. Or rather I knew her. I haven't seen her in two years."

Stoddard tapped a document with his fingers. "That was in San Francisco, right?" he prompted.

"Yes, sir," Gilbert answered, wondering why he was being asked about her.

"According to this," Stoddard went on, "you met her on October fourteen, nineteen forty-eight, in Chinatown. On that day you strolled down Grant Avenue, ate a late dinner at Kuo Wah's. That night you saw her home. The following weekend the two of you went to a movie, *The Emperor Waltz,* with Bing Crosby."

"General, I don't see what my friendship with Lin Su has to do with anything."

Stoddard looked up from the file. "Wasn't it more than a friendship, Lieutenant?" he asked pointedly.

Gilbert hesitated. "I'm sorry, General Stoddard," he said finally. "I don't see why that would be important to anyone but me. I don't see how my relationship with Lin Su has anything to do with the corps."

"Well, it does have something to do with the corps, Lieutenant Bell. And with our country." The general paused, slapped the folder down on top of the other one. "Especially now that you stumbled onto that meeting. God knows who'll want to get into this— the CIA, Truman—I don't know who else. Look, Gilbert . . ." He took a deep breath. "I don't like to pry into other people's business any more than the next man, but this is a special situation."

"I don't see what's so special about it, General."
Gilbert swallowed, cleared his throat. "All right," he
admitted, "I dated her for a while, and I may have
been in love with her. But we weren't lovers. And
I don't see why the U.S. Marine Corps would be interested in her, or why I'd be brought here to talk
about Lin Su just when we may be going to war."

"Are you sure you don't see the connection, Gilbert?"

"No, sir. I don't."

"For all our sakes, I hope that's true," Stoddard
said thoughtfully. After a few moments of consideration, he picked up the file again. "It says here," he
told him, glancing over the report, "you're in love
with Adrian McAllister, a reporter at the Sacramento
Sun. Is that true?"

"Not exactly true. Adrian and I are . . . close
friends." He could have added that they might have
been lovers, if his sister Amanda hadn't told Adrian
about Lin Su, but he kept quiet. Stoddard knew too
much as it was.

The general raised his eyebrows. "My sources say
your close friend is in love with you," he submitted.
"They also say she's beautiful and intelligent. Her
editor claims she's the sharpest reporter he's got on
that little paper of his. A little headstrong, maybe,
and a trifle liberal, but clever. She always lands on
her feet."

"I'm glad he approves of her," he said, growing
restless and uneasy with this strange business.

"I assure you I'm not that interested in your love
life, Lieutenant," Stoddard told him. "I'm just trying
to make a distinction. If you were merely close friends
with Lin Su, then your association with her wouldn't

be important. Do you know where she is now, by the way?"

"No, sir, I don't know where she is. She went back to China with her family two years ago. I wanted her to stay, but she felt she had to go. She was very stubborn about it. She wouldn't even let me talk about it. I couldn't stop her."

"That was eighteen months before Chiang Kai-shek was driven off the mainland," Stoddard observed.

"Yes, sir, about that."

"And you haven't heard from her since?"

"No, sir. I haven't heard a word from her. We ended it the morning she left."

"All right, Lieutenant." His tone hardened as he rose from his chair. "I'll tell you where she is. She's currently residing in Peking—as a high-ranking official in Mao Tse-tung's government."

Gilbert was shocked. "Lin Su? Are you sure? That's hard to believe, General."

"Well, you can believe it. You seem to attract clever girls, Gilbert. Lin Su is now a special advisor to Premier Chou En-lai in the People's Republic of China."

"Advisor!"

"An advisor on American affairs, no less," Stoddard added. "So you see why we're interested in your love life."

The news was so devastating that Gilbert had to sit down. Could what Stoddard was saying be true? Could gentle, loving Lin Su be a Communist? And if she were, had she used him in some way for the party?

He began searching his mind, reaching deep down to recall their conversations, their playful word games,

to see if he could dredge up a mistake he had made—
a secret he had told her. . . .

As Bell was sitting preoccupied in the chair, Captain Hollingsworth entered the room, holding a piece of yellow paper. He eyed Bell a moment, then handed Stoddard the message.

"That's the latest Korean report, General," he announced. "It looks real bad."

The general read the report, then wadded it up in his powerful fingers. "The North Koreans have taken Seoul," he said sadly. "Thousands of South Korean refugees are now trying to break out of the city. I thought the ROK army was supposed to be able to handle this, Captain. What happened to that counterattack in Uijongbu? The report I got said the situation was under control."

"The Uijongbu report was exaggerated, General," Hollingsworth explained. "The South Korean army isn't being all that efficient—"

"Well, what are they doing there?" Stoddard asked, throwing the wadded paper on the floor. "Playing cards?"

"The rumor is the ROK has left the city with everybody else, General. Kaymag is trying to turn them back, but they're scared. They just want out."

"They're not equipped to fight a war," Stoddard observed. "Well, at least MacArthur is evacuating our American citizens out of there. I'd hate to think how Truman would react if a couple of thousand American civilians were killed in a North Korean raid."

Hearing the news of the Republic of Korea's incompetent reaction to the invasion made Gilbert all the more anxious to return to Pendleton. It was only a matter of time, he decided, before the marines would be called into Korea.

"Lucius?" said a strong Midwestern voice from a crack in the office door.

When Bell realized the voice belonged to General Omar Bradley, he quickly snapped to attention. His father, Samuel Bell, loved and respected Bradley, who was once group commander over the First, Third and Ninth Armies in Europe and was a member of the 1915 West Point class that included Eisenhower and Lieutenant James A. Van Fleet.

Bradley's down-home ways put men at ease. He said a few friendly words to Captain Hollingsworth as he was leaving, then exchanged greetings with Gilbert. He grew very serious, though, when he looked at Stoddard. "Lucius," he said, "it's not looking too good. We may be headed for Korea before morning. I warned the Joint Chiefs about this two years ago. I told them we needed to keep our troops in Korea, as a stopgap to the Chinese. But they didn't listen to me. Now it's erupting like a volcano over there."

"It looks like it," Stoddard agreed.

"They're saying forty, maybe fifty thousand ROK soldiers are dead at Seoul. And there'll be more if somebody blows those bridges on the Han River. It's time to ask a favor, Lucius."

"Just name it, Omar," Stoddard replied. "I owe you quite a few."

Bradley paused a minute, looked at Bell, then back at Stoddard. "Truman is sending MacArthur over to Suwon to check out the situation," he told him. "He's taking General Almond and General Stratemeyer with him. Since both of those fellows worship the ground Douglas MacArthur walks on, I'd like for you to be there, too, to balance the picture we get back here. In other words, keep your eye on him; don't let him get out of hand."

Stoddard nodded. "I'll arrange for a plane to Tokyo."

"Never mind that," Bradley told him. "It's already arranged. Get there before he does, Lucius." He looked at his watch. "Your plane is leaving in forty-five minutes."

Stoddard hesitated. "Omar," he said, "I'm satisfied Lieutenant Bell wasn't aware of the Chinese woman's Communist connections. I've talked to him, and as far as I'm concerned, Gilbert is above reproach."

"What about that business of the meeting a while ago?"

Stoddard sighed. "I don't know about that. He saw and heard plenty. But I still stand by him. I think he can be trusted."

Bradley turned toward Gilbert and scratched his chin thoughtfully. "Exactly what did you hear in that conference room, Lieutenant?" he asked.

"I didn't hear anything that I could understand, sir," he replied quickly.

"Good. How much of it are you going to repeat?"

"I'm not going to repeat any of it, General."

"Not even to me?" Bradley pressed him.

Bell paused, swallowed hard. "If a marine superior officer should ever ask me to repeat what I heard, I will, General Bradley. But since only General Stoddard and you know I was there—"

Bradley held up a hand. "All right," he said, "that's a good answer. Lucius tells me you're a loyal marine, from a good fighting family. I trust his judgment about as well as I trust anyone's—and so I'm going to have to trust you too, Lieutenant." He looked back at Stoddard. "Lucius," he said, "get going. I got an army plane out at the airport right now, cranked up and ready to go."

The general hesitated, glanced at Bell, then snapped the two file folders from his desk and stuffed them into his briefcase. "I'm on my way," he said.

"Keep in touch, Lucius," Bradley said, going toward the door. "I want a personal report as soon as possible. If you'll watch MacArthur in Korea, I'll keep an eye on Truman here."

"I'll get back to you as soon as I can, Omar."

When Bradley had left, Stoddard looked directly at Bell. "You can go back to Pendleton, Gilbert," he said. "From the looks of things, it won't be long before you'll be landing in Korea."

"Yes, sir."

"Gilbert," he said apologetically, "the reason we're so sensitive about reports like the one on Lin Su is that national security happens to be a damned precious thing right now. We're trying to watch the Chinese Communists closely. There's a possibility they may be behind the invasion of South Korea two days ago. And since our Atomic Energy Commission has started work on the hydrogen bomb, we may find ourselves in an atomic war if we're not careful."

"I can be trusted, General," Gilbert told him.

"I know you can. And I know you had no idea Lin Su was a Communist. But I also know we're all human, and it scares me that even one of us possesses information that in the wrong hands could light up the world with a thermo-nuclear flash. The world's awfully fragile now, ever since Nagasaki and Hiroshima."

"General, no one knows—" .

"I know they don't," Stoddard interrupted. "No one knows except the other people in that room. All I hope is that none of us ever find ourselves in a position where we're forced to tell somebody. Because when we do, it won't matter how many of the enemy the UN forces kill in Korea—we'll all be blown to bits by a nuclear explosion."

2

MINUTES LATER in the newsroom of the Sacramento *Sun*, Adrian McAllister sat at her desk and shuddered under the stare of Wayne Hunter, who was eyeing her over the top of the new copy he was reading. Hunter was one of the few people in the world who made her uncomfortable. He always seemed to be watching her, his small, penetrating eyes burning holes into her skin, like piercing beams from a ray gun in a science fiction movie. His eyes seemed always to be fixed on her breasts or her legs.

Not that Adrian wasn't used to being stared at. She was an extraordinarily beautiful woman, with a perfect figure—small waist, full, high breasts, rounded hips—and under rich, thick, black hair, a classic model's face that attracted every man with an ounce of life in him. But Hunter's stares were different. His whole bearing made her feel uneasy.

She turned away from his stare, tried to fix her attention on the story she was writing. It was a feature article on civil rights, a description of America's racial progress since the report by the President's committee on civil rights in 1947. She had written up Jackie Robinson, the first Negro to sign with a major-league baseball team, and would move next to Ensign John W. Lee, the first black officer commissioned by the navy, and then end the story with Dr. Mary T. Sproul, the first woman doctor in the U.S. Navy. But she couldn't concentrate enough to come up with a catchy angle. Too much else was happening. The South Korean capital of Seoul had been taken by the North Koreans. Activity on the newspaper was in a holding pattern now; everyone was waiting to see what was going to happen next. And the information seeping out of Korea was painfully slow.

"Here's the stuff you wanted, Adrian," said a tall, young blond man, Kevin Jones. He thrust a piece of paper in front of her. "America now has a standing army of a little over a half-million men—and women, I hasten to add. Five hundred ninety-three thousand, to be exact."

"Is that enough?" she asked, glancing at the typewritten note.

"If you mean enough to fight a war, unh-unh. Not nearly. Not when they've grown fat and lazy, the way ours have since the war. A half-million is the lowest it's been since the thirties. We had over eight million in forty-five."

She put down the paper. "Then I hope there won't be a war," she said.

"I wouldn't count on it, Adrian. It looks to me like war is definitely brewing over there."

"Kevin, if the president does send American troops to Korea, would the First Division Marines be the first to go?"

He shrugged. "I have no idea," he replied. "I could find out."

"Would you do that for me?" she asked. "Without making too much of a deal about it?"

He shook his head and gave her a sly smile. "Let me guess—that's Gilly Bell's division, right? What's going on here? I thought you two split up over that Japanese girl a couple of years ago."

"There was nothing to split up, Kevin," she said firmly. "Besides," she added, "she wasn't Japanese. She was Chinese."

"I see," he said knowingly. "It looks like you're still carrying the torch."

"I am *not* carrying a torch, Kevin," she insisted. "I just want to know, that's all. Aren't reporters supposed to be curious?"

"Well, I'll say this—old Gilly is a hell of a lucky man," he sighed. "I'm all envy. So is Bud Thomas over there, and Wikins, and Somerville. And Douglas—"

"All right, Kevin," she said, a little embarrassed. "I'm just concerned about him—as a friend of the family, that's all. There's nothing between us any more. All right?"

He smiled, not believing her. "I understand. You break off with a man everybody in Sacramento thinks you're going to marry and that makes him a friend of the family. Makes a lot of sense, Adrian."

"Oh," she said, a bit exasperated, but not angry. "You listen to gossip too much, Kevin. It's bad for you." She got up and walked toward the water fountain next to the elevators.

With most of the men in the room in limbo, waiting around for a break in the South Korea story, she got more than the usual number of approving looks as she made her way through the row of desks. She smiled pleasantly but not warmly as she passed through. It was always nice to be appreciated, for men to gaze approvingly at her body; but sometimes, like now, she wished she weren't quite so noticeable to them. It often made her job much harder to do.

She took a Dixie cup and held it under the water stream and looked around the room. She wondered what Gilly would have said a few years ago about her working in a room full of men. . . .

"Rivers!" a voice boomed out of the editor's glassed-in office. It was Ed Mallory, summoning the assistant editor. Mallory was a tough, middle-aged journalist of the old school. He had pushed his way up through the ranks from selling newspapers on the Bay in 1910 to his current job in Sacramento by virtue of his instinct for what made a story. He wasn't progressive or philosophical or farsighted, but he was usually sound and clear.

Bill Rivers didn't move. He called back from his desk, "What is it, Ed?"

"Where's that report on the evacuation of Seoul?" Mallory was standing in his doorway now. "We're still waiting for it."

"I'm tired of waiting," Mallory growled. "Looks

like I'm going to have to send somebody over there after all," he announced, then slipped back into his office.

Adrian came over to Rivers's desk. She liked the assistant editor; he was a calm, competent man of about thirty, unattractive, but pleasant and businesslike with her.

"He's been saying for two days he's going to send a correspondent to Korea," she said. "Do you think he actually will?"

Suddenly a delivery man burst into the room with a bundle of papers under his arm. "Here you go, folks," he called out as he dropped a copy of the latest edition of the *Sun* on each desk. "Read 'em and weep."

Adrian absently took up Rivers's copy and flipped it open to the second page. She scanned the columns, then turned over to page four. What she saw there stunned her.

"Bill!" she exclaimed, pushing the paper in front of him, on his typewriter. "What do you mean. . ." Her voice trailed off. She was too outraged to speak coherently, so she swallowed her words and tried to remain calm.

She stared at the paper through watery eyes. All of page four was taken up by her story of Sacramento's public transportation system. There was Evans's picture of the bus depots, the interview with the old man whose father had ridden with Buffalo Bill on the Pony Express—everything. But it was not under her name. There it was, in black and white. "Sacramento—City on the Move" by *Wayne Hunter*.

"I didn't use his byline," Rivers protested. "When

it came across my desk, it had both your names on it. Somebody downstairs must have changed it."

She took a deep breath to try to calm herself, and to prepare to face Wayne. Then she plucked Rivers's paper off his typewriter and walked slowly, holding her anger down as much as she could, to Hunter's desk.

When she placed it carefully on his neatly sorted desk, he looked up and smiled. "Well, look who's here," he said. "You don't mean you're actually stooping to speak to me," he said sarcastically. "I'm honored."

Adrian looked at him a moment and tried to understand why he always seemed so defensive, so on edge with her. Tall and lean, with strong regular features, he could have been an attractive man and popular with women, the way the Hunter men before him had been. But there was something about him that put her off. It wasn't apparent what it was, but she felt it. Just something about him that was off-center.

"Wayne," she said, lowering her voice, "that transportation story was mine. You know it was. I did every bit of that research. I spent two weeks putting that feature together. How could you just take the credit like that?"

"Mallory assigned that story to me, Adrian," he reminded her.

"But you gave it to me. You said you didn't have time to do it."

"Women always seem to have more time than men," he answered. "You did a good job, though, I'll say that. You're a good little researcher."

"I'm not a researcher, Wayne—I'm a reporter."

"Well, we all want to be something, Adrian. I don't hold that against you. But you know as well as I do, when a story's assigned, it's assigned. It's like an apartment that can't be sublet."

"All right, but don't you think the decent thing would have been to give me credit, too?"

He smiled. "Come on, Adrian, let's don't fight, okay? Unless you want to fight with pillows, the way the Japanese do it," he grinned. "Real imaginative, the Japanese."

"You could've had your name on top, Wayne, you know," she said. "You didn't have to cut my name out entirely. That was the biggest story I've ever had—"

"And you did well, Adrian."

"Why do you do things like this to me, Wayne?"

He shrugged his shoulders. "Maybe I do it to get your attention."

"Well, there are better ways to get my attention, believe me."

"I'll use them," he said, then grinned and extended his hand across the desk toward her. "No hard feelings?"

Adrian felt every eye in the room staring at them. Every man there was curious as to what she would do. Would she shake his hand, slap it, or leave it poised in the air?

She decided that her job mattered more than her pride. If she rebuffed a senior reporter, the others would say, "That's just like a woman." No matter how right she was, they would hold it against her. She had to respond professionally.

She took his hand and gave it a quick, polite shake. "I'll be more careful next time."

"Next time we'll just have to work closer, Adrian," he told her. "To keep from getting our wires crossed."

She let go of his hand. "Yes," she said. "We'll have to do that."

"Adrian," he said in a more personal tone. "I heard you talking to Kevin about the marines."

"What big ears you have."

"About Gilly, right?" he persisted. "You still love that gung-ho bastard, don't you?"

"No," she insisted. "I don't. Though it's hardly any of your business who I love."

"You know if this war breaks out, the marines will be the first to go. And a man as gung-ho as Gilly will be dead in a week. It never fails. And if they don't die, the first ones usually come back with something less than they went out there with, if you know what I mean. An arm, a leg—"

"I don't want to hear any more about it, Wayne. Just forget it," she said.

Back at her desk, she picked up the civil rights piece and tried to turn her notes into prose, but she couldn't concentrate on the task. She looked up at the clock on the south wall. Next to it was another clock, put up two days ago, representing the time in Seoul, South Korea. She wondered what those thousands of people who were evacuating Seoul now were feeling at this moment. How could anyone, she wondered, sanction war? It was insane for men to go out on a battlefield and get themselves maimed or killed.

Rivers, on his way to the AP machine, paused at her desk. "You handled that business with Wayne rather well," he said. "He can be a pest."

"I was so mad I could have screamed," she confessed. "How could he do that?"

"He has a friend downstairs, I guess, Adrian. Who
knows? But you have to admit—technically, he was
right. It was his story. Mallory assigned it to him."

"I know," she said grudgingly. "But why does he
do things like that to me?"

"Isn't it obvious, Adrian? The guy loves you."

Adrian closed her eyes, ran her fingers through her
thick black hair, and sighed. And thought of Gilly.

The next few hours at the *Sun* were quiet. As the
staff waited to put together the Korean news for a
special evening edition, once in a while someone
would beat out a quick paragraph on his typewriter,
or call for a copy boy, but mostly everyone sat around
and waited. The room became still as the sky outside the window of the *Sun* building began to turn
gold with the setting of the sun. But in the stillness
there was tension. The entire staff felt it, although
no one mentioned it.

It felt like the eve of a war.

Then, suddenly, the teletype machine cranked up
and began spurting out a single ribbon. Rivers hurried over to it, lifted up the running tape to read.

"This is it," he called out to the others.

Everyone took a deep breath, held it, and waited
while Rivers read the dispatch to himself. Then the
machine stopped and the room was plunged into deep
silence again. Ed Mallory eased open the door of
his office and looked over at Rivers.

The assistant editor wore a pained expression as
he read the report again. "This is incredible," he
said. "Absolutely incredible."

"What is it, Bill?" Mallory called out.

Rivers swallowed. "The South Korean army head-quarters has apparently blown the bridges on the Han River—*before* the evacuation was complete."

"The *South* Korean army?" Kevin Jones said, astonished. "Are you sure?"

"That's what it said. The bridges were blown and most of the ROK soldiers are now trapped inside the city. They're holding off the North Koreans, but their backs are to the river."

The reporters were dumbfounded by the report, but before they could read it for themselves another message ticked in. Snapping it off the machine, Rivers read, "Estimated four thousand refugees perish in the explosion of one Han River bridge. The ROK army is trying to wade across the Han, leaving their weapons behind."

"Dear God," moaned David Maxwell, the society editor. "They're really not ready to fight over there, are they?"

"No," Kevin agreed, "they're not. But I'm wondering, are we any more ready over here? Our men aren't prepared. They've gone soft in five years."

"Why do our men have to be ready anyway?" Adrian asked. "It's their war, isn't it? It's not us the North Koreans attacked."

"Is that it, Rivers?" Mallory asked. "Any more coming in?"

"That's it, Ed."

"All right, that settles it. Hunter, McAllister—get in here."

Adrian involuntarily shot a glance at Wayne as she heard the words, saw that he seemed cold and strangely unmoved by what was happening. Grabbing a steno pad off her desk, she hurried into Mallory's office, with Hunter following.

Mallory invited them to sit down as he closed the door behind them. As soon as they were settled, he went over to the map on the wall. "This," he said, pointing at a spot on the map, "is North Korea. It's about the size of Pennsylvania. Right below it is South Korea, about the size of Indiana. Both countries used to belong to Japan, but Japan gave them up after the war. The country was then divided into two zones, Soviet and American; the thirty-eighth parallel marks the division."

"We know all this, Ed," Hunter said wearily.

"Maybe you do, but I don't know you do. So listen, okay? Now. When the North Koreans crossed the thirty-eighth parallel a few days ago and invaded South Korea, what happened was the Soviet Union entered our space. It's like when you're a kid: you draw a line and tell the other guy he can't cross it. If he does, he's asking for a kick in the ass. Well, they're asking for it."

"Yes, but we didn't draw a line," Adrian protested.

"Oh, yes we did. We agreed with the Russians to the thirty-eighth parallel, and that line became a line of freedom. That's the same as drawing it. Cross it, you have us to contend with."

"But it isn't our war, Ed," Adrian contended. "It's *theirs*, parallel or no parallel."

He looked at her closely. "So you don't think we should fight the people who cross the line," he said.

"No, I don't think we should. War is insane. It accomplishes nothing."

He nodded. "What about you, Wayne?"

"War is inevitable," he stated. "It's the human condition."

"Ed?" Adrian asked tentatively. "What happens if America does decide to get into this war?"

Mallory liked the question. "All right, what happens is this: we currently have thirty thousand troops under General MacArthur's command stationed in and around Tokyo, which is maybe a couple of hundred miles from Seoul. They'll probably be sent in first, to hold back the North Koreans until the marines can go in."

"God, I hope President Truman doesn't declare another war," she said involuntarily.

Mallory sat down on the edge of his desk and rolled his sleeves up, displaying thick, hairy arms. "I figure that's pretty much inevitable, Adrian," he said. "In any case, what I want is somebody to cover what's going on over there."

Both Adrian and Wayne stirred, but it was Wayne who spoke. "Just who did you have in mind, Ed?"

"I have in mind one of you two. Only I have to decide which. Tell me, how would you cover this war?"

Wayne paused a minute, then answered simply, confidently. "I'd report what happens."

"What do you think of the fact that the North Koreans have Soviet weapons? Bombers, Yaks, T-34s?"

"They're all weapons of war," Wayne said. "Who makes them doesn't matter."

"Adrian? What about you?"

"I think it's disgraceful," she declared. "The Soviets have no right to interfere."

"How would you handle the reporting, then?"

Adrian remembered what Rivers had told her earlier. "I'd tell the story from a different point of view," she replied coolly.

"Different how?" Mallory asked, interested.

"Different like from the point of view of a woman," she said. "For women back home. Wives, mothers, girl friends. Those women don't want to hear about tactics and strategy, Ed. They just want to know what's happening to the *men*. Where they are, what they're doing, how they're feeling. Let them follow the strategy in the national news, or in the *Union*, or something."

"I like that," Mallory said after a pause. "That's good thinking." He stood up. "Of course you realize the majority of our readers are men—"

"Thirty-seven per cent of them aren't," she put in. "And anyway, I won't be writing about cakes and pies, Ed. Men will read it, too. The hard news will all be there, but it will mean more to *all* the readers if it's humanized."

Mallory ran his fingers through his thin gray hair. "Have you thought about conditions over there? It's a rough country, Adrian."

"I don't care how rough it is."

He considered the idea a little longer, then made up his mind.

"All right," he said. "You've got it. Go pack your bags."

"Do you mean it?" she asked happily.

"Now wait a minute, Ed," Hunter said, surprised. "I've got seniority here."

"Seniority has nothing to do with it, Wayne. Adrian has the job." He turned to her. "McAllister, go home and get ready. I'll make the arrangements. For the first time in its history, the *Sun* is going to have its own war correspondent. Let me tell you, you'd better do a good job with this; I'll replace you if you don't."

"I will, don't worry," she said confidently.

"I've already got you booked on a commercial flight to Japan. At Tokyo, you'll board a transport plane and fly to Suwon, a few miles south of Seoul. Wayne," he said to Hunter, "you'll be on that commercial flight with her."

"With her as what? A chaperone?" Wayne said.

"No, as a colleague. Adrian will send her reports to you in Tokyo, you'll send them to the paper."

Mallory looked curiously over at Adrian. "You'll have to go by the consulate in Tokyo," he told her. "They'll be arranging office space for you. Fortunately, we have a contact there, a clerk named Amanda Bell."

"I know her," Adrian said, crestfallen.

"I know you do," he said impishly. "She's that marine's sister, isn't she?"

"Yes, and she despises me, Ed," Adrian protested. "Couldn't we do it another way? I really don't want to run into her again."

"Force yourself," he said.

She nodded.

"All right, go, go! I'll be in touch with you."

Adrian disliked the idea of working with Wayne and Amanda, but the possibility of covering the biggest story in the world was too thrilling for her to complain about anything. All she wanted to do was go.

"Ed? Thank you." On an impulse, she leaned over and kissed him on the cheek.

"Get out of here," he said, embarrassed.

As she was leaving the room, Mallory motioned for Wayne to remain seated. When the door was closed, he came around to the front of the desk and leaned back against it. "You're unhappy about this, aren't you, Wayne?"

Hunter glared at him. "You made a fool of me, Ed."

"Look, Adrian's a damn good reporter. She lands on her feet. She's a quick thinker. Besides, I know the military. They'll break their backs accommodating her."

"And a 4-F like me they would ignore—is that what you're telling me?" Wayne asked bitterly.

Mallory crossed his arms. "I was telling you why she got the job, Hunter, not why you didn't get it. But if you want to get into that—I considered sending you, until a while ago. Until I read the *Sun* and saw your name on Adrian's story."

"Who told you about that?" Wayne snapped.

"Nobody told me about it, Wayne. I know things like this aren't reported to the general editor. Fine, what reporters do to each other is their business. But it just so happens I know that old codger Adrian interviewed for that piece. He called me up, told me about this good-looking reporter I've got. I figure that's not you, so I investigate and find you farmed out your story to her. I was waiting to see if you'd steal the glory, and damned if you didn't."

Hunter looked at Mallory with a coolness that covered the detestation he had for the editor. "It was nothing, Ed," he told him. "It was just something between Adrian and me. We straightened it out. We shook hands on it. Ask anyone."

"I saw you did. The girl's not only a good-looker, she's got class."

"Is that what it is you like about her, Ed?" he said accusingly. "Class? Or is it something a little more basic than that?"

The only hint of Mallory's anger over the remark was a slight tightening at the corner of his mouth. "Let's leave me out of this, Hunter. Let's look at you. Ever since World War II, you've been slipping away, losing control of yourself. What's wrong? You're a good reporter all right, but where's that old Hunter fighting spirit?"

"Ask the army, navy and marines," Wayne replied.

"That's no reason to be bitter, man. Anyway, you're going to have to shape up here. I can tell you for sure if you do anything like this again, anything that even smells unethical, you're out. And I mean *out*, with no references, no handshake, no gold watch, no nothing. Do I make myself clear?"

"I think so."

"Good. Now get out of here. Hang by your home phone. I'll be in touch." Mallory held up his finger as an afterthought. "One other thing, Wayne," he said. "I'd be careful about whom I associate with, if I were you."

Wayne stood up. "I'll do that, Ed," he said angrily, then stepped out of the office. Pausing only long enough to pull a plastic cover over his typewriter, he walked through the now-busy reporters and editors and stopped at the elevator.

Adrian was already standing in front of the doors, waiting. She shifted her weight nervously and punched the down button again.

Wayne grinned. "This is some situation, isn't it?" he said. "The beautiful Adrian McAllister being sent over to watch her boyfriend die in the rice paddies of Korea. *Reader's Digest* would love it."

"Look, Wayne," she said, struggling to maintain her composure. "Since we're going to be working together, why don't we try to get along for once? Could we do that? I have a feeling it's going to be hard enough as it is."

"Hey, that sounds fine to me," he said. "I'm a peaceable man. Ask the army. They wouldn't even let me fight."

She looked at him as the doors opened.

Wayne made a gesture for her to go ahead, and the two got on the empty elevator. Seconds later, she felt his body standing too close behind hers. She moved slightly, but he moved with her. She shuddered as his hot, moist breath fell on the back of her neck.

Then, without warning, she felt his cupped hand pressing against her buttocks. She stepped forward quickly, but the hand squeezed. Quickly she wheeled around and swung her hand at him with all the strength she could muster.

His reaction was immediate. He caught her hand and tightened his grip on it. "What's the matter, Adrian?" he chided. "Does a man have to wear a military uniform to get your attention?"

"Let me go!" she exclaimed, jerking her hand back.

Just as he released her, the doors opened. "We'll pick this up later," he told her.

"No, we won't. Don't you ever touch me again! I mean it."

"Hey, would I touch a sweet thing like you? Look, I'm sorry, okay? I just bumped up against you, that's all. No harm done, I hope."

She stood fuming at him for a moment, then hurried through the lobby toward the front doors.

Hunter watched her go out the doors, then turned to the right and entered the coffee shop. At the bar, he ordered a cup of black coffee, took out a Camel cigarette and lit it with a paper match, cupping his hands around the flame as he touched the cigarette to the heat.

The room was light and airy, with elaborate hand-painted murals of Sacramento in the Gold Rush days surrounding the room on all sides. There were only two other customers, each sitting alone by the window, drinking coffee and listening to Frank Sinatra droning out a song on the hidden speakers throughout the room.

A few mintues after he got his coffee, a medium-sized man in a well-cut charcoal gray suit walked in and sat down at a table in the back of the room. He ordered in a soft voice, then thanked the waiter politely when the waiter brought him his tall glass of Coke.

Hunter waited about five minutes, long enough to get a refill. Then he walked over to the man's table.

"Who is he sending?" the man asked him, sucking his Coke through a straw, not bothering to look up.

Hunter set his coffee down and took a seat. "He's sending Adrian McAllister," he answered in a sullen voice.

"You told me you would do this for us, Wayne." The man looked up with cold, forbidding eyes. "I put myself on the line for you."

"Not wait a minute—I'm going, too. She's going to be in Korea, but I'll be in Tokyo, transmitting her dispatches back here."

The man pushed the Coke next to the salt and pepper shakers and touched a paper napkin to his lips. "That might work," he said. "You can 'edit' her material in Tokyo. I'll go there myself, to help you."

After a minute, Hunter angrily slid his coffee cup to the side. "Damn it, Elliott," he said. "Why'd Mallory have to give her that job?"

Elliott's cold eyes locked onto his. "Forget Edward Mallory, Wayne," he said. "You don't owe him anything. You dont' owe any of them anything. Least of all the United States Government. You weren't even born here, didn't become a citizen until your mother brought you here from France. Why did they turn you down, Wayne? What was it—fallen arches? A man whose father flew in the Lafayette Escadrille in World War I turned down by every armed force in this country because of fallen arches!"

"You don't have to remind me," Hunter said, ashamed. "I've had to live with that for ten years. I hate the armed forces. Every one of them."

"You hate them because they rejected you, Wayne. Just like Ed Mallory just rejected you—in favor of a woman."

"Damn them," Wayne said. "They can't say I haven't tried. Ever since I was little, I've tried. My dear mother brought me up on all the legends of my father's family, like the great John Langley Hunter who fought with George Washington, and of course my sainted father, killed in a dogfight with a German ace. Everybody expects you to join the military, live up to your family's name—well, I'm tired of it. Nobody's ever just let me be me."

Elliott approved of his indignant tone. "That's the difference between our way and theirs, Wayne. The Communist party rejects no one. To the party, every man is important. No one cares who your ancestors were. All they care about is you. You as a person, not you as somebody's son."

Hunter looked vacantly across the room, thought of Adrian. Even the woman he loved couldn't stand him. She was in love with a marine who didn't even want her. "All my life," he complained, "everybody has always said, 'You're not much like your father, are you?' Or, 'You're not much like the Hunters I know.' I get sick of it."

"Then do something about it, Wayne. Help us. All we want you to do is help us discredit the Sacramento *Sun.* This one paper. That's all we ask. Do it, and you'll be doing yourself and your world a favor. You'll be helping to bring this country to its knees. Believe me. The revolution is starting right now in Asia, Wayne. And it's starting all over America right now, too. There's no way to stop it."

"I don't want to stop it," Wayne declared. "America deserves it."

"Then you'll help us," Elliott asked.

"Yeah, I'll help you. Why not? I don't owe my country a damned thing." I'll show them, he thought. I'll show them all.

3

WHEN ADRIAN ARRIVED home from the newspaper office half an hour later, she expected to see her whole family, her parents and twelve-year-old sister Cathy, gathered tightly around the radio waiting to hear more news of the Korean invasion. Instead she found Cathy alone in the living room, slumped across the sofa, eating potato chips and watching television with a bored look on her face.

"Where is everybody?" Adrian asked her, putting down her purse.

Cathy shrugged her shoulders, popped in another potato chip. She was tall for her age, and slim, but as yet she hadn't begun to blossom into womanhood. She seemed most of the time to be hanging around, waiting for something, possibly puberty, to happen to her.

Adrian walked into the carpeted living room, stood next to the sofa and glanced over at the snowy television screen. The set was new, an Emerson twenty-one inch, one of the first in the neighborhood. The show coming in was "Texaco Star Theater." She watched the four Texaco servicemen burst joyously out of the wings in front of the camera and begin singing proudly, "Oh, we're the men of Texaco, we work from Maine to Mexico. . ."

"I thought daddy loved Milton Berle," Adrian said, wondering where her father could be on a Tuesday night.

"He had to go talk to some client or other," Cathy answered indifferently. "Some old man got his leg caught in an elevator, or something. Mamma's ironing in the kitchen."

"Is she angry at me for missing dinner?" Adrian asked.

Cathy looked up at her, flicked a lock of her blonde hair off her forehead. "She's too angry at me to be angry at you," she said. "Just because I wanted to go see this picture, *The Asphalt Jungle.* She wouldn't let me go—just like that. She said I was too young to see such things."

Adrian watched almost in a daze as Milton Berle came on the screen in one of his absurd costumes. "If you want, I'll talk to her about it before I go," she said absently.

"Go where?" Cathy looked at her. "Are you and Gilly eloping?"

"God forbid."

"Well, what then?" Cathy said excitedly. "It must be something great for you not to call mamma and tell her you'd miss dinner. It *is* Gilly, isn't it? I know it!"

"It's *not* Gilly, Catherine. Gilbert Bell is the farthest thing from my mind. I'm going on an assignment. I'll tell you about it later—after I've talked to mother about it."

Cathy brought her knees up to her chest and shook her head skeptically. "Well, whatever it is you want to do, Adrian, you'd just as well forget it. She's not going to let you do it. Not the way she's acting tonight."

Adrian stayed a few minutes longer, ostensibly to hear a few of Berle's jokes, but mostly to build up her courage to face her mother. Mrs. McAllister wasn't an unfair or uncompromising woman, but she was, Adrian thought, overly practical. With Alice McAllister there had to be "good reason" for everything, or it wasn't worth doing. She was generally a warm, loving, sympathetic person, but she wanted her family close by, where she could see them. She would have kept them all right there in the house with her all day long, if they each didn't have good reason not to be there.

Mrs. McAllister was poised behind an ironing board in the kitchen, dampening a shirt with water from a Coca-Cola bottle capped with a sprinkler-stopper. She set the bottle upright when Adrian entered the room. "Your father said you'd be late," she said, glancing at the clock over the window. "I said since you weren't calling to say otherwise, you'd be here the usual time for dinner."

"I'm sorry," she apologized. "I didn't get a chance to call. We were waiting for more news on the North Korean invasion."

"Your father had to go talk to Mr. Tomlinson," Mrs. McAllister said, picking up the electric iron. Unconsciously she wet her finger and touched the bottom of the iron to see if the metal was hot enough. Satisfied that it was, she laid it down on the cotton shirt and began pressing out the wrinkles it had gathered that day hanging out on the clothesline.

"Mother," Adrian blurted out all at once, "I'm going to Korea."

Mrs. McAllister's hand froze on the iron. "You'll do no such thing, Adrian," she stated flatly.

Adrian swallowed hard. "Mr. Mallory's assigned me to Korea," she continued. "As a war correspondent. He wants me to write articles for the women here in the States—"

"Adrian, I don't want to hear about articles or anything else. The whole thing is ridiculous. And believe me, I'm going to give Edward Mallory a piece of my mind for suggesting it."

"It's not ridiculous; it's important. Haven't you heard what's happening over there? There may be another war breaking out."

Mrs. McAllister turned the iron up on its side, flipped over part of the shirt, then went on with the ironing, as if she hadn't heard what her daughter was saying.

"Mother, I'm sorry you disapprove . . ."

"Adrian, honey," she said, looking up with patient eyes, "I don't even know where Korea is. If you put a globe right there in front of me right now, I couldn't find it. Surely you don't expect me to let you go traipsing all over the world, just because one Edward Mallory says you ought to."

"There may be a *war*, mother. President Truman may be sending in American troops."

"Then let the troops report to the Sacramento *Sun*. Let Mallory pick somebody who can protect himself."

"I'm not defenseless, mother," Adrian declared. "I can take care of myself."

Mrs. McAllister shook her head stubbornly. "I'm sorry," she said. "It's out of the question, Adrian. I can think of no good reason for you to be going off to some terrible place like that. No good reason at all."

Adrian reached out and laid her hand on her mother's, stopping the movement of the iron. "Will you stop ironing and listen to me, please? I'm going, mother. I'm leaving in the morning. Don't you understand?"

"Oh, no, Adrian—"

"I'm not going there to shoot anybody, mother," she tried to console her. "I'm going there to write. I'll be fine."

"No." Her mother shook her head, tears in her eyes. "It's wrong, Adrian. Wait till your father comes home to decide. Will you just do that for me? He knows about these things. He'll show you it's wrong."

At that point Cathy stuck her head into the kitchen. "Phone, Adrian," she announced.

Adrian took a deep breath. She hated to see her mother cry, but she wasn't going to be talked out of the most important job she might ever have. She would have to be firm. "Who is it, Cathy?" she asked her sister.

"It's Mr. Mallory."

Adrian nodded, hesitated, searched her mother's eyes for understanding, but didn't find it. Then, reluctantly, she left the kitchen to answer the phone.

Ten minutes later she was upstairs in her room, packing. Although Cathy usually didn't bother to announce herself, she had knocked on Adrian's door before coming in. Once inside, she had become fidgety, then visibly nervous, as they talked rather disjointedly about why Mallory had happened to choose her to go.

Finally, Cathy got serious. "Mamma's downstairs crying, Adrian," she said.

"I know she's crying," Adrian said. "I can't help it. She doesn't want to let go."

"I can sure understand *that*," Cathy grumbled. "I get it from her all the time. She won't even let me go to the roller rink, Adrian. The *roller* rink. What can you do wrong on skates?"

"Well, she's right about that," Adrian admitted, tightening the cap of her shampoo bottle. "The roller rink is a rough place."

"Rough place! And you're talking about going to Korea?"

"I *am* going to Korea," Adrian corrected. "My boss just told me, Wayne Hunter's picking me up tonight. In a few minutes. We're driving down to San Francisco to catch a plane to Tokyo."

"Tokyo!" Cathy brightened. "I knew Gilly was in this some way. You're running off to be with him, aren't you?"

"No, Catherine," she answered impatiently. "I'm not running off to be with Gilbert Bell."

"His sister's in Tokyo, isn't she? The one that told you about the Chinese girl?"

"Yes, Cathy, Amanda is in Tokyo. In fact, she's probably processing my papers right now. But contrary to what other people say, Gilbert Bell isn't always where his sister is."

Adrian stared down at the open suitcase on the bed. It was hopeless. She had no idea what to pack. All kinds of questions rushed into her mind. Would she be allowed to take a suitcase into Korea? Would someone provide her with a special uniform? How much shampoo? How much perfume? How many changes of underwear?

She felt so warmly excited about the trip she had to sit down on the bed to catch her breath. Then she thought, what on earth was she worried about? How could she tell what to take when she didn't even know how long she would be there?

"Oh Lord, Cathy," she said with alarm.

"What is it?" Cathy asked.

"It just hit me. I could be over there for years. If we do have another war, I may have to stay there the whole time."

Cathy eased down on the bed beside her. "You've been wanting to leave anyway," she reminded her. "Ever since you threw Gilly over—"

"I didn't 'throw Gilly over.' It was obvious he loved somebody else, that's all. I saw it myself. I saw him kiss her before she got on the ship."

"And you saw him do it because sweet Amanda brought you there to see it," Cathy said sarcastically.

"I don't blame Amanda, Cathy. It was Gilbert. He loved her; I could tell from the way he was kissing her." She paused. "He never kissed me that way."

"That's only because you never let him, Adrian."

"Well . . ." She got up. "What I let him do doesn't matter now. It's all over. I'll probably never see him again."

Suddenly a man's voice called out from the other side of her door. "Adrian?" it said with a deep, resonant sound.

"Come in, daddy." She sighed, walked over to her dresser and opened the top drawer.

"Well," he said feigning cheerfulness. "I haven't seen you two ladies cooperate in years. I like it. You ought to do it more."

Adrian looked at her father and smiled. He could always bring that out of her. He was a sweet, loving man, tall, still attractive in a rugged sort of way, still thin and healthy looking. "She's not being that much help, daddy," Adrian said. "Mostly she's just sitting there."

"Adrian . . ." Her father's voice became serious. "Let's talk about this, okay?"

"I have to pack," she said firmly. "Wayne Hunter's coming for me in a little while."

"Wayne Hunter!" he exclaimed.

"He's going, too, Daddy."

"Wait a minute, now," he said grimly. "Just hold on here, young lady. Let me get this straight—Wayne Hunter and you are hopping a plane for Korea— tonight?"

"Excuse me," she said, passing in front of him with a handful of underwear.

When Sam McAllister saw his daughter obliviously folding thin nylon panties and cotton bras to put into the suitcase, he cleared his throat nervously and said, "Adrian, come downstairs. I want to talk to you."

"I have to pack, daddy."

"*Now*, Adrian."

She looked straight at him. "I'll be through in five minutes."

He hesitated, then grunted out, "Okay. Pack. But don't you leave this house till I've talked to you."

A while later Adrian came downstairs with her suitcase. Her mother was in the living room, sitting on the edge of the sofa, sniffing into a Kleenex. Adrian set down the case, walked to the front screen door and opened it.

The air outside on the porch was warm and heavy. It seemed to surround her as she stood for a moment, looking at the clouds passing rapidly in front of the bright moon. She couldn't help but wonder how different her new world would be from this one—this comfortable two-story frame house in a manicured neighborhood in a neat, well-run city of one hundred and forty thousand.

"Adrian?" her father called out from the swing. When she eased down in the swing beside him, he could smell her perfume. It disturbed him slightly. He looked at her and smiled. "All packed?" he managed to say.

"All packed. Wayne should be here in a few minutes."

"You know your mother's upset, Adrian," he said.

"I know she is, daddy. I wish I could say something to make her feel better, but I can't."

"You can tell her you're not going," he suggested.

"No, I can't, daddy. I am going."

He shifted positions, making the chain on the swing

squeak. "Adrian, I'm afraid you don't realize what you're getting into here. You're a very attractive girl, and boys in battle . . . well, they let their emotions run away with them. You won't be safe over there. It won't be anything like Sacramento. You won't have a community there to protect you."

"I'll be fine, daddy. I'm a big girl now."

"That's what I'm talking about, Adrian," he said. "You're asking for trouble, going over there. Here in Sacramento it's all right to wear your sweaters and jeans, but Adrian, there . . ." His voice trailed off.

"I don't plan on wearing tight sweaters or jeans, daddy," she assured him.

He was impatient now. "You know what I mean. I don't have to spell it out for you."

"No, you don't," she said, getting up. "I'm not as innocent as you think, daddy," she said. "I am twenty, after all." For one terrible second her fear of leaving home for the last time almost made her want to clear the docket with him—to confess that she truly wasn't his little girl anymore, that she had made love before . . . twice. But she let the feeling pass over her.

"What are you saying, Adrian?" he pressed her.

"Never mind, daddy."

"Look, sweetheart, if it's adventure you're looking for, we could plan a trip to Europe. What would you think of that? We could take one of those whirlwind tours—"

"I'm not looking for adventure, daddy. I just want to do my job."

He didn't understand. "There are other jobs, Adrian," he told her. "You don't have to do this. I can get you a job in the law firm, if this newspaper business isn't working out. It's all temporary anyway."

"It's not temporary, daddy," she said, going back to the swing. She took his hand in hers and looked straight into his eyes. "Don't you see? I hate and detest wars. If I can *be* there, report what I see, maybe . . ." She gave up; there was no hint of comprehension in his eyes. He had always assumed her job at the *Sun* was just something a woman would do to pass the time, not something that either she or her employers would take seriously.

"I disapprove of this, Adrian," he said. "I strongly disapprove of it. If you do this, you'll break your mother's heart."

"Then please make her understand. It's important for me to go."

McAllister was silent for a few minutes. He sat on the soft cushion in the swing and looked straight ahead, out across the lawn to the street. In just a few minutes a car would pull up and take his daughter away—before he had to tell her how he felt about her. Finally he reached out and touched her soft flowing hair. "Will you be careful, anyway?" he asked softly.

Adrian burst into tears and embraced him. "Oh, daddy," she said. "I'm so scared."

"I know you are, sweetheart," he comforted her. Then, in a broken voice, he said, "I'm scared, too. scared I won't ever see my little girl again."

She sobbed into his shoulder for a while, until the headlights of Hunter's car flashed their beams onto the porch. Then Adrian stood up, wiped the tears from her eyes and straightened her skirt. "Well, I guess this is it," she said. "I've got to go."

"I don't care for that Wayne Hunter," McAllister

commented. "I don't trust him. I don't like the way he looks at you."

"Oh daddy," she sniffed. "He's not going to rape me or anything."

"Adrian!"

Just then the screen door opened and slammed shut and Cathy appeared under the porch light with her sister's suitcase. Adrian walked over, hugged her tightly, and whispered in her ear, "If you look in the bottom drawer of my dresser, you'll find my old training bras wrapped up in a plastic bag. Have fun."

Cathy squeezed her hand. "Will you write to us, please?" she pleaded.

"Just read the *Sun*," Adrian told her.

"Why doesn't he come up here," McAllister complained, staring intently at Hunter's car. "You'd think he'd have the decency to come up here on the porch."

"He'd be embarrassed, daddy," Adrian explained.

"Well, I like to see the faces of people," he mumbled.

Adrian was about to go inside to see her mother when Mrs. McAllister stepped out onto the porch. For a second she seemed dazed, as if she were sleepwalking. Then she held out her arms. "Come here, Adrian," she said affectionately.

"I'm sorry, mother," Adrian said as she wrapped her arms around her.

"Never mind," she said. "I don't understand why you're doing this without good reason, and I guess I never will understand it. But you're doing it, so I'll just have to live with it. But for God's sake, Adrian, be careful. Will you, please?"

"I will, mother. I promise."

Tears were clouding her eyes as she reached down for the suitcase. It seemed impossibly heavy as she picked it up. She had forgotten already what she had put in it. She gave each person on the porch another quick kiss, turned, and walked slowly toward Wayne's Plymouth sedan.

Before she even reached the end of the sidewalk she heard Wayne turn on the ignition and start the engine. As she touched the handle of the door, she looked back toward the porch, then ducked quickly into the car.

She couldn't bear to wave.

4

THE MONOTONOUS ROAR of the four engines of the C-54 transport plane was so loud that Adrian couldn't hear the other correspondents talking to each other. She was so preoccupied she might not have paid any attention even if she had been able to hear. Her heart was pounding, her mind was spinning, her whole body was charged up with fear and anticipation.

Below her the bright blue waters of the Sea of Japan turned into the desolate wastelands of South Korea. They were flying in an army evacuation transport to Suwon, south of Seoul. The only other passengers in the large belly of the plane were Bud Ayers and Edmund Kohler of the wire services, two grizzled old veterans in the news world, and Robert Kowalski of the *New York Times,* a tall, formal, aloof

man of about forty who had won the Pulitzer Prize
in 1943 and 1944 for his on-the-line stories in World
War II.

For the eighth time she adjusted the loose-fitting
fatigues she was wearing. That morning a gruff supply
sergeant in Tokyo had laid a stack clothes in front
of her, ripped off all the insignia, and advised her,
"Better wear your own shoes, ma'am. And I wouldn't
recommend high heels, neither." She had dutifully
put on the shirt and pants ("the littlest we got ma'am,"
the sergeant had said) but had to apply a great
deal of finesse with a needle and thread to make them
fit enough to be seen in.

"Got everything?" Bud Ayers called out to her
over the noise of the engines.

"I think so," she shouted back. "Thank you!"

"Nice," he said, pointing with exaggeration at the
new compact Royal typewriter positioned between
her feet.

"Thank you," she responded again.

"Brand new, right?"

She nodded, tried to end the little interrogation by
looking somewhere else. But Ayers persisted. "You
did get one without punctuation keys, didn't you?"
he asked her.

When she gestured that she didn't understand, he
told her, "War dispatches are typed without punctuation. Didn't you know that?"

"Why don't you leave her alone, Bud?" Kowalski
admonished. "This is hard enough as it is. Don't kid
around with her."

"Are you sure you got everything, Miss McAllister?"
Ayers asked, after a hard look at Kowalski. "Tooth-
brush? Kleenex? Hair brush? Kotex?"

She stared at him. "I have all I need," she said. "I'm as prepared as any man."

"Are you prepared, Miss McAllister? What about your camera, hunh? Don't tell me you forgot your camera?" He held up his own bulky box camera to illustrate his point.

She sat erect and flushed, trying hard to ignore their laughs, making a mental note not to go anywhere again as long as she lived without a camera.

Half an hour later she could hear loud booming noises, explosions, above the roar of the plane engines. Suddenly the fusilage began to shake violently around them.

"Enemy Yaks," the pilot, Lieutenant Coleman, yelled back to them. "We must be getting close to Suwon. Hang on tight, folks."

Another massive vibration of the plane nearly shook her off her bench. For some reason she snapped up her typewriter and brought it up to her lap.

Ayers laughed. "Just like the Loop-the-loop at the California State Fair, hunh, Miss McAllister?"

"One under us, folks," the pilot hollered. "Make sure your chutes are fastened. You may have to make an unexpected personal appearance down there."

A seemingly endless ten minutes passed before the pilot announced that the Yaks were gone and they had the airfield at Suwon in sight. They all breathed better then, and after landing they began arranging their gear to leave the plane. As Adrian was preparing to climb down to the airstrip, Ayers snapped a picture of her. "For my own files," he explained as he slipped in front of her and stepped down out of the plane. "The fellows back in New York won't believe it."

When Adrian's feet hit the landing strip, she had to

stop and assure herself that what she was seeing was real. Less than a hundred yards away an American fighter plane was engulfed in flames. Part of the runway was torn apart. Five or six jeeps lay overturned in the mud. Above her head, out of sight behind the heavy cloud cover, she could hear what sounded like a hundred planes headed north, toward, she assumed, the thirty-eighth parallel.

Suddenly, out of nowhere, an army lieutenant was standing in front of her. "That's a squadron of F-51 Mustangs," he explained, looking up into the air. "They're just looking, right now. Wait till we get into this thing full force. We'll hit them with the F-80 Shooting Star. They won't know what hit 'em."

"What's an F-80 Shooting Star?" she asked.

He stared at her in amazement. "That's a jet, young lady," he replied haughtily. "Best jet on the face of the earth."

"Oh," she said, shifting her typewriter to her left hand.

"I'm Lieutenant James Metz," he said. "I've been assigned to take care of you."

Metz seemed to her a proper Lieutenant. He fit his uniform; he was trim, compact, ramrod straight. He was rather attractive, she thought, with blue eyes and blond hair, but much too rigid in demeanor to interest her romantically. "Do those Mustangs mean we're under attack, Lieutenant Metz?" she asked him.

"No, ma'am, we're not under attack," he reassured her. "May I take that for you?" he asked, nodding toward the typewriter.

"No, thank you," she replied quickly. "I can manage."

They began walking over the rough runway toward

a jeep. "My orders are to take you to Seoul," he said, almost through his teeth. "So, unless you have to, uh, take care of something before we go, we'll get started."

"You don't sound as if you approve of me."

He stopped, let his eyes scan her body. "Nothing personal, ma'am," he said. "It's just that you're a woman."

"Well, I know that, Lieutenant," she teased him. "My mother's very modest, but she never kept that from me."

"What I mean is," he went on, undaunted, "this is no place for a woman. It's dangerous. You could get hurt. Besides . . ." He paused, searched for a word.

"Besides what?" she asked him.

"What I mean is, there are no, you know, bathrooms in Korea."

She put down her typewriter and stared at him in amazement. "We're standing here with fighter planes buzzing over our heads and guns going off over the hills, and you tell me there are no bathrooms in Korea?"

"Well, I'm aware that women have a greater need for such things than men."

"Lieutenant," she said, astounded, "don't you know what's going on here? We're facing a war."

"War or no, ma'am, you'll find out here a soldier carries out his orders. And my orders are to make you comfortable."

"I don't want to be *comfortable*, damn it. I just want to do my job. And I certainly won't be able to do my job if every time I turn around you're asking me if I need to use the bathroom."

"Suit yourself, ma'am," he bristled. "I don't like

this assignment any more than you do. I'd rather be doing K.P. than ministering to a . . . woman."

"Then don't minister to me, Lieutenant," she told him and moved briskly ahead.

Just as they reached the army jeep, it began to rain. Adrian scrambled into the passenger seat, put down her typewriter, and curled up tight to shield herself from the torrents of water beating down from a black sky.

"Here, put this over your head," Metz said as he handed her a poncho. "That is, if you don't mind my ministering to you."

"Thank you," she responded formally. "I appreciate your thoughtfulness."

"No thanks needed," he grunted as he clambered into his seat. "It comes with the job."

The rain lasted half an hour. They proceeded slowly up the road to Seoul, parallel to the railroad, which, the lieutenant explained, ran all the way up to Wonsan, in North Korea. At first the way was clear, then all of a sudden they began passing Seoul refugees by the hundreds, trudging slowly toward them in the thick mud, in single file, headed nowhere in particular—just as long as it was away from home.

Soon she could hear gunfire off in the distance, followed by sporadic explosions. On the road now appeared South Korean soldiers, wounded or scared or both, moving past the refugees as if some great invisible horror were chasing them. Then from behind their jeep erupted a stream of American army vehicles of various kinds, a sergeant or corporal and two officers riding in each. They sounded their horns, passed by without the slightest expression on their faces.

"There they go," Metz grumbled. "And here I am, escorting a woman correspondent."

"This is all insane," Adrian observed, looking around her. "It's so chaotic. How does anyone know what's going on?"

"No one does know right now," Metz conceded. "Anything's liable to happen. That's why I don't think it's such a good idea for you to be here."

"You've made your point, Lieutenant," she said impatiently. "You don't have to keep harping on it."

"Yes, ma'am," he said stiffly. "Anything the lady wants."

Five miles out of Seoul, the jeep began to sputter and kick. "I think this may be as far as we go," Metz proclaimed, shaking his head.

"Why? What's wrong?" she asked.

"What's wrong is that we're out of gas," he replied as he directed the jeep toward the side of the road. There it spit, coughed, and died. "I guess Sergeant Willis didn't fill it up after all."

"Oh great." Adrian threw up her hands. "No bathrooms, no gas."

"I guess you'll have to write your story here," Metz said, leaning back in his seat."

"Oh no I won't," she said. "My story is in Seoul, and that's where I'm going, gas or no gas." She peeled off the poncho, climbed out of the jeep, and went around to the front of the hood.

"What are you doing?" he demanded. "You can't stand out on the road like that. It's dangerous."

"I'm going to thumb a ride," she explained.

He laughed. "Thumb a ride! You're kidding."

"I assure you I'm not kidding, Lieutenant," she told him, and positioned herself for a hitch. At first

she got a great deal of attention, standing in the
road bed with her thumb up. American soldiers whis-
tled at her, begged her to show her legs, asked her
for dates in Tokyo. But no one stopped for her. Finally she got desperate. She decided to flag down the
next north-bound vehicle that appeared and make it
stop.

That vehicle was a jeep, loaded with men. Boldly
she sprang out into the middle of the road and waved
her arms. "Stop, please!" she yelled.

"Miss McAllister!" Metz screamed out in great dis-
may. "Not *that* jeep!"

"Hey, lady!" the driver, a sergeant, bellowed as
the vehicle slid to a halt. "Get out of the way!"

"Could you give me a ride to Seoul?" she pleaded,
coming around to the driver's side. "The lieutenant's
jeep is out of gas."

"Sir!" Lieutenant Metz appeared next to the jeep
and snapped to attention for the officer. "The lady
is my responsibility—"

"It's all right, Lieutenant," said the tall dark man
in the back seat.

Adrian gasped. The jeep was full of army generals!
And the one who had spoken she recognized from
wire photos in the newsroom—it was General Douglas MacArthur himself. She felt her blood rushing
to her face; she knew it beamed like a red beacon.
"I'm sorry, General," she apologized. "I had no
idea . . ."

"Never mind. Go ahead and get in, miss," Mac-
Arthur said. "Let's go, Sergeant," he prompted the
driver as she climbed in.

Adrian had to squeeze in between MacArthur and
General Almond, his chief of staff. Both men felt

like trees next to her, hard, immovable, strong. She couldn't help noticing that they seemed a bit ill at ease at finding themselves next to a woman's soft body on the way to the front. In fact, they were nervous.

MacArthur cleared his throat. "Are you a journalist, Miss . . ."

"McAllister. Yes, sir. Sacramento *Sun.*"

"I thought war journalists carried typewriters these days," he said.

"Oh Lord!" she exclaimed. "I left my typewriter in the other jeep!"

MacArthur looked straight ahead. "Just between you and me, Miss McAllister, that's pretty much the whole story over here. Everybody is unprepared for this. The ROK Army, especially."

"I've been watching them come down the road," she said, nodding. "The fear on their faces couldn't be more obvious. Fear, and confusion. They don't seem to understand what's happening to them."

"That's very astute, Miss McAllister," MacArthur replied. "The truth is, they *don't* understand what's happening to them. I'm not sure they even know what the word *freedom* means. The word as we know it isn't in their vocabulary. So how can they be expected to lay down their lives for it?"

"But it's not up to *us* to defend them, is it?"

MacArthur took a corncob pipe out of his khaki shirt pocket and tapped the bowl on the side of the jeep, knocking ashes out into the wind. "You don't think we should?" he asked in almost an accusing tone.

She winced, but said determinedly, "No, sir, I don't, General. I don't believe in war."

"I don't 'believe' in it, either, Miss McAllister. That's why I do everything in my power to end one, once it starts." He paused, then softened his tone of voice. "Tell me something," he said. "Do you have a boyfriend back home?"

"I had a boyfriend, General. It didn't work out, for some reason."

"What does your young man do?" MacArthur asked. "Besides make a fool of himself by letting you go?"

She smiled at the compliment. "He's a marine. Camp Pendleton, California."

"Good. Now what would you think of that marine if some Neanderthal of a man attacked you and he stood by and said, 'It's your battle, Adrian. You fight it'?"

"Now that's not fair, General," she said. "Gilbert is not a country, he's just one man."

"That's why I try never to talk to correspondents," he responded glumly. "All you're ever interested in is confirming your own ideas."

"Well, isn't that what you're doing?" she asserted boldly.

He frowned thoughtfully, took out a tobacco pouch and began stuffing the bowl of his pipe. "Maybe so," he admitted. "Maybe it is."

A while later the city was in sight. Refugees and ROK soldiers were still periodically trying to ford the Han River. On the south side of the blown bridges hundreds of civilians were standing, sitting, even lying about, aimless, lost, dazed by it all.

MacArthur's jeep pulled up next to two officers standing near the road. One of them was a marine major; the other was Brigadier General Lucius Stoddard.

"Lucius," MacArthur greeted him. "What're you doing here?"

"Well, you know how old marines are, Douglas. We have to get there first, if we can."

"Have you been here long enough to tell what's going on, Lucius? I've never seen such confusion."

Stoddard had been looking at Adrian. Now he shifted his eyes back to MacArthur. "The ROK headquarters is estimating forty-five thousand dead," he answered. " 'Guessing' is more like it. Nobody knows yet who gave the orders to blow the bridges. Most of them might've gotten out easy if that hadn't happened."

"What about equipment?"

"Equipment's lost. Most of it, anyway. The ROK soldiers just threw down everything and ran when they realized the bridges were blown and they were trapped."

"Looks like it's left up to us," MacArthur said. "What we'll do is continue the air raid over North Korea, and mount a counter-offensive of American troops. We'll bring in a regimental combat team, then two divisions from my forces in Japan."

"We don't know how strong the enemy is, Douglas," Stoddard warned him. "Are you sure two divisions will do it?"

"They'll do it easily," MacArthur replied. "Now, General Stoddard, if you'll do me a favor . . . if you'll take care of this young lady here, I'll have a closer look."

After saying her thank-yous, Adrian slid down off the jeep, extended her hand to Stoddard. "Adrian McAllister, General," she identified herself. "Sacramento *Sun*."

He smiled, thought of Gilbert Bell. He wondered how a healthy marine officer could regard such a beauty as Adrian McAllister as a close friend. Seeing her confirmed what he had expected: there was more to it than that.

"What did you think of the great man?" he asked her.

"He was nice," she said evasively.

"*Nice?*" he laughed. "MacArthur? I've never heard him called that. Somehow I don't think he'd like that."

"Well—what I meant was, he wasn't as stuck-up as everybody says."

"Maybe you struck the right chord with him. There's no telling with Douglas MacArthur. He's a hard man to figure, sometimes. He's a great leader, and a powerful man. Sometimes I think he's just itching to see how far his power extends, and just how great he is." He cleared his throat, wiping away the subject. "I've got a tent over here," he said to her. "You're welcome to it. Looks like it's going to rain again in a few minutes."

"Thank you. What I wouldn't give for some dry clothes—You wouldn't have any extra fatigues, by any chance?"

"Sorry," he said, walking with her toward the tent. "No fatigues." A few steps later, he said to her, "You're a friend of Lieutenant Gilbert Bell, aren't you?"

She stopped. "How did you know?" she said, puzzled.

"I just saw him in Washington," he answered. "We sort of crossed paths."

She was silent for a moment before suddenly asking, "General Stoddard, I know this will sound silly, since we just met, but . . . did he happen to mention me?"

"Well, as a matter of fact, he did mention you. He said you two were close friends. Yes, I believe that was the way he put it."

She was disappointed. "That's all? Close friends?"

"That's what he said. But then Lieutenant Bell is a man who keeps his own counsel. At least that's how I see him."

"What does that mean?" she wondered.

"I'm sorry, it doesn't mean anything. Come on, let's get inside; the rain's coming again."

The rain arrived suddenly and in heavy sheets. And for three hours Adrian and the general were forced to remain inside the tent. During the time they were together, Stoddard talked about many things—the North Korean invasion, World War II, his wife, food —but he never returned to the subject of Gilbert Bell.

She ached to know about him. She wanted to know if he was coming to Korea, if he still loved her, even a little. But she was too proud to bring up the subject again. And a little defiant: Lieutenant Gilbert Bell wasn't the only one who could keep his own counsel.

When the weather finally cleared, it was dark. General Stoddard signalled to a marine major to get his jeep ready; he was going to return to Suwon to catch a plane to Tokyo.

"I'm going back to report to Bradley," he told her. "You can come along and file your story in Tokyo, if you want to."

She considered the invitation a minute. "Do all the other correspondents file theirs from Tokyo?"

"I suppose so."

"Then I want to report mine from here. It'll beat theirs by a couple of hours at least, if I can do that."

Stoddard was amused in spite of himself. "Yes, but just how do you expect to do that?" he asked her. "The only phones are in Seoul, and you're not about to go into Seoul, I can tell you."

She thought a while. "What about HQ's phone in Suwon?" she suggested.

"*MacArthur's* phone? My God, you *are* plucky. You can't just barge into MacArthur's quarters and use his phone, Adrian."

"I'd only use it for a minute," she promised.

"You'd take a chance like that just to scoop your colleagues?"

"Some colleagues! They act like I'm a high school reporter."

He rubbed his chin, raised his gray eyebrows, shook his head, reconsidered, then finally said, "Well, why not? We can look into it, anyway. No harm in that."

Suwon was bustling when they got there. South Korean women were wandering around moaning sad, soulful stories to anyone who would listen. American army officers were scurrying about trying to track down rumors of an enemy air strike on Suwon. Native children were hanging onto the arms of noncoms, begging for food and candy.

And there was gunfire. Every few seconds the sky lit up in orange or white, and a deep rumble of artillery shells unloading upon fighter planes shook the wet ground. Once Adrian heard the blood-curdling whistle of what sounded to her like a bomb passing overhead, followed by a deadly silence that sent chills tingling down her spine.

General Stoddard let the major off at the airstrip, told him he would be back soon, then drove off in the jeep with Adrian. When they reached headquarters, he parked the jeep and shut the engine off.

"That's it," he said, nodding ahead. "MacArthur's sanctuary."

Adrian examined the building. It was a hastily erected hut, but large enough to serve MacArthur and his retinue of generals and other officers. It looked empty, except for a stiff and proper lieutenant standing outside with his arms crossed—a lieutenant she recognized.

"That's my old friend Lieutenant Metz," she told Stoddard.

"I suppose he's out here protecting the place," Stoddard said sarcastically.

" 'Ministering to it' is more like it," Adrian noted.

"Well, look, I'll leave Metz to you. All I can do is keep MacArthur and Almond busy for a few minutes. No more than that. Do you think you can swing it?"

She nodded, charged her lungs with air, then got down from the jeep. "I'll think of something," she said.

"Good luck," he said and drove off.

It took a while for her to build up her courage. She didn't want to think about it too long. If she were to consider where she was and what she was doing—*really* consider it—she would probably find a hole somewhere and crawl into it. But she had to have a plan of some sort. Everything had gone wrong this day. She had forgotten her camera, she had been assigned to Lieutenant Metz, the jeep had run out of gas, she had left her bags in it, she had flagged down one of the greatest generals who had ever lived, for God's sake—and, the worst of it all, she had seen misery, fear, pain, suffering in the thousands of South Koreans leaving their homes in search of sanctuary. She needed to think very carefully about what she was doing.

An idea occurred to her as she watched the two red taillights of Stoddard's jeep fade into the dark. She would call her story "There Are No Bathrooms in Korea." It would be a description of the place and the people. The angle would be to depict for the average American woman the kind of battleground into which she could be sending her son or husband. A place unlike anything in the United States. A poor, foul-smelling place. A destitute, end-of-the-earth place. A place with no bathrooms.

The story seemed to block itself out automatically in her mind, paragraph by paragraph. It was a natural—and, if she could get to that phone and call Tokyo, a scoop.

She let more of the heavy damp air into her lungs and marched confidently across the field to the HQ building. As Metz drew himself to attention, she said casually, "Excuse me, Lieutenant."

But he reached out and stopped her. "Just a minute, young lady. You can't go in there. Nobody less than a colonel can go in there."

"I have to, Lieutenant," she said, pretending to be very uncomfortable.

"Ma'am?" he said, eyeing her suspiciously.

"I have to *go*, Lieutenannt," she told him flatly. "If you know what I mean."

"I'm sorry, ma'am," he said, his voice strained. "That facility is reserved solely for high command officers."

She was happy to hear there *was* a facility there. "Lieutenant," she said. "I'm not kidding. I must go in there. Now."

Metz was flustered. "It's against regulations, Miss McAllister," he said defensively.

"Lieutenant, there is something about women you don't understand—"

"I don't want to know," he interrupted her.

"When something like this happens—"

"Okay, okay, go on in," he said. "But be quick about it."

Adrian hurried into the room, grabbed the phone. Using the pass words Stoddard had told her to get through, she managed, after a few minutes, to contact Tokyo, then, after five minutes more, Wayne.

"Here it is," she said and quickly dictated the whole report. "Did you get it?" she asked when she had finished.

The phone crackled in her ear. "I didn't . . . all . . . report," Hunter's voice sputtered in the static.

She was just about to respond when General MacArthur walked into the building. Quickly she replaced the phone and looked up at him sheepishly. He looked like a giant standing over her.

"Couldn't you have waited, Miss McAllister?" he asked her.

"I'm sorry, General, but I couldn't. I just had to file my story first."

He looked at her a minute. "You're a persistent person, aren't you?" he said. Then, "Well? Did you get through?"

"Sir?"

"Did you get through to Tokyo?" he said, taking a seat on a folding chair. "I have a devil of a time getting through to them on that thing."

"Well, yes, sir, I got through," she answered, surprised at his casualness. "There's some static, but you can hear most of what's being said."

"Good. Then why don't you get back on it and get me command HQ in Tokyo? Maybe they hear a woman's voice better."

"Yes, sir," she said, picking up the phone.

He took out his pipe. "You see, Miss McAllister," he said, "what you've done here is to illustrate the difference between an American and everybody else. Four hours ago you were totally unprepared for this war. Now look at you. Sneaking in to use the high command's telephone to call in a story."

"I apologize for that, General MacArthur—"

"Well, don't apologize," he said. "You weren't ready for this experience, but you got ready for it. You can be proud of that, because it's that kind of thing in an American that makes an old soldier like me have to fight back the tears."

"General—"

"Get me command HQ in Tokyo, Miss McAllister," he said. "There are people I want there when I report to Truman that we have no choice but to enter this war."

She took a deep breath. His words chilled her to the bone. What she was afraid of was going to happen after all. The president was going to send American forces into Korea. And that meant, as always, the marines would be the first to go.

And the marines meant Gilbert Bell. Could any war, any battle, be worth the death of such a man as Gilly? "Close friends," he had said. Didn't he know she would never love anyone else as long as she lived? How could she ever face seeing him lying dead on the foul-smelling ground of Korea? It would kill her.

"Miss McAllister," MacArthur prompted.

"Yes, sir," she said, and with tears filling her eyes, put in the call. "I'll see if I can get them."

5

In Osan, South Korea, a few miles south of Suwon, the first American soldier fell dead on July 5, 1950. The Korean War had begun.

The dead soldier had been part of a force of five hundred Americans which General MacArthur sent into the country to delay the movement of the North Korean army. The group, called "Task Force Smith" after their leader, Lieutenant Colonel Charles Smith, landed in the southern coastal town of Pusan and moved toward Seoul. At Osan, they found themselves surrounded by an entire Korean division.

A third of Task Force Smith perished on that ground as the ill-prepared troops dug in against the enemy. Eventually, unable to cope with the odds, they retreated.

To the south, Major General William Dean tried

to use the delaying action of Task Force Smith to gather the Twenty-fourth Infantry Division around Taejon. For two weeks Dean's men managed to delay the onslaught of the North Korean People's Army.

But at the Battle of Taejon, Dean's men were overpowered. After five days of fighting in and around the city, the general was captured, and the division pulled back, defeated again. . . .

By this time the army and the marines were beginning to arrive at Pusan. At the rail of one of the ships pulling into the Pusan harbor in mid-August Lieutenant Gilbert Bell stood looking out over the calm water at the approaching dock. It felt good to him to see so much activity there. Army vehicles with great white stars on their hoods were dashing about, crates by the thousands were being hoisted off the huge ships, men in army, navy and marine uniforms were hustling around doing their jobs.

It also felt good to know he was a part of an armed strength now gathering in South Korea—a part of a marine brigade that numbered 6500 well-equipped men and a host of M-26 Pershing tanks sporting 90mm guns that could blow a Soviet T-34 into black dust. Smith and Dean had done their part, holding back the enemy. Now it was time to deal from strength.

"Lieutenant," a marine corporal standing next to him said in a low voice. "How are we supposed to know them when we see them?"

Gilbert smiled, patted his friend on the shoulder. Bell thought of DeWitt Baruchi—"Chick," everyone called him—as his closest friend. The truth was, he had always felt protective toward Chick, but not only because Chick was four years his junior. Chick, who was blond and had a broad, muscular physique, had all the natural abilities to become an officer in the corps—except for two things.

One was the respect of the other men. Chick was the best marksman Bell had ever seen, but he had never established any camaraderie with the other men. His voice was too soft, his manners too gentle. His finesse with a rifle was more like that of a concert pianist executing a concerto than a professional soldier wielding a death weapon.

The other was confidence. Chick had never truly belonged anywhere. He was illegitimate, the son of Everett DeWitt and Lucy Baruchi, brought up by his mother in Italy. He had never felt he had a family. Until he had joined the marines—and met Gilly.

"You'll know them, Chick," he assured him. "Don't worry. You won't have time to think about it."

"But what about the South Koreans?" he wondered. "These people all look the same to me."

"We probably all look the same to them, too, Chick. But I think the North Koreans will be the ones shooting at us."

"Yeah, I guess so," he agreed.

"And if there's one thing in the world you can do better than anybody else, it's to shoot that Browning Automatic of yours."

Chick smiled, nodded. "Yeah, that's right. Barbara's going to be right there with us, isn't she?"

"Yes, she is. Look, Chick, why don't we go get our gear ready? We'll be landing in a few minutes."

"Yes, sir."

"One thing, Chick," Gilbert cautioned him. "I wouldn't call the BAR Barbara in front of the other men, okay?"

Baruchi frowned, not understanding. "*You* don't mind, do you?" he asked.

"Unh-unh. I don't mind. I think of her as Barbara, too," Gilbert said as they moved off the bow. "To tell you the truth, Baruchi," he said in a serious voice, "I call my carbine Milly."

"Do you really?" Baruchi said, relieved. "As long as you understand, I don't care what the other fellas say."

Twenty minutes later, they came down off the ship onto the dock. Gilbert looked around. The place was busy, but otherwise it seemed peaceful. It was hard to believe the fighting was so close. He could feel the adrenalin building in his body, getting him ready to fight. He was anxious to see action, to put into practice all the training the corps had given him.

"I wish I could've brought the BAR," Chick said as they walked over the wooden walkway in front of the supply sheds. "I'd feel better with it along."

"You'll have a chance to use it," Gilbert assured him. "More chances than you'll want."

"Not me," he asserted. "I'm ready . . ."

Baruchi said something else, but Bell didn't hear him. He was engrossed in what was happening down the walkway. A crowd of army men had gathered noisily around someone. They were laughing, joking, and moving against each other excitedly.

As he and Baruchi drew closer, they could see that the center of attention was a tall woman with long, flowing black hair, outfitted in army fatigues. She was laughing with them, asking questions and busily jotting down notes on a steno pad.

As Gilbert stepped to the edge of the crowd of

army men, the woman turned around and he could see her beautiful face. It almost paralyzed him.

"Hey, Gilly," Baruchi nudged him, forgetting Bell's rank. "It's Adrian!"

"I know who it is," Gilbert replied stiffly.

"Wonder what she's doing here?"

"Making a big hit with the army, obviously," he snapped.

One of the army men, a private, called out above the others to Adrian, "How about coming over to my foxhole, honey? Any time, day or night."

"Shut up, Collins!" someone yelled.

"Hey, look, honey," Collins hollered, then began pushing his way through the crowd. "We could, you know, make little foxes together. Right, fellas?"

The army men broke into tense laughter.

"Sorry, soldier," Adrian responded nervously. "I can't stand foxes."

"Come on, now," he persisted, "no woman that looks as good as you do would come all the way over here just to look. Now would she, fellas? Anyway, that's what foxholes are for."

Collins took another couple of steps toward her and then ran into a surprise—the hard, straight body of a marine lieutenant.

"You're talking to the wrong woman, Private," Gilly said, looking him straight in the eyes. "Back off."

"Get out of the way, *sir*," he said derisively. "I don't have to listen to a marine."

Gilbert stood firm. "You've got a foul mouth, Private," he said.

The other man glared at him a second, looked about, drew courage from the presence of his buddies around him. "What's it to you, anyway, *sir?*" he challenged. "What the hell business is it of yours?"

Gilbert was calm, collected. "I know the lady. All right?" he said.

"Gilbert," Adrian broke in. "I can handle this—do you mind?"

The private kept his eyes on Bell. "You know her, hunh?" he said. "Well, don't go around feeling like the Lone Ranger, Lieutenant, because she's putting out for the whole Eighth Army—"

"One more word, Private," Gilbert warned him.

The army soldier looked directly at him. "One more word and what, Lieutenant? One more word and you'll hit me? Now how would that look, an officer striking an enlisted man? How about that, fellas?" he called out for support.

Gilbert's face was unmoved. "Keep it up and you'll see, Private."

"Go ahead, *sir*," he goaded. "Hit me. Hit me. I'll have you thrown in the brig faster than you can spit."

Gilbert reached out and in a flash clutched onto the private's collars and gripped them tight. The army man's face turned bright red. "Now you listen to me, son," he said. "You're a big boy, so I'm going to assume you can understand this. Any time you harass somebody weaker than you are—and that includes this woman—you'd better not be so cowardly as to hide behind your rank when somebody steps in to defend her. It won't always work."

"Let go of my throat, damn it," the private gasped.

"What I'm saying is, private or not, son, if I catch you doing anything like this again, I'll break every bone in your face."

"Gilbert—" Adrian called out.

"Do you understand what I'm saying, Private?" he asked, ignoring Adrian's plea.

He gulped, nodded. "I understand. Now will you let me go? I'm choking."

"You understand?"

"I understand, sir."

Gilbert released his collar, the man grumbled something incoherent and the crowd slowly dissipated.

Adrian looked straight at Gilbert. "Well, are you proud of yourself, Lieutenant?" she said. "Beating up on an enlisted man?"

"I thought you needed help, Adrian," he explained.

"And why should *you* help *me*?" she said angrily. She could have kicked herself the moment the words were said, but it was too late.

"Your mother would never forgive me if I let someone slander you," he said.

She sighed, looked at him silently. She wanted so much to reach out, touch him, hold him, kiss him— but she was afraid he would back away, and then she would have no hope at all. She had to hold her love back, somehow.

After a minute, she said, "Well, thank you, anyway. And you, too, Chick, for keeping him from being killed or court-martialled. He can get very violent."

Gilbert stared at her. She was dressed in army clothes, but he could still see the lovely, sensual curves of her body underneath. Her shirt was stretched tight over her full breasts. They seemed to be straining to be released.

"What are you doing here, anyway, Adrian?" he

asked her. "You're the last person I expected to see in Pusan, South Korea."

"It's very simple, Lieutenant," she said, trying to sound independent. "I'm here to report on this mess for my newspaper."

"That's strange. I would've thought you wouldn't go anywhere near a war."

"Well, you thought wrong," she said flatly.

"Yeah, I guess I did . . . Chick," he said to his friend, "let's go. We've got to meet Corelli in a few minutes." He looked at her. "Good seeing you again, Adrian."

She was piqued at his abrupt leaving. Didn't he care enough to exchange a few words?

"Couldn't you. . . ." Her voice trailed off.

He picked it up. "Couldn't I what?"

She hesitated, swallowed. "Nothing," she said.

He paused, looked at her intently, hoping to see something he could move on. But he didn't see it.

"See you around, Adrian," he said and turned away.

As she was standing there watching him walk toward town, Lieutenant James Metz came next to her. He watched Adrian for a while, then said, "Boyfriend?"

"No," she said, turning toward him. "He's not my boyfriend." She whipped out a handkerchief and brought it to her eyes. "I'm sorry," she apologized. "There must be something in my eye."

He waited a decent interval while she wiped the tears away and straightened up. Then he handed her a copy of the Sacramento *Sun*. "The high command doesn't like this, Miss McAllister," he told her.

"Doesn't like what, Lieutenant?" she said, only half-interested.

"They don't like your Korean reports. They're anti-American."

"They are not," she corrected him. "I may not support this war, but I'm certainly not anti-American. That's ridiculous."

"Ridiculous or not, Miss McAllister, this particular column is definitely anti-American. Read it yourself."

She unfolded the paper. "I haven't even seen one in print yet," she told him.

"Well, I'd suggest you read them all in print, young lady," he advised her. "Or lose the cooperation of the United States Army."

She opened to her column on page two. "On the Front: A Woman's View of Korea," by Adrian McAllister. She scanned the article quickly. It was an account of the reactions of the soldiers in Pusan to General Dean's capture, up in Taejon. The piece was hers all right, but it wasn't the way she wrote it. A few words and phrases had been altered; the tone had been changed. What she remembered as a sympathetic view of a navy ensign's reaction to the news of Dean's heroics in Taejon, his blowing apart North Korean T-34s with new 3.5-inch rocket launchers, had somehow come out to be an exposé of American incompetence. The more of it she read, the more infuriated she became.

By the time she managed to get to a phone in Pusan, she had cooled down some, but the second she heard Wayne's voice at the other end, she was boiling over again.

"Just what do you think you're doing over there,

changing my story?" she admonished him. "Who gave you the right to change what I report?"

"All right, take it easy, Adrian," Wayne said. His voice sounded thin and reedy, as usual.

"*Did* you change this story on Dean?"

"Well, yes I did—if you call fleshing it out changing it. I don't hear half your reports, you know. I've told you that. What do you expect me to do, type up all your little notes and send them over the wire, as is?"

"I expect you not to change them, Wayne. Is that too much to ask?"

"I do what I can with what I have, Adrian. But I can't very well give my editorial approval to sketchy outlines, can I?"

She bit her lip, tried to calm herself. "I'm doing the best I can," she defended herself. "Conditions are terrible here."

"That's the nature of war, Miss McAllister," he commented.

"You're so understanding," she said sarcastically.

"Well, I'll tell you one thing, Adrian. Ed Mallory's not so understanding. He's impatient. He wants some front line stuff. When are you going out to the lines?"

"I'm going out today, as a matter of fact," she blurted out, though it was the first time she had thought of doing it. "Lieutenant Metz is taking me," she added.

"Good," he replied. "I'm glad to hear it."

"I'll be in touch, Wayne," she said coolly.

"Uh, Adrian, Amanda was in here today. She wanted me to ask you about her brother."

"That doesn't surprise me much," she said. "She

wants to know if I'm over here seducing him, right? Poor, defenseless Gilly."

"Are you?"

"No, I'm not. I saw him on the dock a few minutes ago, but then he left. Amanda will be happy to know that's all that happened."

"I'll tell her."

"Good. And please, Wayne, don't change my reports . . ."

"Anything you want, Adrian," he said. "Just get out on the lines."

"I'll have a story from the Pusan perimeter tomorrow," she told him flatly. "Tell Amanda *that,* if she's interested."

Adrian learned from Lieutenant Metz the next day that she was now in the only part of South Korea not occupied by the enemy. The Eighth Army was holding the area south and east of the Naktong River by a line of troops along its banks, so the entrance to Pusan appeared secure for the moment.

She managed to get Metz to take her up to the lines because he believed that the area was safe now that the marines had landed. Even the mayor of Pusan had proclaimed to all, when he saw the marine ships coming, "The panic will leave my people now."

But as Metz's army jeep rocked along the rough road to Taegu that afternoon Adrian began to feel vaguely uncomfortable, as if they were being watched. Once she even had Metz stop the jeep and shut off the engine to listen for another vehicle. Listening, looking around, they recognized no evidence of any hostile troops, but somehow she believed they were there, observing their every move.

Then, thirty miles out of Pusan, on the road before them, they saw a jeep that had turned over on
its side.

"I don't like the looks of that," Metz said, slowing
down. "We'd better go back."

"No," she told him, straining to see what they were
doing. "Keep going. We may be able to help."

He nodded, reluctantly pressed on a few hundred
more feet, then stomped the brake. The instant the
jeep skidded, Adrian realized what was ahead of
them. The wrecked jeep was American; lying dead
on the ground were the bodies of its occupants. The
bodies had been stripped of their jewelry and their
insignia, their boots had been removed by a squad
of North Korean soldiers.

"Oh, God," Metz moaned, whipping the steering
wheel around.

Adrian could feel, somehow, the pressence of rifles
leveled at the back of her head. Instantly she knew
they didn't have a chance. Even the worst marksmen
in Korea could hit them at this distance. She could
do nothing about it, though; she closed her eyes and
trembled, and waited to hear the terrible sounds of the
rifles behind her.

But when the shots rang out, they were from another direction. Two, three, four quick sharp cracks
punctuated the damp air. She wheeled around to see
in front of her four dead Koreans in bloody lumps
on the ground and two others groaning loudly, holding their hands high in the air. Off to the right, a
squad of marines approached, each man with a gun
out in front of his chest.

She relaxed her body, heaved a sigh as a young
sergeant walked toward the jeep. "Lieutenant," he

acknowledged Metz, then touched his fingers to his helmet and uttered a guarded "ma'am" to her. "You folks ought not be out here, you know," he warned them. "We've got a few of these guys around here."

"Thank you, Sergeant," Metz said. "We didn't know that."

The marine sergeant watched the other men in his squad make sure the North Koreans were dead. Then he looked back at her. "I'll bet you're Miss McAllister," he said. "The whole line's buzzing about you. They say you're Lieutenant Bell's girl."

"I'm nobody's girl, Sergeant," she informed him. "But we thank you for saving our lives. We were careless. We won't be again."

"Yes, ma'am, you were careless. That's a fact. If I were you, I'd wait a while before coming out here again. It ain't possible for us to patrol every inch of ground out here."

"Thank you, Sergeant," Metz said stiffly. Then he moved the jeep around to face south.

"Nothing to it," the marine said. "Glad to help a lady in distress." As Metz pulled off, he called out to Adrian, "I'll tell the lieutenant we saw you."

Adrian was so tense that she didn't even react to her close call with death until that night in her room in Pusan. Since the fall of Seoul, Pusan had become a place of refuge for thousands of South Koreans. It was crammed with people; outside the city the bare hills were speckled with hundreds of dark wood lean-tos, discarded army tents, and flimsy, temporary shacks. The population had swollen by the thousands in a matter of weeks.

In all this confusion Adrian had been assigned to an apartment above the house of Yang Sin, a merchant who had run a shipping service from Pusan to Shimonoseki, Japan, for most of his life. During the three days she had been in Pusan, her rooms had become nothing more than a place to sleep; now, though, six hours after her frightening encounter with the enemy, they were a sanctuary.

For an hour she sat quietly on the bed, stared out the window to the gloomy wet streets. Nothing could calm her, not making tea, or writing or pacing the floor. For the moment she had lost control of her emotions. Her palms were wet with perspiration, her forehead was cool, her cheeks were burning as if with a fever. For the first time in her life she was really scared.

She went to bed early, but she couldn't sleep. She kept feeling those rifles behind her, pointed at the back of her head. . . .

At about eleven o'clock, she heard a noise, a bumping sound downstairs. Startled, she raised up in the bed, listened intently for a few minutes, but she detected nothing but the rumbling sounds of people outside her window. Then, as soon as she eased back down, she heard footsteps clicking up the stairs toward her door.

She jumped up out of bed, threw her robe over her thin nightgown, and backed up against the wall. She knew it was irrational, but she was terrified that the North Korean soldiers she had seen on the road had escaped somehow and come to take out their brutal revenge on her.

Then came a knock—three firm, solid raps on the thin door.

"Mr. Sin?" she called out hopefully, but got no answer. She swallowed hard. "Mr. Sin—is that you?"

"Adrian?" came back a male voice.

Her heart seemed to leap up into her throat at the sound of Gilbert's smooth, comforting voice. Instinctively, she hurried across the room and snapped the door open. It was almost like a dream, seeing him standing there.

"Good evening," he said. He was poised at the top of the stairs, holding his helmet and carbine by the straps.

"I . . . don't know what to say," she stammered.

"You could say 'Come in.'"

"Oh," she caught herself, "do, please."

"Thank you," he said, coming in, looking about the room. It was bare, a bed, a table and chairs, a dresser and mirror, and Adrian's suitcase open on a thatched basket. "Mr. Sin downstairs said it would be all right to come up," he said.

"Mr. Sin thinks all Americans are kin to each other," she told him.

He smiled, laid his rifle and helmet on the table and peeled off his jacket. When he looked at her, she unconsciously pulled the collar of her robe together at the throat. "You're amazing, Adrian," he complimented her. "You're right at home here, aren't you? You seem to be able to fit in anywhere."

"Oh no," she said nervously. "It's not like that at all. I may as well be on another planet. Everyone in Pusan is so polite, but they don't understand a word I say . . . Would you like some tea?" she said nervously, abruptly changing the subject.

"No. Thank you," he answered calmly.

She crossed her arms. "We're very polite, aren't we?" she observed. "For two people . . ." She let the sentence hang.

"Adrian," he began, changing his voice. "You know that was dumb, don't you? Coming out on the road today. You could've been killed."

She looked at him closely. In the dim room, lit only by the lamp next to her bed and the moonlight outside her open window, he looked mysterious and romantic. The cold fear that had seized her body earlier was seeping away now; she was beginning to feel warm again. "Yes," she responded, "you're right. I admit it. It was dumb. But then so is being in Korea to begin with, isn't it?"

"Why are you in Korea, Adrian?" he asked. "Ever since I saw you on the dock, I've been worrying about you."

"I'm flattered," she said, laughing lightly. "I didn't think you ever thought about me."

"Oh, Adrian," he said, coming closer. "I never stop thinking about you."

"Gil—"

"No," he said, taking her wrist. "Don't turn away from me. I let you do that once before. I'm not going to do it again."

His fingers seemed to burn into her flesh. She wanted so much for him to take her into his arms, protect her, keep her from trembling. "Gil," she said sadly. "Don't do this. Please."

He brought her close. "When I saw you being ogled by all those men the other day, I almost went crazy," he confessed. "I had to come here tonight."

"Oh, Gil—"

"Adrian. God I want you," he said softly, squeezing her against him.

They kissed, slowly, tentatively at first. Then, as

their bodies began to surge with desire, the kisses became passionate, almost frantic. They couldn't shed their clothes fast enough.

"God, you're beautiful," he said, backing away and looking at her naked body. He reached out and caressed her breasts tenderly, kissed her again, and eased her down to the bed.

"Gil," she said softly, touching his face. "I love you so much. I've never loved any man but you."

He laid her back, touched her breasts with his rough, unshaven face as he ran his strong fingers over her stomach and thighs, down to the dark area between her legs.

She smelled the dried mud and grass clinging to his body, but even that tantalized her, as he moved his fingers about, making her ready to receive him.

"Oh, Gil," she moaned. "Why were we ever apart? I love you so much."

"You're so exciting, Adrian," he said, moving on top of her, and then into her. "It's incredible how exciting you are."

They made love as they had kissed before, slowly at first, then more and more rapidly, building their passions up to a feverish pitch until both of their bodies exploded with pleasure and they collapsed together, wrapped tightly in each other's arms.

A while later, as they lay on their backs in bed in the warm room, she said in a low voice, "Gil? Do you love me?"

"Yes," he replied without hesitation. "Of course I love you. I love you, and your body. It's the greatest body God ever gave a woman."

"I'm serious, Gil."

"So am I," he said. He didn't want to hurt her feelings, but he wasn't sure of his own yet, not completely.

She raised up on her elbow and looked at him. "Then come away with me," she said, playing with his dog tags.

"Anywhere you say, love," he replied lightly. "Where to? Paris? Rome?"

"I mean it, Gil. We're crazy to be here, risking our lives for no good reason. This isn't our war."

He stirred uncomfortably, then sat up. "Don't talk like that, Adrian," he said. "You know I have to be here. You may not, but I do."

"But you don't. Don't you see? What good is doing your duty if you're killed doing it? I came close to being killed this afternoon. It was terrifying, Gil. It happened so fast! It could happen to you, and then where would I be? I've never loved anybody but you. I couldn't live without you."

He got up off the bed, began putting on his trousers. "I've got to go, Adrian," he said. "I'm AWOL as it is. I'd better get back before I'm missed."

She sat up. "You haven't heard a word I said, have you?"

He turned, looked at her. "I hear the words," he said sternly. "But I don't want to hear them again. What you're saying is treason. I don't like it."

"It's not treason to have your own life, Gilbert," she declared.

He slipped his undershirt over his head. "I came here to fight a war, Adrian," he said. "Not to run off and hide behind your skirts."

"But it's not your war," she said calmly. She wanted to scream it.

"It is my war, Adrian," he said, grabbing his shirt and jacket. "And yours."

"Gil—" she called out to him as he scooped up his other gear and made his way toward the door. "I'm sorry. I didn't mean it. I was just talking."

"Well, that kind of talk bothers me, Adrian," he said. "I don't want to hear it."

"Gil—" she called out, but he was gone. A minute later, she got to her feet and walked naked over to the door and fastened the lock. "Damn it," she murmured softly, leaning her head against the facing. "What am I doing?"

She listened to his footsteps down the stairs, then rushed over to the window to see if she could spot him on the street. But he wasn't there. No one was there. Lieutenant Gilbert Bell had gone as quickly as he had come.

The next morning it all seemed like a dream.

6

Adrian's and Wayne's temporary office quarters in Japan were located on the second floor of an office building in the Marunouchi district, in the heart of Tokyo. It was a new structure, part of the massive post-war rebuilding effort conducted by prominent Tokyo businessmen. The two rooms had been assigned to them by the American consul general the day they arrived in Tokyo.

Early one morning, three days after Adrian left Pusan, she was standing at the window, gazing absently out across the moat at the Imperial Palace, when a young woman stormed brusquely into the room without knocking.

Adrian braced herself. She knew the shapely woman stylishly dressed in a tan European-tailored suit very well: it was Amanda, Gilbert's sister. She was tall and attractive, like most of his family, but unlike most Bell women, she was unattached. Adrian had never known her to be romantically involved with a man; in fact, she seemed to ignore men altogether.

"Good morning," Adrian said cheerfully. "How are you, Amanda?"

The other woman's face was rigid. "Just what do you think you're trying to accomplish, Adrian?" she said accusingly. "Are you trying to get him killed, chasing after him all over the world this way?"

"Why don't you sit down and tell me what you're talking about, Amanda?"

"I'm not going to even try to be civil with you, Adrian," she said dourly. "I think you and I are beyond that, aren't we?"

"Yes." Adrian sat down behind her desk. "I think we are. Ever since you led me to San Francisco harbor just so I would *happen* to see Gilbert put Lin Su on a boat for China."

"Well, Adrian, I thought if you saw them together, maybe you'd begin to see the light," Amanda said staunchly. "Obviously I was wrong. You're still running around all over Asia, trying to hang onto him."

"I'm not trying to 'hang onto him,' Amanda. Gilbert Bell is not somebody a woman can hang onto. Not even a sister."

"Don't try to throw it back on me, Adrian. I know what happened at Pusan. I know you saw him."

"How would you know that?" Adrian asked, surprised.

"I have . . . sources," she said haltingly.

"Your sources consist of one Wayne Hunter, don't they?" Adrian quickly guessed. "He's been telling you everything I've been doing, hasn't he?"

Amanda paused a minute, then said, "It doesn't matter in the slightest where I get my information, Adrian —I get it. All I want to say to you is, leave him *alone*. He needs a clear head out there. He's only a man; if you go swishing your hips around him, you'll probably manage to get him into bed with you, but you'll also manage to get him killed."

"You don't give your brother much credit, Amanda. And you might remember, he is your brother. Not your son. Or your husband."

Amanda glared at her. "And just what is that supposed to mean?"

"It means leave him alone yourself, Amanda. The man is a free agent, he's not your personal property. He doesn't belong to me or to you. So why don't we both let him alone?"

"He doesn't want you," Amanda said coldly. "I should think that would be obvious. He just wants to sleep with you."

"I don't know about that, Amanda. All I can know is how *I* feel. And I love him. All right?"

"If you really love him, you'll go home and leave him alone." Amanda slipped into a pleading voice. "He gets crazy around you, Adrian. He always has. You're no good for him."

"You don't think any woman's good for him, do you? Every time he's been interested in someone, you've turned him against her."

"That's a lie."

"Is it? Isn't that what you're trying to do now?"

"I'm trying to save his life, Adrian," she declared, bearing down on the pronunciation of her name. "And I'm going to continue to do that, whether you stay here or not. But you'd help him if you went back to Sacramento and did your 'reporting' there."

"I'm not going anywhere," Adrian stated flatly. "I'm willing to be friends if you want me to, or I'm willing to continue being enemies. Either way, I'm staying."

"Well, we'll see about that, won't we?" Amanda said, and left the room as abruptly as she had entered it.

Adrian blew a heavy sigh of relief when the door slammed behind her. It was as if a tornado had touched down and then left. She almost looked around the room to see what had been damaged.

An hour or so later she had to leave her desk to answer the phone in Wayne's office. He hadn't been around much since she got back from Pusan, but she didn't particularly mind that. She always felt uncomfortable around him.

As she was waiting for the overseas operator to put through the call, she noticed a note on Wayne's desk with the previous day's date on it. "Adrian: General Stoddard wants to pick you up for lunch tomorrow: one o'clock." It was odd that he hadn't mentioned that; but then, now that she thought about it, Wayne had become more and more strained over the past few months. She wondered what could be happening to him—

"Adrian?" a voice came over the phone.

"Ed?" she spoke out, recognizing the editor's voice. "How are you?"

"Don't you how-are-you me, Miss McAllister. Tell me something: do you actually read these things you send in?"

She was puzzled. "What do you mean, read them? Of course I do."

"I'm sorry to hear it, because they're *bad*, McAllister. Bad journalism. We've got people all over us about these reports. We're losing readers. A hundred more went over to the *Bee* yesterday."

"I don't understand," she said, alarmed. "What's so bad about them? That's the way it is over here."

His voice was hard, insistent. "There's a big difference between calling the UN forces 'unprepared' and calling them 'incompetent'—"

"You're talking about my second piece, Ed. Wayne and I straightened that out."

"All right, then, let's talk about your last one. Tell me about this company of army men that can't trust their commanding officers."

"What?"

"I'm looking at it right here, Adrian. This kind of stuff creates low morale back here. It's bad. I can't trust you anymore; and if you think I'm here to rewrite everything you write, you're crazy."

"You don't have to rewrite anything," she said, thinking of Wayne. She knew he was responsible. For whatever reason, he was wrecking her career by altering her reports. "I'll straighten it out," she promised.

"You do that, Adrian. This paper all of a sudden has a reputation of being un-American, and I don't like it. Neither does Sacramento. I don't have to tell you we can't stay in business with that kind of press."

"I'll get back to you, Ed."

"You'd better shape up, Adrian, or I swear I'll have you back in Sacramento so fast your ears will pop."

There was nothing to do for a while, until lunch. She listened to a Tokyo radio station, but she couldn't use any of the information being reported. She heard that the marines had destroyed the Fourth Division of the North Korean army, that a marine underwater demolition team had slipped off the U.S.S. *Horace A. Bass* and blown up a line of bridges and tunnels on the east coast of Korea. For a moment, the war seemed well in hand.

Then she heard the announcer declare that, with the enemy pushing down against the Pusan perimeter north of Taegu, the Eighth Army and First Marines would probably bow out and retreat to Pusan. "We can only wait and see," he said.

She saw nothing to write on. The war was holding.

Precisely at one o'clock, General Lucius Stoddard knocked on the door of her office; at two they had finished eating at a restaurant a few blocks away; at two-fifteen, he was walking back to her office building with her. They paused near the moat and he explained to her that where her office was now situated was once the location of the homes of the Japanese feudal lords, the *diamyō*. Their residence, he told her, formed the *marunouchi*, the inner circle, which was the current name of the district.

She listened to these historical facts and others like them attentively, as she had listened to him throughout their meal together, but all the while she wondered what he was up to. Although he hadn't been forward with her, he had fenced with her, asked a number of indirect questions about Gilbert and her relation to him. At times she even felt she was being interrogated, however gently and skillfully.

"General," she said when there was a pause. "Would you tell me something?"

"I'll try," Stoddard answered, smiling at her. "What do you want to know?"

"I'd like to know why you've been pumping me for information for the past hour." Her voice wasn't accusing; it was tentative.

"Have I been doing that?" he said evasively.

"You know very well you have. You've asked me a hundred questions about Gilbert, and fifty about China."

Stoddard colored. "I didn't mean for you to put those things together, Adrian," he said. "All I was doing was making conversation—you know, talking about someone we have in common." He took out a pack of cigarettes, offered her one. When she declined, he put them back into his pocket.

"You're in Tokyo for some reason," she speculated. "What could it be? Could it have anything to do with Admiral Sherman, Chief of Naval Operations, Major Smith, General Collins, Army Chief of Staff, Admiral Doyle . . ."

Stoddard's face grew suddenly pale. "How did you know about . . ." He was astonished that he couldn't finish the question.

"I heard it on the radio," she said. "A couple of hours ago."

"The radio!" he exclaimed, astounded. "What kind of security does MacArthur have around here, anyway?"

"I assume there was a meeting. What was it about, General Stoddard?" she pressed. "Is MacArthur stepping up the effort? Are we pulling out? What?"

He waited a while to answer. Then, after some consideration, he said to her, "I want you to go home, Adrian. Back to Sacramento. Would you do that for me?"

"No! I've told two people today already, I'm not going home. Why should I?"

He hesitated, then went on. "You and Lieutenant Bell were . . . together in Pusan, weren't you?"

"I don't think that's any of your business, General," she said, offended.

"Well, never mind admitting it, Adrian. I know it for a fact. I have Lieutenant Bell watched everywhere he goes."

"Watched? Why? What's he done?"

"I'm not sure he's done anything, Adrian. That's why I'm talking to you. I have to know if he revealed to you any . . . confidential information while you were together. I'm sorry I can't be any clearer than that, but if he said anything at all about . . ."

"One doesn't talk much about war in situations like that, General Stoddard," she said.

His face showed embarrassment. "Okay," he said, "I believe you. He told you nothing. Only he knows. Which means I can give you a choice. You can either go home, or you can—" He stopped.

"Can what?" she prompted him.

"Follow him. I can't use my own men to spy for me anymore; they're getting suspicious. But I can use you. He knows you, he'll let you get close. You can find out if he's revealed anything to anyone, or, if he's captured—"

"General, damn it—what could he reveal to anyone? Tell me!"

He stalled a minute, then said, "I can't tell you Adrian. I can tell you, though, that Lieutenant Bell possesses information that could make this war explode in our faces. It could mean millions of lives. He probably doesn't know how important a man he is right now. If the Chinese Communists ever get hold of him . . . but thank God they're not in this thing."

Adrian was confused, angry, apprehensive. All of a sudden the man she loved was a walking bomb and she had been assigned to monitor him! She didn't know whether to do it, or run to Gilbert.

"I'm sorry, General," she said finally. "I just can't tell how serious you are about this."

They began to amble toward the office building. After a few minutes of reflection, Stoddard said to her, "All right. I'm serious enough to tell you what went on in that meeting. I'll tell you about Operation Chromite—if you'll keep it to yourself."

"What's Operation Chromite?" she asked excitedly.

"It's one hell of a plan, Adrian. It's risky, but MacArthur says it's possible. If it works, it could turn the tide for us. If you'll do what I asked you to do, I'll see to it you're put right in the thick of what may turn out to be the greatest story in the war."

She was hesitant. "If I keep my eye on Gilbert?"

"Just watch him."

"You're tantalizing me, General," she said.

He smiled. "I know I am, Adrian."

As they mounted the steps to the building, Adrian stopped, looked over at two men walking to the north of them.

"Is that Wayne Hunter?" Stoddard said. "The man who works with you?"

She nodded. "You have a sharp eye, General," she remarked.

"Who's the man with him?" he inquired.

Adrian squinted against the sun. "I have no idea. I've never seen him before."

"He looks familiar," Stoddard commented as they approached the doors.

Upstairs, Stoddard stood stiffly in her office in front of a world map on the wall and waited for her to make up her mind. He looked strong and capable, standing almost at parade rest, in his dress uniform, examining the features of the map.

Finally, she walked over and stood next to him. "Well, what'll it be?" he asked her.

She looked at the map. "Tell me where it happens."

7

ADRIAN'S ORDERS came to her folded neatly in a brown manila envelope, delivered by messenger two weeks later. Attached to the official-looking document inside was a note in Stoddard's hand. "Adrian. Your transport (the *Cavalier*—see attached First Marine Division Embarkation Order 1-50, 31 August 1950 for description of supplies) will leave Pusan on 11 September. I have alerted Capt. Daniel Sweeney of the *Cavalier*. He knows who you are. Good luck. B.G. Lucius Stoddard, USMC."

She caught a C-54 transport plane to Pusan on the tenth, paid a short visit to Yang Sin, then walked around the docks for a while. The air was crackling with excitement. She could feel it charging through her body. Soon the harbor would be stuffed with transport ships loading up for the move around the peninsula and up the western coast to Inchon. It had already started, in fact. The military population of Pusan was swelling by the minute.

One of the arrivals was someone she half-expected: Lieutenant James Metz. He appeared at her side as if he had just materialized out of the air. "Ma'am," he acknowledged her, touching the rim of his helmet.

"Lieutenant," she said, smiling in spite of herself. "And here I was afraid I'd miss you."

"No, ma'am," he said. "General MacArthur himself gave me orders to stay with you."

"Does that mean you're going to Inchon?" she said, surprised.

"If they go," he said, gazing up at the sky. "I hear there's a typhoon expected here tomorrow."

"Oh, I imagine they'll go, Lieutenant, after all this planning and trouble."

"May I see your orders?" he asked politely.

She unbuttoned a breast pocket and brought out the folded papers. "I'm supposed to hitch a ride on the *Cavalier*," she told him.

He perused her papers. "The *Cavalier*'s anchored down that way," he said, gesturing with his head. Then, with a move that was unusually assertive for him, Metz pressed his hand against the small of her back and pushed her gently in the right direction. She couldn't help but smile when he left it there longer than was necessary.

On board the *Cavalier*, they were shown to the captain's cabin. Captain Daniel Sweeney dutifully checked their orders and looked curiously at Adrian. "Miss McAllister," he said, "you know of course you'll be the only woman aboard a vessel filled with men."

"I won't mind if they won't."

"Yes, well, what I mean is, it will take us four days to reach Inchon. Most of that time you'll be thrown together with the enlisted men, since I have my own duties to attend to and can't look after you."

"That's my job, Captain Sweeney," Metz reminded him.

But Sweeney's eyes were locked on Adrian. "You'll eat standing up," he went on, "sleep in a corner somewhere—though I don't know, we may be able to come up with a cabin or something of the sort for you. There won't be any entertainment, you'll have to handle the looks and stares from the men yourself—"

"Captain Sweeney," she interrupted, "I think I'll be able to survive four days all right."

"And if you get sick," he went on, "you get sick. Only God and General MacArthur can turn this vessel around once it's headed toward Inchon."

"I understand that," she assured him.

"Good. Now if you'll excuse me, I'll get back to my work."

Adrian surprised herself the next four days on the transport: she found Lieutenant Metz to be agreeable company. His attitude was still that of a lioness protecting a cub, but as the harsh reality of the mission became clearer and clearer in her mind, she began to find that comforting.

The other men on the ship were strangely indifferent to her. For the first time in her life, she wasn't stared at and attended to by the men around her. They were calm enough, none of them seemed out of control, and none of them had the look of horror she had seen on the ROK soldiers leaving Seoul. And yet there was a kind of dread evident in their eyes. It preoccupied them. It made them react to her as if she were one of them . Or worse—as if she were nothing at all.

On the evening of September 14, Sweeney called her and Metz into his cabin to explain what was going to happen beginning at dawn the next day. He stood with a pointer in front of a map of Korea. "I'll try to make this as clear as possible," he said. "Your lives may depend on it." He struck the points on the map. "At dawn tomorrow, marines will attack and secure Wolmi Island and provide a cover for the other landings. The transports will stay out in the Yellow Sea while the cruisers and aircraft carriers and amtracks move in to 'Red Beach' to the north, here, and 'Blue Beach' to the south, here."

"That will give us control of the tidal basin," Adrian said.

He looked at her with surprised interest, then said formally, "That's correct. We'll have a way to move our cargo in for internal fighting at Seoul. Our biggest advantage is surprise. Since the tides rise and fall thirty feet, we'll have only four hours to get in. Otherwise we're stuck in mud flats. The North Koreans won't be expecting anything this bold, so we may get away with it. If our timing's right."

"When do we go in?" Adrian asked.

"I suggest you stay on the *Cavalier*, Miss McAllister," he said seriously. "You can watch the landing from here."

"I can *watch* it on Movietone news later," she reminded him. "I'm here to report it."

"All right," he said, shrugging his shoulders. "I know better than to argue with a reporter. We'll call you when it's time."

Later that night she heard the naval warships pummeling the shoreline in the distance. The deep, heavy booms of the big guns grew louder as the *Cavalier* inched slowly toward the rendezvous point in the Yellow Sea. Out in the darkness she could hear the roar of another transport, or a cruiser, invisibly cutting its way through the choppy water, toward Inchon.

Few of the men slept that night. They went through the motions, but their eyes were open, their bodies too tense to allow them any sleep.

When they reached the rendezvous point several miles off the coast, the distant rumble of the naval guns had ceased. The sixty war ships firing away at the shore were silent, their guns drawn in and waiting for the operation to commence.

Adrian stood looking out to the east, as the sun began slowly to brighten the sky over Inchon, and beyond that, Seoul. Gradually the huge metal objects around her became visible and only then did she realize the magnitude of the invasion. The sea was filled with nearly three hundred ships. Guns were ready to resume their pounding the beaches, marine Corsairs were high in the heavens, ready to strafe the beaches.

Adrian wrapped her arms around her breasts. "I'm scared, Lieutenant," she said. "Look at me, I'm shaking."

Metz nodded, said nothing. He looked calm; she wondered if he was scared, too. Did everyone feel the icy grip of fear that was holding her now?

Soon the word came over the radio that Wolmi Island had been taken by the marines. There was no turning back now. The landing was on. But the tide was out, and in its place was nothing but a sea of mud. They had to wait for the afternoon tide to go in.

The delay was excruciating for her. All around her marines talked, smoked, ate candy bars, joked about the peculiarities of the men or other services. But still on their faces, in their eyes, she could detect the tense, cold fear of death. All morning she kept seeing Gilbert in her mind, first standing at her door in Pusan, then lying in a pool of blood on the Inchon beach. She knew he too would be calm, confident-looking. Would she, she wondered, ever see him again?

Then the tide began to move in. Shortly after three o'clock, the small landing crafts were briskly lowered to the rocky sea and the marines began spilling into them. "This is it, Miss McAllister," Lieutenant Metz said as they moved closer to the edge of the deck, awaiting their turn.

"Will you please call me Adrian," she asked, watching a Corsair pass over.

"Yes, ma'am."

"All right, you guys," a sergeant yelled out. "All assault waves on the beaches by six-thirty. You hear me? If we gum it up, those LSTs will be stuck in those mud flats like sitting ducks."

No one bothered to help her into the landing craft. Drawing a deep breath for courage, she crawled down the cargo nets and on the side of the ship, and dropped like a stone down into a mass of hard marines. One of them, a corporal, caught her. But as soon as he realized he had clutched one of her breasts in the process, he snapped back his hands. "Sorry, ma'am," he apologized in a Southern accent. "I didn't mean to . . ."

Metz was jumping down now. He hit the deck, found his balance and straightened his helmet. "Don't get lost, Miss McAllister," he called out to her.

Lost. How could she get lost on a boat with forty

men? "I wondered if you were coming," she said to him as he made his way toward her.

"You're my responsibility," he declared.

She took a deep breath, nodded, and took his hand and squeezed it gratefully. "I'm glad you're here, Lieutenant."

He lowered his eyes, puffed up a little in embarrassment.

While guns blew away at the beaches, the landing craft met with the other boats in its particular assault wave. Since the tide was rapidly reaching its peak, it was nearing time to hit the shore.

Suddenly the naval guns tapered off, then stopped completely. Adrian looked around her, stunned by the spectacle of seventy thousand men concentrating their minds and bodies to one gigantic effort. She was awed by the power of General Douglas MacArthur, who stood poised like a statue on the bridge of the flagship, giving an order that would silence a hundred 16-inch guns.

The tense quiet seemed unreal, somehow, as if someone had shut off the sound in a movie. Then she heard a low, dull groan of engines somewhere in the skies. As it grew louder, a few men began looking up, straining to see through the gathering clouds.

"Here they come, boys," the sergeant announced. "That's a Corsair, I'd know that sound anywhere."

All eyes in the boat turned to the sky, which seemed to be filled, all of a sudden, with marine planes. Adrian couldn't explain it, but when she saw the many formations of Corsairs majestically roaring in over their heads, she felt chills. And when they commenced dropping their bombs over the Inchon beaches, her whole body trembled, and she wanted to cry.

But there was no time for that. Soon the planes were circling back toward the Yellow Sea and the assault was on.

"All right, let's do it!" someone yelled out.

The men steadied themselves as the landing craft, abreast with five others, surged ahead, through the channel, around the pulverized Wolmi Island, through the destroyers and cruisers and amtracks, toward the beach.

When the huge stone sea walls along the beach came into view, Adrian felt a surge of panic rising in her. What, she wondered, lay behind those walls? Would they be mowed down by North Koreans when they plunged over?

But the landing was so abrupt, she didn't have time to consider turning back. Out into two feet of water jumped the marines, weighted down by shovels, packs, and rifles. Without a word they rushed ahead, dug into the beach in front of the sea wall.

"Come on!" a lieutenant yelled from the beach. "Bring those ladders!"

Adrian found herself knee-deep in the surf, stumbling next to two marines carrying ladders with hooks on the ends on their backs. Then her feet were on dry ground in front of the stone wall.

Up went the ladders and instantly a hundred soldiers began pouring over the wall, ducking whizzing bullets and grenade shrapnel as they hit the ground on the other side. "All right, you guys," she heard someone say behind the wall, a few minutes later, "bring it on. Bring it on."

In the confusion of clearing the sea wall, Adrian lost touch with Lieutenant Metz. Even with the beach being stormed by thousands of men now, she felt alone.

"Get down!" someone shouted at her. "Get your ass down!"

She hit the ground, lay on her belly as soldiers rushed past, firing their M-1s and BARs at targets she couldn't even see. Behind them, on the other side of the wall, the great LSTs were pulling in with their loading ramps down, ready to spew out the heavy back-up artillery and vehicles.

Minutes later a grenade exploded nearby and she scrambled to her feet and ran. Then, in front of her, a handful of men were exchanging fire with a squad of North Korean soldiers. A tracer bullet shot over her head and she dived down again.

Only then did she realize the sun was setting. The beach was bathed in a warm, glowing orange light. The sun setting behind her cast moving shadows on the ground as the assaults pushed ahead. She closed her eyes and breathed deeply, her face pressed hard against the rough sand.

All around her, boots were crunching down into the beach. She had her courage back now. She sprang up and raced forward. Twenty yards in, she saw a young marine on the ground, writhing in pain. She dropped down next to him.

"Corporal?" she said. She recognized him as the boy who had accidentally grabbed her breast as she was boarding the landing craft. She flipped off his helmet, touched his face with her fingers, then saw the wound in his chest. It was open; blood was spurting out in streams. Instinctively she placed her hand on the blood vessels and held the blood back.

"Ma'am?" the soldier said. "I'm sorry about . . . you know."

"Oh for God's sake, Corporal," she said, almost in tears.

"I didn't mean to . . ."

"Medic!" she screamed. "Medic!"

But it was too late; the blood had stopped pumping. He was dead.

In a daze she wiped the blood off her hands and tried to stuff her hair back into her cap. Anything to be *doing* something. This was the first man she had ever seen die—and he had died with her hand on his exposed heart.

"How is he?" the medic asked, kneeling down beside them.

"He's dead."

"Then leave him. We'll get him later."

She nodded, let him take her arm. "Come on," he said, "it's safer if you keep moving. They're everywhere."

For the next fifteen minutes, the enemy fire began to dissipate; by the time it was completely dark, a marine sergeant proclaimed the place "secure as it'll ever be," and the fighting stopped.

She found respite near a jeep, in range of a squad of soldiers gathered near a lantern, eating C rations and smoking cigarettes. The place was quiet, but there was a war still raging inside her head. Images of guns, planes, bombs, and the Southern corporal flashed again and again before her eyes until she began to shudder all over.

A while later she relaxed a little when she saw Lieutenant Metz. He was a stuffy and officious man who seemed to have very little use for women, but she was beginning to like him anyway. There was a kind of loyalty about him she could respond to.

"I've looked all over for you," he said, plopping down beside her. "I told you not to get lost."

"I'm not lost, Metz," she said quietly, "I'm just kind of sick to my stomach. Why do people have to fight wars, anyway? It makes no sense, shooting at each other, one innocent man trying to kill another—getting paid to kill another. It's sick."

"Sometimes you have to fight, Miss McAllister."

"Adrian," she corrected him. She brought her knees up to her chest, thought about the corporal—and Gilbert. "I hope that's not true," she said thoughtfully.

"Are you ready to go?" he asked after a while.

"Go back?" she asked, then shook her head. "No. I'm not."

"General MacArthur wants you to return to a navy medical ship and wait there until he comes ashore."

"When will that be?"

"Two or three days. When the marines take Seoul."

"I want to wait here."

"The other correspondents will be phoning in their stories from the medical ships," he told her. "If you wait for General MacArthur, your report will probably be the last one in."

She smiled. "Wouldn't Ed Mallory hate that?" she said. "I can hear him now. 'I send you into the thick of the battle and you get your story in three days after everybody else. What do you mean, wasting the *Sun*'s money like that!"

Metz was impatient. "Miss McAllister, you can't stay here. There are no bunks, no proper sleeping facilities—"

"No bathrooms."

"That's right, no bathrooms. And no showers or hot food or anything a woman needs. I suggest the medical ship. It'll be more comfortable for you."

"I'm staying, Metz," she said firmly. "I want to go with them to Seoul. There's someone I want to see there."

"Oh come on, Adrian," he pleaded, forgetting himself.

"You go on, Metz. I'll stay here. I'll be all right. Really. I just want to make sure a certain marine lieutenant is all right."

"Is that all you want? Just to know that?"

"That's all. I don't want to stay out here any more than you do. It's going to rain."

Metz sighed, looked at her, and smiled grimly. "All right, who is he?" he asked. "I'll see if I can find out anything."

"His name is Bell. Lieutenant Gilbert Bell. He was with the First Provisional Marine Brigade down at Pusan."

"They've joined the First Marines now," he said. "Under Major General O.P. Smith. They were moving through Inchon a while ago. I'll get on the radio and find out what's happened to them."

She had to wait nearly an hour for him to return. During that time not one person spoke to her. Every soldier she saw looked like a phantom moving about in the dark. She wondered how anyone ever knew who to shoot in such conditions.

Finally Metz came back with the information. "The First Marines are out of Inchon and moving along the railroad into Seoul. They expect to be in Yongdungpo in a few days."

"What about Lieutenant Bell?"

"Alive and well, according to the radio man. And he claimed to be looking right at him."

She heaved a sigh of relief. "Thank God," she said, rising. She found her legs wobbly when she stood, but she didn't say anything. They walked on past the men playing cards around the lantern and made their way back across the conquered beach.

Three days later, near the main highway west of Yongdungpo, a suburb of Seoul, Gilbert Bell lay crouched in a gully with the rest of his command, surrounded by North Korean soldiers. The radio man, Banner, hurried up, dived into the trench as a spray of bullets swept over their heads.

"Did you get through?" Gilbert asked.

"Yes, sir," Banner replied. "I got through. The Fifth has taken Kimpo Airfield. They're moving across the river now."

"That means they'll be hitting Seoul soon. What about the army regiment?"

"They should hit the city from the south, the same time the Fifth comes in from the north."

They ducked as mortar projectiles scorched a path in the air over their heads and exploded twenty yards behind them. "That means we've got to get past Yongdungpo right now," Bell told him. "How's the captain?"

"He's pretty bad, Lieutenant. He's lost a lot of blood."

Bell pulled his helmet down low. "Stay here, Branner," he ordered, then crawled carefully back through the trench to where Captain Marshall lay on his side, curled over in pain from two bullets in his lower abdomen. Bell knelt down beside him. "Sir," he said, "we're going to have to get out of here. We can't stay pinned down like this forever. Their mortars are getting closer."

"I can't move, Gil," Marshall grunted.

"You've got to, sir."

"All right. I'll tell you what. Just leave somebody here with me and move the company out with the rest of the division."

"I can't do that, Captain."

"Why the hell can't you?" Marshall growled, then grunted in pain.

"They've isolated us here. We're cut off. Let me take a BAR man and cut in behind their lines. We can knock them out before they know what hit them."

Marshall grimaced in pain. "Okay—do it. Take what you need."

"I'll need three men, with one BAR: Corporal Baruchi."

The captain tried to sit up, but moving was too painful. He had to lie still. "Not Baruchi," he said. "Take Peters."

"Baruchi's a better shot, Captain."

"I know he's a better shot, Lieutenant. But take Peters. Some of the men don't trust Baruchi."

"Damn it, Captain, he's a good man."

"Don't argue with me, Bell. Take Peters. That's an order."

"Yes, sir," he said reluctantly.

"Do you know where the seam is? Can you get through?"

"They're spread out pretty far," Bell answered. "If we can make it to that hill over there, we can come up behind their lines. What we need is a diversion."

"What've you got in mind?"

"That dead Korean tank on the road."

Marshall nodded, understanding. "Good. Go to it."

Bell got down low again, crawled back through the gully, collecting his men along the way. "Peters," he said to a stocky, smooth-faced corporal. "You come with me."

"Lieutenant—" Chick began.

"Next time, Corporal," Bell cut him off. He looked at a private he had yanked off the line. "Davis," he said, "I want you to blow that T-34 out there."

"Yes, sir," he said crisply.

"I don't mean with grenades. Get an armload of that dynamite we were using back at Inchon. I want it blown into powder."

"Yes, *sir*," he said, scurrying off.

"Edwards?" He motioned to another marine. "Can you get inside that tank and get it moving by itself?"

"Yes, sir. I can get the dead guys in it to drive it if you want."

"That's exactly what I want, Private. Let's go."

"Gilly—" Baruchi grabbed his arm. "Can't I go?"

"I'm sorry, Corporal," Bell answered stiffly. "Stay here and give us some cover. We're going to stuff that tank like a Thanksgiving turkey. When it blows, you'd better have your face in the dirt."

"Yes, sir."

A few minutes later, the four men rushed the enemy tank; Bell and Peters covered while Edwards and Davis scrambled up the tank and into its belly. Then Bell and Peters hustled across the road, slid down next to the tracks of the tank.

"Lieutenant!" Peters gasped. "Look at that!" He

was staring at a huge truck pulling to a stop down the road.

In its bed were two Koreans manning the largest rocket launchers Gilbert had ever seen. "They must be Russian," he said. "Look at the size of them!"

"They're getting cranked up, Lieutenant. We'd better do something fast."

Gilbert stole a look around the T-34. The rockets were being aimed in the direction of the rest of the company.

"Come on, Davis," Bell murmured under his breath. "Do it. We don't have all day."

"I can't hear them in there, Lieutenant," Peters said.

"Let's hope they see that truck and aim the tank toward it. The second it hits, head for that hill over there, Corporal. If we can get that hill, we've got them."

"Yes, sir. Anything's better than sitting here, waiting for this tin can to blow up."

Suddenly the hatch clanked open, the jeep began to move, and Davis and Edwards piled out onto the ground. "Got it!" Davis said jubilantly. With the others he hit the road bed and covered his eyes with his helmet as the tank moved slowly down the road.

As Gilbert had hoped, it headed straight for the truck and the rocket launchers. For a while the North Koreans seemed to be puzzled by their own tank coming toward them. Then they quickly swung their rockets around.

They were too late. The tank rammed the truck, exploded with the noise and force of a volcano, and the sky was suddenly aglow with burning rockets.

"Go!" Bell ordered, and they dug out across the field toward the hill.

Minutes later, rifles flaring, they blew out a massive hole in the enemy lines and the company moved up. "They're retreating," Peters said, watching the Koreans scramble. "They're going back to Yongdungpo."

"And so are we, Corporal," Bell told him. "We've got a date with the Fifth in Seoul."

For a while Gilbert stood calmly on the hill and watched the men gather together and advance. Then he saw Chick Baruchi come up to him, his automatic rifle poised and ready for battle. Gilbert was about to explain why he hadn't let his friend go along when he detected a sad, pained expression on his face.

"Here, what's wrong, Chick?" he asked. "We did it, man. Cheer up. We're breaking through."

"It's Captain Marshall, Gilly," he replied stiffly. "He didn't make it."

Gilbert stared ahead. It didn't seem fair now to explain that it was Marshall who had objected to Chick. He decided to let it go. "I thought he'd make it," he said hopelessly.

"I guess he lost too much blood."

"I guess so."

"Well," Chick lifted his voice, "it's up to you now, Gilly. The captain's gone, you're the ranking officer. You're in command."

Gilbert took a deep breath, flicked the strap of his carbine over his shoulder. "Then let's move out of here, Corporal. Seoul's dead ahead. Let's see if the Marines can help MacArthur's image, what do you say? Let's see if we can make him famous for the Inchon landing."

8

IN TOKYO, at one o'clock in the afternoon of the following day, Wayne Hunter climbed the last steps to the second floor and paused in the hall. He was surprised to find the door to his office ajar. Adrian was with the marines at Inchon, he thought; she shouldn't be back in Tokyo yet.

He proceeded cautiously down the hall, reached the door and pushed it in slightly. There was a man sitting at his desk, reading his papers. Stunned, Wayne realized that it was none other than Ed Mallory.

His heart pounding, he stepped in, tried to appear cool. "Well, look who's here," he said, affecting an affable tone. "Welcome to the Orient, chief."

Mallory's thick body was hunkered over the desk; his eyes were flying over the papers in his hands. Finally he pitched them down on the desk with a gesture of disgust. "I knew it," he said. "I knew it," he said. "I knew it as well as I know my name."

Wayne smiled nervously. "Knew what? What're you doing here anyway, Ed?"

Mallory shook his head. "I didn't come to see the sights, I can tell you that. Where's Adrian?"

Hunter took a seat on the green vinyl chair and tried to appear comfortable. In truth, he was scared. He recognized the incriminating papers Mallory had been reading. He could only hope they meant nothing to him. "She's covering the war, Ed," he said. "She's probably in Seoul by now."

"Good." Mallory nodded his approval. "McAllister always does her job."

Wayne caught his accusing look. "And I don't do mine, is that what you mean?"

Mallory looked at him. "Oh, you do a job all right, Wayne," he acknowledged. "Only thing is, you're not doing it for me or the *Sun*. What the hell are you up to, Hunter? What's going on here?"

"I don't know what you're talking about. I'm just doing what I'm paid to do."

"You're paid to work for me, Hunter, not against me. Look at this stuff," he said, picking up the papers. "This is Adrian's report on the Pusan perimeter, and this is your version of it. The one *I* got. There's a big difference here Wayne."

He stirred uncomfortably in his seat.

"So I edited her copy; so what? She's only a female reporter, for God's sake. She's not Edward R. Murrow."

Mallory stared at him a moment, then pushed himself up. Keeping his eyes on Hunter, he stalked around the desk, eased down on the edge, and crossed his massive arms. "You want to tell me about it?" he asked. "You want to tell me why you've been subtly twisting Adrian's stuff, making us look like fools for being in the war? Are you trying to get her fired? Or *me* fired? Tell me. What are you trying to do?"

"I'm not trying to do anything, Ed," he protested. "I swear. I'm just doing what I was sent here to do."

"No you're not, Hunter. You're sabotaging the Sacramento *Sun*, that's what you're doing. And I want to know why."

Wayne tried to dismiss the idea with a laugh. "You're crazy."

But Mallory was insistent. "I didn't fly fifty-one hundred miles across the Pacific Ocean because I'm crazy, Wayne. I'm here because I care what happens to my reporters, okay? And that includes you."

"That's not true and you know it, Mallory! You don't care what happens to me any more than anybody else does. You all use me, you, Adrian, Rivers, everybody."

Mallory's eyebrows rose in surprise, and he studied Wayne a moment before saying, "Now look who's crazy."

"It's true and you know it. It was a big joke to you, making Adrian a war correspondent right there in front of me. Wasn't it? It was a big joke to embarrass me like that."

"No. You know it wasn't. I told you then why I didn't give you the job. Obviously, I was right." He got up, went to the window, looked out at the moat.

Wayne Hunter had no idea what to expect now. The fact that Mallory was probably deciding his fate at this very moment made him extremely nervous.

Restless, he got to his feet. "All right," he admitted.

"I changed her stuff. I was just trying to improve it, that's all. I was wrong, okay? Her copy's perfect as it is. I won't touch it from now on."

Mallory turned around to face him. "You won't have a chance to touch it," he stated.

"You're sending me back to Sacramento?"

"No, I'm sending you packing, Wayne. You're fired."

"Fired!" he exclaimed, genuinely startled. "Now just a damn minute, Mallory."

"Get your stuff and leave," Mallory ordered, easing toward the door.

But Hunter reached out and grabbed his arm. "Hey, wait a minute, man. At least give me a chance to explain."

"I gave you a chance, sending you over here. You blew it, all right? Why don't we let it go at that?"

Hunter squeezed the arm. "Don't do this to me, Mallory," he warned.

The editor looked him straight in the eye. "I told you back in Sacramento, Wayne: one more unethical stunt, and you're gone. I don't talk to hear myself make sounds, I mean what I say. This has been building up for a year now. You finally blew it."

"But you don't have to fire me. We may be in another world war here, Ed. I'm going to need a job."

"I'm sorry; there are other jobs. I'll give you a month's severance. Now let go of my arm."

"So you can go get into Adrian's pants, right?" Wayne snapped angrily. "That's what you really want, isn't it? You want me out of the way so you can have her."

"Get out of the way, Wayne," Mallory said wearily.

But Hunter was desperate. He moved his body in

front of the door and tried to stand firm and erect. "You're firing me because of *her*. Admit it!"

"I'll ask you one more time, Hunter. Get the hell out of the way."

Wayne caught the stern, angry look in Mallory's face. It had the effect of sapping his strength. He found himself backing away.

"Thank you," Mallory said as he moved. "Come by the *Sun* when you get back. Alice will give you your check."

"You can shove your check, Mallory," he growled.

The editor paused to look at him one more time. "You've still got time to shape up, Hunter," he said. "You've got good family, good blood. You could be the man your father was—"

"My father can rot in hell, Mallory, along with the rest of my family."

Mallory nodded. Then, without another word, he walked out of the room, leaving the door open behind him.

Wayne went over and plopped down in the swivel chair behind his desk. He looked at the date calendar in front of him and laughed. What good did a calendar do now? He reached down, opened the bottom drawer of the desk, and brought out a pint of Old Crow whiskey he had brought with him to Japan. He wasn't much of a drinker, but now, he figured, was the time to get drunk.

But before he could get through his first glass of liquor, Elliott Stoner, dressed as usual in a neat gray suit, appeared in the doorway with his hands in his pockets. "I take it from that," he said eying the glass of whiskey, "you didn't like what Mallory had to say."

"You don't miss a thing, do you, Elliott?" Wayne said, taking a swig of the whiskey.

"I couldn't miss him," he said, coming in. "He was fuming. What happened?"

"Nothing, he just fired me, that's all. You underestimated the guy, Elliott. He's smarter than we thought."

Stoner's expression remained unchanged. He lowered himself carefully into the vinyl chair, unbuttoned his suit coat, and pulled the sleeves of his white shirt down. Then he very carefully crossed his legs and looked at Hunter. "You know we're part of an overall effort to discredit America's coverage of the war, don't you, Wayne?" he said in a cold voice.

"Yeah, I know that. Only it's *were* now, Elliott, not *are*. It didn't pan out. Besides, from what I just heard on the radio, the landing at Inchon was a big success. MacArthur's famous again. It looks like America's going to win the favor of the world again, in spite of what you do. Cheers." He raised his glass for a toast.

"You're not thinking, Wayne," Elliot said quietly. "We're far from done here."

"Well, *I'm* done. The bastard fired me."

Stoner shook his head calmly. "Didn't you expect that? It's typical. It's the American way. Glory to the few, to hell with the rest. Mallory wants Adrian McAllister to be his star, Wayne. He doesn't care about you or anybody else who doesn't shine. It's the same all over America. A few are glorified, but the good men and women like you are discarded—ground up and spit out by 'democracy.'"

Hunter thought about what he was saying. "Mallory

wants Adrian to be more than his star, Elliott. He wants *her*."

"American Puritan morality," Elliott sneered. "He's willing to sacrifice you for his own lusts."

"Yeah, that's about right. Bastard."

"And what about Adrian? What does she want? I'll tell you: she wants to shame you, Wayne. She's a woman, and we all know women are inferior to men, and yet look at her. She gets the job, she gets the glory, while you get a severance check."

Hunter's anger was building rapidly. He slapped the whiskey bottle with the back of his hand, sent it crashing to the floor. Then, for good measure, he flung his glass, liquid and all, at a Japanese watercolor print on the wall. The glass burst, whiskey spattered all over the pale green wall.

"One day that woman is going to come crawling to me," he declared. "I swear it. One day she'll crawl on her belly to me."

"She should crawl to you," Elliott said, pleased at Hunter's anger. "She's the one who got you fired."

"Her and Mallory. I used to respect that bastard, but now I hate him."

"Then *get* him, Wayne," Elliott said in a hard, penetrating voice. He leaned forward in his chair. "Get both of them."

"I will, some day," Wayne vowed.

"Do it now, Wayne. Stand up and be counted. The world's about to change. Capitalism is dying right now, on the battlefields of Korea. Get them now, while you have the chance."

Hunter looked at him seriously. "How?" he asked. "How can I get them?"

"Think about it."

But Hunter was too angry and impatient to think. He got up, walked a few steps and kicked the broken Old Crow bottle across the room. "Just tell me, Elliott," he demanded. "Tell me. How can I get back at them? How can I get Adrian to come to me on her knees?"

"By the same process, Wayne. Don't you understand the party yet? The war's not the way the party will win over the world. It will win. through information."

"You mean propaganda?"

"Propaganda, information—whatever you want to call it. What I'm talking about is discrediting Adrian McAllister. And Mallory. And the Sacramento *Sun.* Doing our part for the party."

"Yeah, well, I'd love to do that," Wayne confessed. "I'd love to cut Adrian McAllister down to size and make Mallory come begging, too."

"Then do it," Elliott urged. "Get your revenge. You've got the means to do it."

"What means? What've I got to fight them with?"

Stoner stood up, buttoned his coat, adjusted the white display handkerchief in his pocket. "You've got Amanda Bell," he suggested. "She's working in the American foreign service, isn't she?"

"So?"

"And she also hates Adrian McAllister, doesn't she? At least that's what you told me."

Hunter smiled knowingly. Suddenly it all came clear. "I can use Amanda's position in the consulate to discredit Adrian. Why not?" He brightened. "Adrian deserves it. So does Mallory. They all deserve it."

"You're right, Wayne," Elliott agreed. "They all deserve it."

It was several days before Hunter took any action on his plan of revenge. He was hesitant at first, merely savoring the irony of using Gilbert Bell's sister to bring Adrian to her knees. But after a few days of being without a job, of wandering about Tokyo with no purpose, he began to consider the idea seriously. He had been rejected one time too many, he decided. Now he was going to have his way for a change.

On the twenty-first of September he sent Amanda a confidential message: "Amanda. I need your help. Bring your file on Adrian to Shiba Park, noon, the 23rd. Very important to your brother. Wayne Hunter."

On the appointed day, a Saturday, he waited until 12:10, idly watching Japanese and American construction crews working almost frantically to restore the area around the Tokugawa shogun tombs and shrines. Then, as he was checking his watch for the tenth time in ten minutes, he saw her walking up the Zōjōji Temple toward the park.

Amanda Bell was always prettier, it seemed, when you hadn't seen her in a while. Wayne was surprised at how graceful, almost elegant, the woman approaching him was. She carried her tall and shapely body with ease, and she wore her clothes with dignity, even the casual cotton skirt and blouse she had on now.

"Amanda," he said, smiling to see a file folder in her hand.

"Wayne. How are you?" she said coolly.

"I'm fine, considering."

"Considering what? The weather? Your health?" she said sarcastically.

"You're kind of testy today, aren't you?"

She was already impatient. "Look, Wayne, I have no particular desire to be here with you, okay? I'm certainly not going to stand and listen to all your complaints about how life is treating you. I've got better ways of spending my weekends."

"You're a hard-hearted thing, aren't you?"

"Good-bye, Wayne," she said, starting to go.

He grabbed her arm. "Wait a minute. Hear me out, anyway. It concerns Gilly."

He had said the magic word. She turned toward him. "What about Gilly? You said in your note that this is important to him."

"It is," he said, letting her go. "It's important."

"Then what does Adrian McAllister have to do with it?" she asked, holding up the file for him to see. "Whatever Adrian does is of no importance to me."

"Let's walk," he said, and they began to amble toward the temple. After a minute, he said sadly, "Adrian got me fired, Amanda."

"How?" she asked, surprised.

He swallowed hard, began boldly lying to her. "She wanted that job as war correspondent so much, she turned Ed Mallory against me," he said. "The only reason I'm here now is that Mallory's throwing me a bone."

Amanda stopped. There was a look of irritation on her face, but Hunter could also see satisfaction there, pleasure at seeing her opinion of Adrian McAllister confirmed by some hard "facts."

"Just how did Miss Beautiful manage all this?" she asked.

Hunter was finding the going easy. Lies were easy

to tell if the listener really wanted to believe them. "How do you think she managed it?" he said. "She's sleeping with the old bastard. She has him wrapped around her finger. He'll do anything she wants him to." He paused for effect. "Just like Gilly," he added.

She looked off in the distance, her face flushed red. She brought the folder up against her chest. "So she got Mallory to fire you because she wanted all the limelight. Well, she's certainly getting it. Everybody in the foreign service knows about her. Men strain their silly necks to catch a glimpse of Her Grace. But I didn't know, I'm kind of surprised to hear about her sleeping with Mallory. I don't like Adrian, but I never thought she and Mallory . . ."

Hunter studied her face, decided he had better keep going in order to hold her attention. "I saw them," he lied. "That's one of the things she has against me. I caught them in the act. In his office, no less. I came back after work one night to pick up some copy and I opened Mallory's door and there they were."

Amanda took a deep breath and began walking again. For a while she was silent, as she thought about what she had just heard. Finally she asked him what she expected her to do about all this.

"Help me," he replied. "That's all I'm asking for: help."

"Help you what? If you think you and I—"

"No, no," he assured her quickly. "Just help me put Adrian where she belongs. That's all I want."

"I'd like to, believe me. She's no good for Gilly. If she keeps following him around Asia the way she's been doing, she's going to get him killed."

"That's why I'm here, Amanda," he said. "If you help me, I'll help you."

She stopped again, waited until two Japanese men in American-styled suits nodded, bowed, and passed by. "Just how can you, of all people, help me, Wayne?" she asked. "You've never helped anybody in your life."

He gritted his teeth, waited a few seconds until his temper cooled a bit. "I want *her*, Amanda, all right? Satisfied?"

She laughed. "After Mallory and my brother cast her off, you want her? God, men are sick."

"What do you care how sick I am, as long as I get Adrian out of your hair?"

"Gilly's hair, not mine, bud," she corrected him firmly. "All I'm doing is looking out for my misguided brother. I just don't want to see him get hurt."

He held out his hand. "Let's see the file, Amanda."

She hesitated as a group of Japanese women passed by, eyes lowered to the ground. Then she shook her head. "No," she said. "If anybody does anything to Adrian McAllister, I want to be the one to do it."

"Does that mean there's something in her file we can use?" he prompted her. "A little treason, maybe? I'd love to see that."

"No. No treason, but something about as bad." She brushed a lock of hair away from her eye, then placed her hand on his. After a deep breath, she went on. "The thing is, since your boss Mallory and the consul general are old friends, Mallory arranges it so that *we* are supposed to handle Adrian's travel plans while she's in Japan and Korea. Only, a certain general, Lucius T. Stoddard by name, has been complicating that by putting her on whatever plane or boat he wants to. The consul is fit to be tied about it."

"So what?" he said impatiently.

"Well, we were called in to get Adrian an apartment in Pusan when she up and decided to fly over there. We had to use a Japanese connection over there, a Mr. Yang Sin. Mr. Sin's servant reports to Mr. Davis, and everything Mr. Davis hears eventually comes across my desk."

Hunter was interested now. "And what did this servant report?"

"He reported that Adrian flirted with a whole battalion of American soldiers on the docks, that she actually rode out to the Naktong River with one, and that she spent most of the night with a marine officer—in her own apartment."

"By marine officer, you mean Gilly."

She stared at him. "The point is," she said haughtily, "she's making a disgrace of herself. And of her country."

"What does Davis say about this?"

"Mr. Davis doesn't know about it," she told him. "He hasn't seen the report yet."

Hunter liked what he was hearing. "That's just the kind of thing we need, Amanda," he said excitedly. "What would the consul general say if he knew an American correspondent was acting like a . . . whore?"

"I shudder to think," she answered. "I don't imagine things would run quite so smoothly for Adrian McAllister, however."

"Then tell him. Go over Davis's head."

Amanda appeared reluctant. "He's hard to get to."

"Then use your charms, Amanda. God gave them to you for something."

She glared at him. "You can save the innuendo, Hunter."

"No offense," he said quickly. "Just get to the consul general, like you said, and I'm happy. He'll do the rest. Just let him know what kind of woman Mallory sent over here."

She looked at him curiously. "You hate her as much as I do, don't you?"

"I don't hate her, Amanda. I just want to own her," he said with grave determination. "And I want Mallory under my foot." He was moved to tell her everything, that he wanted revenge on the whole country for rejecting him. But he stopped himself.

Amanda nodded. "All right," she decided. "I'll see what I can do. If this General Stoddard doesn't get in the way, we'll have Adrian scurrying back to Sacramento with her tail between her legs."

"Or between mine," he offered.

Amanda stared holes into him. "You're crude, Wayne," she said haughtily. "If we didn't want the same thing, to get Adrian McAllister out of Asia, I wouldn't even be seen with you. You make my skin crawl."

2

9

L IEUTENANT GILBERT BELL led his company into Yongdungpo with the rest of the First Marines on September 24, 1950. A day later, the North Koreans were in full retreat back across the Han River into Seoul. But their access to North Korea, across the 38th parallel, was cut off by the Seventh Marine Regiment. On the morning of September 25, the city was sealed by army and marine regiments on three sides, with the First Marines moving in from the west for the kill.

Ahead of them in the street moved a line of concentrated mobile firepower, Pershing and Sherman tanks, trucks mounted with .50-caliber M2 Browning machine guns, and the UN soldiers themselves armed with a range of weapons from the 75mm recoilless to the light 6.5mm Japanese rifles used by the South Koreans.

Gilbert eased his men slowly, cautiously, into the city behind the tanks and trucks. All around him he could hear the sounds of war—women wailing, men moaning, children screaming as overlapping shots rang out through the streets and alleys, and 90mm guns burst the roofs off solid buildings as if they were made of cardboard.

By midday General Almond proudly announced that Seoul was again in friendly hands, but his announcement was ahead of the facts. Bottled within the city were hundreds of the enemy, lurking, hiding anywhere they could, unable to escape, afraid to get out in the open to face the massive machinery of the UN forces. They were desperate, panicky men, driven into a corner. By late afternoon of the first day as the city began growing dim in the sunset, they began to make themselves known to the UN forces, all over the city.

"They're just sneaking around, picking us off, Lieutenant," Private William Davis said to Gilbert. They were standing inside a partially demolished building, stealing occasional looks outside into the street. Davis, a small, wiry man with dark hair and eyes, held his M-1, bayonet fixed, out in front of him as he talked. "If we could just see them . . ."

"If we keep moving, we'll see them, Davis," Gilbert declared.

"I saw a guy from the Fifth a while ago, Lieutenant," Davis said, pushing his head back against the wall, out of sight of the street. "They lost twenty on one hill, coming in."

Gilbert started to speak, but an explosion nearby

rattled the foundations of the building and light debris from the ceiling crashed down on top of them.
A minute later Bell took off his helmet and shook
the dust off. "Where the hell's Baruchi?" he asked.

"He's still in the church, sir," Davis answered, stealing another glance outside. "Protecting our flank, he
says."

"What do you mean, 'he says'?"

"Nothing, sir."

Bell looked straight at him across the hall. "I think
you'd better explain that, soldier," he said seriously.
"If you don't trust the man to do what he says, tell
me. We're not playing games here."

"I trust him, sir," he replied unconvincingly.

"Damn it, Davis. If you're lying to me—"

Another explosion cut off his words, rocked the
building so hard that both of them were thrown to
the floor.

"Sergeant!" Gilbert yelled as soon as it was still
again.

"Sir!" came a clear voice from somewhere behind
him.

"See who's doing that," he commanded, getting to
his feet.

"Will do, Lieutenant."

"You come with me, Davis," he said to the private.

"Yes, sir. Where to?"

"Let's see if we can make it to that three-story
up the street. I figure you and Edwards need a view
of the city tonight."

"Yes, sir."

By nightfall most of Gilbert's company had gathered
in the house, and the streets were quiet. Private Edwards was up on the loft, on watch, and most of

the other men were sprawled about in the six rooms
of the old building. Some of them were playing cards,
most of them lounging, listening for the enemy, waiting for something to happen.

At midnight, Gilbert stuffed a pack under the small
of his back, leaned against a crumbly wall, and closed
his eyes. He was exhausted, more tired than he had
ever been in his life. He tried to stay awake for a
while. With his eyelids drooping, he took one look
around at the strong, uncomplaining men in the room
with him, then drifted off to sleep.

At some time during the dark early morning hours,
he was startled out of a peaceful dream by the
touch of a warm moist hand on his chin. Instantly
he sprang up, grabbed the bayonet lying next to his
leg, and pinned the intruder to the floor.

Almost before his eyes were completely open, he
had the edge of the blade pressed against the soft
flesh of a throat. But when a high, soft voice screamed
out in terror, he realized he was holding down a
woman.

He eased back, pulled her up. She was Korean,
small, dainty, dressed in a loose, heavy cloth skirt
and loose white blouse. And, understandably, she was
crying. "Davis!" he called out to the private.

"Yes, sir," Davis snapped to attention when he appeared.

"Davis, what is this woman doing here?"

Davis looked curiously down at the Korean. "I
don't know, sir," he answered, puzzled. "I didn't
know she was here."

"Well, who let her in?"

"I don't know, sir."

"Find out, then, Private," he said impatiently.

"Yes, sir," Davis replied and hurried off.

Gilbert slipped on his helmet, watched the woman out of the corner of his eye as he waited. She sat absolutely still, and stared at him with sad, tearful eyes. A few minutes later, he offered her some C rations, but she shook her head no, and continued to stare. Finally, Davis came back, accompanied by a Korean soldier.

"Sir, this is Private Yon Ku, of the ROK. He can ask her what she wants."

Gilbert shook his head, almost laughed. "Okay," he said, "go ahead, ask her. Never mind how she managed to slip through a company of crack marines."

"Yes, sir," Davis said, and pushed the South Korean soldier forward.

Yon Ku's first few words to her ignited a pitiful, sometimes hectic harangue that seemed to Gilbert to go on forever. He finally had to raise up his hand to make her stop.

"What's she saying, Private?" he asked Ku. "What is it she wants?"

"Lieutenant," Ku said in clear, but heavily accented English, "she is the wife of a farmer. She says she sneaked in while all the white faces were asleep."

Bell nodded. The South Korean soldier spoke English extremely well. Leave it to Davis. He could not only handle explosives, he could get just what you needed, when you needed it.

"Ask her why she's here, Private," Bell said, trying to be patient.

The South Korean nodded, spoke to her again. A while later he translated: "Lieutenant, she says her daughter is in the hands of the enemy."

"I'm sorry about that, but what does she expect us to do about it? All we do around here is follow orders."

"She says the lieutenant is leader of men. The lieutenant must help."

Gilbert thought a minute. "Davis," he said, "you and Ku give her a hand—"

At those words, the woman began shaking her head violently.

"She wants you—"

"I know, Private Ku. I understood that much. She wants *me to* help her."

"She says lieutenant is General MacArthur."

Gilbert sighed. "Where is her daughter now?"

"She will lead you to her."

He looked at his watch, then glanced over at the other lieutenant, David Poe. It was quiet. Poe could handle the company while he was gone. He stood up. "All right. Davis, go wake up Baruchi and bring him along. Ku, let's go."

The streets of Seoul at three in the morning were as still as a cemetery. They could hear the muffled sound their boots made as they shuffled across the dirt streets, and the low moaning of a light tank easing past rows of sandbags on the perimeters of the city. The streets were as dark as they were quiet. Most of the houses were open and vacant, no lights, no sign of life anywhere.

They found themselves in the center of the city now, shut in by buildings, artificial palisades, and the line of military vehicles encircling the whole area. Once there, the woman indicated where they were going. She pointed specifically to a slate-roofed two-story house a hundred feet away.

"Chick?" Bell said to Baruchi after a minute. "I don't see anything moving in there. See if you can slide around by that side window and look in."

"Yes, sir," he said, then spurted out into the street, crouching down low as he ran. Seconds later he was peering into the window. After a minute, he turned and waved a no to Bell.

"All right, Davis," Gilbert said, "follow me. Ku, keep the woman out here till we see what's going on in there."

They approached the house cautiously, alert to any strange sound or movement, but they met no obstruction whatever. Even the house was empty. Gilbert was surprised to find that it was actually luxurious. As yet undamaged, it was spacious, attractively decorated, and comfortable. He called the others in to see it.

"Is this the place they had her?" he asked the woman.

But he could see that it was. With a worried look on her face, she began wandering around, touching vases and tables and chairs with her dainty fingers, shaking her head, as if she were tracing her daughter's steps in the main room. She spoke softly in Korean under her breath, but Gilbert needed no interpreter to tell him what she was saying.

Suddenly they heard a noise coming from beneath the floor, then recognized it as footsteps, moving upstairs, toward the floor. Without a word, Gilbert jumped across the room, grabbed the woman, jerked her back behind a screen in front of the window. "Shh," he whispered. "Be quiet." He motioned for Baruchi, Davis, and Ku to find some cover fast."

The footsteps moved up, stopped, then a trap door

opened up out of the floor, and the mingled voices of men joking and laughing seeped out into the empty room. A small man in a plain uniform and cap eased the door down on the floor and walked past the screen into the kitchen.

While he was out of sight, Baruchi stole quickly across the room. Bell wanted to call him off, but he couldn't risk it. He had to stand behind the screen, holding the woman in his arms, and watch as Chick got down on his belly and looked into the cellar. When Baruchi heard the opening of the kitchen door, he rolled away from the edge of the opening, dived under a table nearby. He watched unnoticed as the soldier returned to the trap door and stairs.

When the door was secure, Gilbert quietly gathered the others and went outside. He looked at Chick. "I don't remember telling you to look down into that cellar, Corporal," he admonished him, though without anger.

"The lady was right, Lieutenant. They do have a girl down there. Looks like she's about fifteen or sixteen."

The woman nodded, said something in a sad voice.

"Lieutenant, she says her daughter is a virgin," Ku translated.

"*Was* a virgin," Gilbert corrected him. "Not anymore. Okay, Ku, get her out of here. Chick, how many are down there in that hole?"

"Ten, fifteen, maybe. They were spread around, playing cards or something. It looked like the girl was serving rice to them."

"I can drop a couple of eggs on them, Lieutenant," Davis volunteered, patting a grenade on his belt.

"Sounds good to me," Gilbert said. "After we get the girl out."

"Lieutenant?" the ROK soldier interrupted.

"You stay with the woman, Ku," Gilbert told him.

"Uh, there's something the lieutenant should know," he cautioned.

"All right, Ku," he said wearily. "What should I know?"

"She says she's not sure they're North Koreans."

Gilbert frowned. "Now just what does that mean?"

Ku asked her a couple of questions, nodded as she answered. He looked at Bell with a perplexed expression on his face. "She *thinks* the men who have her daughter are not North Koreans," he said.

"Then who in the hell are they?"

"She thinks Chinese."

"Chinese," Bell repeated in a low voice. "I hope she's wrong."

"Lieutenant," Davis said in a concerned voice. "They've been telling us the Chinese Communists aren't going to enter the war."

"We don't know if they have yet, Davis. Don't jump to conclusions."

"No, sir, but if those men down in that cellar *are* Chinese Communists, this whole city could be surrounded by them right now. They have *millions* of men, Lieutenant."

"Take it easy, Private. Even she's not sure."

"Yes, but if they are in the war, we've got to have more than a couple of divisions in here. They'll slaughter us."

Gilbert took a deep, halting breath. What Davis was saying disturbed him. Was the success of the

Inchon landing going to bring the Chinese into the war? Was the small North Korean army now going to swell its ranks by hundreds of thousands, maybe millions of Chinese?

"Why don't we go find out who they are?" Gilbert said.

Leaving Ku in an alley, holding onto the woman, the other three raced across the street, lined their backs against a wall outside the front door. Then they eased slowly inside and began moving softly across the wood floor. The room was warm; it smelled vaguely of wine and tobacco as they trod the carpet and finally came to a stop near the door to the cellar.

"Sir?" Davis whispered from his position on the other side of the door. "I think they heard us."

"Get down, Davis!" Gilbert whispered back.

Again they heard footsteps, then suddenly the door flung open with a clack and the barrel of a rifle slowly protruded into the room. Then a head with a cap on it appeared, the same man they had seen earlier, this time ominously holding out an automatic rifle in front of him. The man looked around but couldn't see anyone in the shadows.

Bell held his breath as the soldier spoke to someone in the cellar. He could feel his hands sweating on the wood of the rifle stock. If he could draw all of them out, he thought, they would forget about the girl.

But then, without warning, the front door blew open with a crash and the Korean woman burst into the room, Private Ku chasing. The man at the cellar door immediately whirled around and opened fire. But before his rifle flashed in the dim light, the woman had dived to the floor and the bullets blew over her head. The South Korean private was almost caught by the shower of bullets, but he managed to quickly disappear into the shadows out of the way.

It took only a second for Davis to aim and fire his M-1 at the man; the .30-calibre slug burst into his heart and he tumbled back down the stairs. At the bottom of the steps came garbled sounds of confusion. The men below panicked, someone yelled out a command, another grunted out a response, the girl screamed, and all of a sudden one of them was firing a bazooka into the floor boards.

The floor exploded under the violent impact of the bazooka projectile; splinters, hunks of wood and metal burst into the air. Then, seconds later, another blast, and the hole in the floor had cracked open wider.

"Let's get them!" Chick yelled out and charged the cellar.

"Chick! Get back!" Gilbert yelled.

But the corporal didn't hear the command. He darted through the smoke, dust, and debris made visible by the light from the cellar, and plunged into the hole. A second later Davis hollered "Geronimo!" and scrambled down the stairs after him.

By the time Gilbert reached the steps himself Baruchi was wielding his automatic rifle like a water hose, dousing the enemy with bullets as calmly as if he were spraying them with water. Davis was jabbing one man in the chest with his bayonet as Gilbert hurried down the steps.

Before he reached the bottom step, though, a man lunged at him with a machete. Instantly he jerked up his rifle in front of his face and caught the blow on the breech. In a sharp, quick move, he rammed the stock into the man's groin, then plunged his bayonet into his heart.

The cellar room was quiet all of a sudden. The three Americans left standing were surrounded by bodies—twenty-five of them—bloody, riddled with bullets, and very still. "Where's the girl?" Gilbert asked, looking around.

"Over here, Lieutenant," Chick answered. He walked over to a corner, led her out.

She was clinging to her bare chest with her arms, trying desperately to cover her breasts with part of her skirt. Her small dark eyes were full of terror at what she was expecting to happen to her. But then she heard a familiar sound at the top of the stairs. As soon as she heard her mother call out to her, she raced past Gilbert, up the steps, and into her arms.

"Good shooting, Baruchi," Bell complimented the corporal. "I never saw anything like it."

"Yeah, Chick," Davis agreed. "You handle that BAR like it was a hot lady on a dance floor."

"You were a bit lucky, though," Bell told him. "That girl could have been hit."

"I saw her over there, Lieutenant," Chick said. "I wasn't going to let her get hurt."

"How could you see her? You just dived into the hole—against my orders, I might add."

Baruchi looked at him seriously. "Lieutenant, I swear. I didn't hear any orders. I swear. I just knew the next time they fired that bazooka, one of us was going to be dead, so I dove in."

"And singlehandedly killed twenty-five of them," Davis added. "First-rate shooting, Baruchi."

"You got your share, Davis," Chick asserted. "Don't pretend you didn't."

Gilbert looked around at the dead men. The question remained. He couldn't tell if they were Chinese or Korean. "Ku!" he called out through the hole in the floor. "Are you up there?"

"Lieutenant!" an exuberant voice rang out.

Gilbert grinned. "I wonder if the ROK would let us have that guy?" he said to the others. "I like him."

"Lieutenant," the Korean said, saluting, looking down through the hole.

"Get down here, Ku."

When Ku reported to Bell down in the cellar, he saluted again, then stared at the bodies and shook his head. "Damn," he said, gazing at the corpses.

"What are they, Ku? Chinese or Korean?" Bell asked.

Ku shrugged his shoulders. Then, with great patience, he examined the face of each body. "Lieutenant," he said finally, pointing with both his hands. "These two are Chinese."

"Sir?" Davis broke in. "Look at this." He showed Bell a coarse cloth sack, then with a flourish he turned it upside down, emtpied the entire contents out on the black dirt of the cellar floor. The papers were made up of leaflets, pamphlets, and pictures by the hundreds.

Bell reached down and picked up a handful. He held out one of them to Ku. "Korean or Chinese?"

Ku whipped out a pair of pince-nez glasses, put them on, and read the script slowly. A long time later, he peeled off his spectacles. "Lieutenant, it is *hankil*—Korean—but written by Chinese."

Bell nodded, handed him a photograph. "Correct me if I'm wrong, but isn't that Mao-Tse-Tung, Chairman of the Communist Party, People's Republic of China?"

Ku nodded.

"And this cheery face," he said, holding up another, "belongs to Joseph Stalin, Premier of Russia."

Davis sat down at the table. "Then the Chinese Communists *are* in this thing."

"It looks like it." Bell shook his head. "All this time we've been told the revolution in China had nothing to do with the rest of the world, it had nothing to do with Russia's plan to spread Communism over the face of the earth. Well, it doesn't look that way now."

"Couldn't these Chinese be here as advisors or something, Gilly?" Chick asked hopefully. "Couldn't they have been visiting and then were caught by the occupation of Seoul?"

"That could be, Chick, but I doubt it. I'm afraid what this means is that China is just about ready to show itself in Korea and proclaim to the world that its aim is to engulf anything in its path."

"Which could mean an all-out war. Us against them," Davis finished the thought.

Gilbert took off his helmet, ran his fingers through his damp hair. "Which also explains what I saw in Washington," he mumbled to himself.

"Sir?"

"Nothing. Look, Davis, bring that sack of propaganda with you. We'll see if we can get somebody to look at it."

"Yes, sir."

"Somebody with clout," he said stuffing the papers into his jacket.

They left the cluttered cellar and went up top, where the Korean woman was hanging close to the door, waiting for them. She was holding tightly onto her daughter and sniffing loudly. Gilbert stopped, touched the woman's cheek with his hand. "I'm very sorry, ma'am," he said. "I wish we could've gotten to her sooner. But she'll be all right." He looked back at the ROK private. "Won't she, Ku?" he asked.

"Lieutenant, the woman wishes to bring you bowl of rice. That's all she has."

He smiled at her. "Fine," he said. "Tell her to bring her family. We'll all eat it." He turned to the others. "Baruchi? Davis? Are you guys coming? I'm tired, I need some sleep."

"Yes, sir," Davis replied, then made an elaborate gesture with his hand to Baruchi. "You first, Corporal," he said. "If we run into any more unfriendly fire, I want you and that BAR where you can do your stuff."

Two days later Gilbert found himself being led by an army major into the sanctuary of a half-demolished church in the middle of Seoul. There, sitting erect at a desk, looking through a sheaf of papers, was General MacArthur. He curtly acknowledged Gilbert's salute, took a final glance at the pictures and leaflets, and raised his eyes.

"You marines are tough customers," he said. "They tell me you wiped out twenty-five North Koreans to get these pictures."

"My men more than me, General," Bell answered.

MacArthur nodded, leaned back in his chair. "And all this happened right here in Seoul. Is that right?"

"Yes, sir," Gilbert replied quietly. "It happened a few blocks from here."

The general nodded again, thoughtfully. "You know, Lieutenant," he said, "every day we hear on the radio that the Chinese Communists are on the verge of entering the war. But as of right now, nobody really believes it. Now what I want to know is, do *you* believe it? Does finding these Chinese Communist papers here in Seoul convince you we're at war with China, too?"

Gilbert spoke without hesitation. "General, sir, I'm convinced that two of the men we killed were Chinese. And that they were distributing Communist propaganda."

"Don't evade the question, Bell," MacArthur said flatly. "Answer it."

Gilbert swallowed, took a deep breath. "All right, sir, I'll answer it. Yes. I think we are at war with China. Or will be soon."

MacArthur tapped his fingers on the desk, looked at Gilbert closely, as if he were sizing him up. Finally he stood up, flicked a piece of paper off his desk. "Lieutenant," he began in a more casual voice, "I want you to hear something—a message I received on the radio two days ago. It's from George Marshall, Secretary of Defense. He's giving me authority to cross the 38th parallel into North Korea."

"I'm glad to hear that, General. We have Seoul now; we should keep going."

"Yes, we should. Unfortunately, this information you uncovered may create a wrinkle in my plans."

"I don't understand, sir."

MacArthur looked at the paper. "Marshall gives me permission to cross the parallel—provided, he says, 'there has been no entry into North Korea by major Soviet or Chinese Communist forces, or no announcement of intended entry.'"

"He's afraid of a retaliation by China," Gilbert observed.

"He's afraid, Truman's afraid, the JCS are afraid. They're all quaking in their boots, Lieutenant. And now this turns up," he said, picking up the pictures and throwing them back down. "And you tell me two of those twenty-five men were actually Chinese."

"Yes, sir, they were."

"What do you think that would mean to Marshall or Truman, Lieutenant?"

"I suppose it would mean an entry by Chinese Communist forces, General."

"But Marshall did say entry into *North* Korea," MacArthur reminded him.

"Yes, sir. I know, but—"

"Tell me, Lieutenant, what would you do?" MacArthur asked him. "Would you ignore the existence of those two Chinese and move into Wonsan while we have them on the run, or would you back off and let them regroup while we figure out what to do about China?"

Gilbert shifted his weight uncomfortably. He felt as if he were suddenly thrust between two great forces—the men he'd seen at the meeting in the Pentagon, Stoddard, Bradley, and Eisenhower, on the one hand, and the great General Douglas MacArthur on the other. Should he tell MacArthur about the secret meeting in Washington? Or should he keep the vow of secrecy he made to Bradley?

"Well, Lieutenant," MacArthur pressed, "what do you·say? Don't tell me you don't have an opinion; marine officers always have opinions."

Just as Bell was about to speak, an army major entered the sanctuary and saluted. "General," he said in a crisp voice, "President Syngman Rhee is at the National Assembly. He's ready and anxious for the presentation."

"How anxious?" MacArthur asked.

"He's beside himself, General. He's over there leading cheers. He's calling you the savior of South Korea."

"Well, he's right. I am," MacArthur said in a matter-of-fact voice, with no display of conceit.

"But he says he can't claim victory until you officially give him the city, General," the major stated.

"Go tell him I'm coming." He looked at Bell, changed expression. "You're not afraid of China, are you, Lieutenant?" he asked. "Marines aren't afraid of anybody, are they?"

"I'm not afraid, General MacArthur."

"Sir?" the major interjected impatiently.

"All right, Major, I'm coming. Lieutenant," he said to Bell, "I want you to think about what I said. We'll talk about this later."

"Yes, sir," Bell replied. He watched MacArthur leave with the major, on his way to present the key to the capitol of South Korea to Rhee.

That evening the word came down from general headquarters: the First Marines were returning to Inchon. From there they would go around the tip of the peninsula and proceed to Wonsan, on the east coast of North Korea.

MacArthur had made his decision: for the first time in the war the UN forces were crossing the 38th parallel.

10

T HE FIRST THREE weeks in October were difficult for Adrian in Tokyo. Since Mallory hadn't given her a replacement for Wayne Hunter, she was having to work alone. That wouldn't have bothered her ordinarily, but since Wayne had been fired, he had begun to follow her everywhere she went. He was never within the sound of her voice, but he was always near, in alleys, on street corners, in cabs, or outside her office, sitting on a bench. If she'd thought him a little off before, she now thought he was definitely a strange one. Each time she saw him, his presence made her more nervous.

On October 23, she arrived at her office more apprehensive than usual. She had seen Wayne, as usual, loitering near the palace to watch her, but this time he had someone with him—the man she and Stoddard had seen before. As she hurried up the steps to the front door, she saw out of the corner of her eye that Wayne was gesturing toward her. It made her shudder all over.

When she reached her office, she discovered a manila envelope that had been slipped under the door. As she opened it and read the message, she felt anger rising within her. She wanted to scream in protest. Quickly she snapped up the phone and called the consulate.

"Mr. Davis's office," a woman's voice answered. "Amanda Bell speaking. May I help you?"

"Amanda," Adrian said, trying to hold down her temper, "this is Adrian McAllister. I want to speak to Tom Davis."

"I'm sorry, Adrian," she said in an affectedly friendly voice, "Mr. Davis won't be receiving calls today. He's out of his office."

"Out where?"

"Out of touch, Adrian," Amanda said firmly. "Why don't you try again tomorrow?"

But Adrian was persistent. "Amanda, I assume you know about this note preventing me from going to Wonsan."

"Yes, I know about it. It's just terrible, isn't it?"

"He can't do this, Amanda. You people are over there to help us, not hinder us. You can't keep me from going."

"It's done, Adrian. You aren't going. Why fight it?"

"You're behind this, aren't you?" she accused her. "You don't want me to go to Wonsan because Gilbert is there."

"Mr. Davis is here," Amanda said. "He wants to speak to you."

"Miss McAllister?" said a deep, resonant voice. "This is Thomas Davis. Can I help you?"

"Yes, you can help me," she answered. "You can get me on an army transport to Wonsan, North Korea."

"Well, I'm sorry. We can't do that. We have no power to do that. The military is in charge of transportation—"

"Mr. Davis, you know what I'm talking about," she said, trying to keep her patience. "I have a note right here, signed Thomas R. Davis, which says women correspondents are to be prevented from going into North Korea."

"Yes, that's correct. Do you have a problem with that, Miss McAllister?"

Adrian clenched her fist and closed her eyes, then proceeded calmly, but with strong emotion in her voice. "My problem is I don't accept it, Mr. Davis. I know Amanda had something to do with this."

"Miss Bell certainly doesn't make policy, Miss McAllister," he informed her stiffly. "For that matter, neither do I."

"But somebody made *this* policy!"

"What you received is a directive from the secretary of state himself, Miss McAllister. It's a very clear directive: no women correspondents are to be allowed in North Korea. I'm sorry. And please, leave Miss Bell out of this."

"What!"

"If I can speak off the record, miss, let me say we were all shocked to hear of your conduct with the men who are fighting the war in Korea. We've all been quite embarrassed by it—"

"Now just a minute!"

"And we would be obliged if you didn't try, out of some desperation to bring any of our employees, such as Miss Bell, into your situation."

"Miss Bell is the reason you're doing this—isn't she?"

"Good-bye, Miss McAllister. I'm sorry we can't help you."

"Mr. Davis—"

"Adrian?" Amanda's voice came in on the line.

"Amanda—"

"Tough luck," Amanda said smoothly. "Maybe you'd have better luck with the boys back in Sacramento."

The *click*! on the phone as Amanda hung up almost sent Adrian into a rage. She stood for a moment, holding the receiver, tempted to fling it out the window. No one could infuriate her the way Amanda Bell did.

A few minutes and a drink of water later, she had calmed down. She thought about the situation, patiently weighed her alternatives. She then decided that she had to do something to change a situation she considered intolerable. And she knew only one person who could help her do that: General Lucius T. Stoddard.

Getting through to the Pentagon on the phone was difficult. The Japanese operator could barely speak English, the operator in Washington was reluctant to give out information, and the woman on the switchboard in the Pentagon declared that she would try to get through to General Stoddard; and, as she said, "get back to you there."

In the meantime Adrian listened to the radio. The war, according to Japanese reports, was close to an end. The ROK army was mopping up in central Korea, north of the parallel, the Eighth Army had seized Pyongyang, the Seventh Division was landing at Iwon. It was just a matter of time before the enemy surrendered.

"Unless," the announcer always added, "there are unexpected developments in Korea." To everyone in the Press Club in Tokyo, that code phrase meant, "Unless China enters the war." The fear of the Chinese lay under every report, every optimistic rally of the pro-American press. The closer the UN forces got to the Manchurian border, the deeper that fear cut into every member of the correspondent corps in Asia.

After a half hour of listening to news reports and Japanese music, Adrian picked up the phone and heard the comforting voice of Stoddard at the other end.

"Adrian?" he said. "What's up? What can I do for you?"

"You're being very kind to talk to me, General, after the way I finked out on you. When it came right down to it, I just couldn't spy on Gilly—and as I said, I don't believe there's any reason to suspect his loyalties. But you must have thought it was pretty rotten of me, after you got me in to cover Operation Chromite."

"Are you kidding? I quite understood. Besides, talking to you will brighten my whole day. It already has."

"General," she said soberly, "I hate to ask, but I need your help. I need to get to Wonsan."

"The First Marines are in Wonsan harbor now, aren't they?"

"Yes, they are. They've been there four or five days, waiting for the navy demolition team to get the mines out of the harbor. They're saying around here they'll be stuck there for another couple of days."

"You know Gilbert's there?"

"Yes, I know. And so is the end of the war, General. I have to be there. In Wonsan, or wherever it happens."

There was a smile in his voice. "That decision doesn't surprise me, Adrian. Any woman who'd steal MacArthur's phone isn't going to sit around watching other people do things. But what's keeping you from going to Wonsan?"

"The secretary of state is keeping me."

"Acheson? He doesn't want anybody in Korea, Adrian."

"But they're preventing me from going, General Stoddard," she said pitifully. "On his directive. Or so they're saying. Could you do something to help me?"

Stoddard paused. "Maybe I could," he said. "But there's something you'll have to do for me first."

"Watch Gilbert, you mean," she anticipated him.

"Adrian, I told you once Gilbert had certain information that could become explosive—especially if the Chinese enter the war. Well, I guess you knew that in spite of what MacArthur told Truman on Wake Island the other day, that could happen any day now. The situation with Gilbert is more crucial now than ever. It's not that we suspect his loyalties, mind you. It's just that anyone who knows what he knows is in a sensitive spot."

"What do you want me to do?" she asked, forgetting her own problem for the moment and thinking of Gilbert. "I'll do anything."

"All right. We know he talked to MacArthur three weeks ago. And we know what they talked about had something to do with the Chinese. I want you to find out if he gave out that certain information to Mac-Arthur."

"Aren't you people on the same side, General?" she asked, puzzled.

"Never mind that. Just find out. Now, if he did tell MacArthur, we'll be able to anticipate his next plan. If he didn't, then see if you can get him out of there before they move toward Manchuria."

As far as Adrian was concerned, this whole business was becoming more and more perplexing. But she stifled her doubts and simply asked, "How?"

"I don't care how, Adrian. Just get him out. This whole war could blow up in our faces if we don't."

"I can try, General, but I warn you, Gilly doesn't listen to me. He goes his own way."

"You're my only chance, Adrian. I can't jerk him out myself. Too many people are watching. It has to be unofficial. Make him go AWOL. Shoot him in the foot if you have to, but get him out of Korea."

Adrian felt her heart pounding rapidly inside her chest. "You're scaring me to death, General."

"I hope so. At least think about it."

"All I want to do is get to Wonsan."

"I'll get you there. I'll go see Dean Acheson as soon as I get through talking to you. It may take a couple of days, but count on it. I'll have a liaison officer there in Tokyo take you over."

"I'll be waiting. Could you make it Lieutenant James Metz?"

"Well, Metz is army, but I think I can arrange it.

Look, Adrian, promise me you'll think about what I said. It's very important."

"I promise, General. And thank you."

On a cool, clear morning four days later Adrian and Lieutenant Metz landed at the Wonsan airfield in a supply transport plane and hurried to the dock where the First Marines had been stranded since October 15. But to Adrian's surprise, the docks were empty.

"They got off yesterday," Colonel Porter, an intelligence officer, told them later at his desk in a temporary quarters. "The navy took two thousand mines out of the bay, can you believe that?"

"Colonel," Adrian said anxiously, "I'm doing a story on Lieutenant Gilbert Bell. I wonder if you could tell me where he is."

"He's down at Kojo," he answered quickly. "Only it's Captain Bell now, ma'am. General Smith got him promoted a couple of days ago. Bell's a good man. He knew you were coming, by the way."

"Where is Kojo?" Metz inquired.

"It's about forty miles south of here. General Smith sent a battalion down there yesterday to protect the supply dump. We don't have any reports of any major Communist troops in that area, but it pays to be careful."

"What about Chinese? Are any of them in the area?"

He looked at her curiously. "What makes you ask that?" he said.

"I just wondered, Colonel. Reporters hear rumors."

He looked at her a while, then said, "Well, there are no Chinese here, Miss McAllister. None at all, rumors to the contrary. Now if you and Lieutenant

Metz want to go down to Kojo to meet Captain Bell,
we have no objection, so long as you don't get in the
way. You can get on the supply train leaving Wonsan
in a few hours, if you want to."

They thanked him, went to the railroad to wait for
the supply train to be loaded and sent down to Kojo.
The air seemed to be getting cooler by the minute as
they stood out in the sunshine and waited. Adrian
buttoned her jacket at the collar and wrapped her
arms around her chest to keep warm, but she still felt
chilled to the bone.

The railroad was bustling with activity as marines
began to pack the cars with fuel and supplies, and
reinforcements began to report in an orderly fashion
to the commanding officer of the project. Adrian
watched with excitement as the train became organized under his direction.

Then a train carrying refugees from Kojo appeared.
Adrian had never before seen so many people and
animals packed into one place. Then open gondola
cars were crammed to overflowing with women,
babies, dogs, even chickens. They were all cheering
madly, deliriously waving their arms as the train
pulled slowly into Wonsan.

An hour later, after the refugees had dispersed, a
corporal hoisted her up into one of the open cars
already packed with marines. She felt their eyes
immediately lock onto her as her feet touched the
wood floor of the car. Unlike the men at Inchon, these
soldiers were obviously relaxed and happy. They were
convinced the war was over, so their minds could
easily be turned to other things—such as a beautiful
woman.

"Allow me, please," said a handsome, muscular man as he placed a heavy wool coat over her shoulders.

"No, thank you," she said. "I don't need it. Really."

She knew all the men in the open gondola car were watching her. She smiled, touched his elbow lightly and thanked him. Every marine in the car reacted to her gesture—with whistles, cat calls, and loud, energetic cheers.

"Do you want me to shut them up, Miss McAllister?" Metz whispered.

She shook her head. "If I can't trust the marines after Inchon, there's no hope for any of us, Lieutenant," she said good-naturedly.

The man who had given her the coat grinned at her. "If any of these guys gives you any trouble, Miss, you just holler for McCoy. Okay?"

"Thank you, Sergeant McCoy. I'll remember that."

"You just holler. I'll be up front here."

The air became cold as the train coughed, sputtered, and then eased off toward Kojo, but Adrian was snug in the warm coat; it didn't matter to her that winter was coming. All she wanted to do was get Gilbert out of Korea and go back to Tokyo and write her story. If only she could get him to come. . . .

Adrian found Kojo a curious place. It was a small seaport, unspoiled by the war. Surrounded by slopes and hills, it had a bay the color of a clear blue sky and beaches that looked like fine white powder. It could have been a resort area in California, she thought, with a little work.

And yet all around her were the evidences of conflict. The battalion commander, Lieutenant Colonel Hawkins, was in the process of setting up the defenses of the village when the train pulled in. All over the little seaport men were being sent this way and that with deadly weapons—machine guns, 3.5-inch rocket launchers, 75mm recoilless rifles, 81mm mortars, even flame throwers. Seeing the terrible guns of war in peaceful Kojo was very disturbing to her.

When Adrian and Metz got down off the train at the railroad station south of town, a marine corporal stepped briskly up to them and identified himself as David Paxton. "You're a *reporter?*" he said with surprise when Adrian told him she was from the Sacramento *Sun.*

"That's right."

"They told me one was coming, but they didn't say it would be . . . a woman."

"Careless of them not to mention it, wasn't it, Corporal?" she said with a smile.

"Uh, Miss . . ."

"Adrian."

"Miss Adrian, begging your pardon, but you can't stay here. This is no place for a woman."

Metz shook his head. "I've tried that, Corporal. Save your breath; it won't work. She doesn't pay any attention."

"Yes, sir, but we could be attacked at any time."

"We were told by a G-2 back in Wonsan that the enemy was nowhere around," Metz said.

Without a word Paxton gently pulled Adrian out of the way of an approaching rifle squad. "We haven't *seen* the enemy, sir, but that doesn't mean he's not here."

"Corporal," Adrian said as he let go of her arm, "could you get someone to take us to Captain Gilbert Bell, please?"

"You'll have to talk to the colonel about that," he answered promptly. "He's in charge here."

"Good. Then would you take us to see the colonel?"

He nodded, led them away from the station toward the village. For an hour he kept them standing in the cool air while he went to see the colonel. Finally, at five o'clock in the afternoon, as the temperature was beginning to drop with the bright sun in the west, the corporal returned to them.

He reported that they were to stay in Kojo until all defense troops were deployed. Then, he would personally take them out to Captain Bell's company, west of town.

They waited a while longer while refugees from below Kojo began to file into the railroad station by the thousands, in a line that stretched south for as far as anyone could see. Adrian watched in amazement as they moved slowly and calmly up into the peninsula northeast of town, where they would wait for a morning train to take them to Wonsan.

Finally, an hour after dark, the corporal led them out west of town into the defense manned by Gilbert. After a flurry of shouting out passwords and scuffling around through the dark, they were rushed through the line and stuck into a foxhole and told to wait.

Adrian snuggled down in the hole, wrapped in her wool coat, and tried to keep warm. Metz stood up and waited. In what seemed to Adrian to be only a few minutes' time, the silence of the night was broken by a thin little voice calling out, somewhere in the blackness.

"Friend," it said. "Please. Friend."

She stood up. "What was that?"

"Shh," Metz hushed her.

The small voice spoke again, this time closer. "Don't shoot. Please. Friend."

Adrian glanced over at a foxhole nearby. She could see rifles out, over the lip of the hole, but no sign of men behind them. "Who is it?" she whispered to Metz.

"Get down," he ordered.

"Is it one of our men?" she persisted.

He put his hand on her shoulder and shoved her down into the hole. At that second a grenade exploded ten feet behind them and dirt blew over their backs. Then rifles began cracking in the dark, toward where the voice had come from. In seconds the place was lit up with flaring guns as a band of North Koreans began plunging across the line and diving into foxholes.

Adrian kept her head down for a few seconds, looked up in time to catch Metz tumbling over backward into her arms. There was a deep gash in his forehead, and blood was streaming down his face.

"Metz!" she exclaimed.

But before she could get out from under him, a North Korean soldier bounded over the lip of the dugout and planted himself in front of her. Even in the dim light she could see his bright, burning eyes glaring at her as he lifted a long knife next to his ear, ready to plunge it into her chest.

Frozen by fear, she couldn't move a muscle, not even when a shot rang out and the Korean's body abruptly curled, twisted, and then crumpled over onto Metz. She remained stiff as a statue as Gilbert reached in and with one powerful swoop yanked the body of the Korean up and out of the hole.

Then he was in it with her, holding her down, firing

away into the darkness. "Davis!" he yelled out. "Give us some light!"

Seconds later a flare burst in the sky and the landscape was bathed in bright light. Adrian could see little knots of men moving about, guns blasting, arms cocked to throw grenades. Suddenly machine guns began splattering and the Koreans began to fall and, finally, retreat.

Gilbert bent down to look at Metz. "He's got a head wound," he said in a matter-of-fact voice.

"How bad is it?" Adrian asked.

After a minute, he answered, "He'll be all right." He looked up and yelled over the hole, "Banner! Get us an ambulance up here."

"Yes, sir!"

"Gil—"

"Adrian," he said flatly, "I want you to keep your head under the line of this hole, okay? Will you do that?"

"I'll do it," she said weakly.

"Good. We don't know if they're coming back. Anything could happen."

"Gil—"

He gestured toward Metz. "See if you can stop his bleeding."

She nodded, turned her attention to the wounded lieutenant. After that, Gilbert said practically nothing to her the rest of the night.

When she awoke the next morning, she was shaking with the cold. The sky was clear and bright over Gilbert's head as he stood with his carbine poised and ready to fire. She straightened up, checked on Metz for the hundredth time. He was unconscious, but the bleeding had stopped, and he was breathing easily.

She stood up, looked about cautiously. She felt drained, weak, as if she had been working for a week without pausing. The gripping fear that had seized her when her eyes met those of the Korean in her foxhole was gone. But now, as she watched the ambulance move in and load up the bodies of American marines, she felt something almost as bad—a great sense of loss. And futility.

"Will he be all right?" she asked Gilbert as Metz was being carefully lifted up and out of the foxhole.

"Yeah, he'll be fine."

"Gil," she began tentatively, "I know what you're thinking. You don't believe I have any business here."

"Your business is writing about the war, Adrian," he said indifferently. "Other correspondents are out on the lines, so why not you?"

She was surprised at his words. "I'm glad you understand that," she said.

"I don't like it, but I understand it. What I _don't_ understand," he added, looking at her, "is why you're following me. You don't approve of what I'm doing. Why are you out here? Are you making fun of me in that paper of yours?"

"No! Certainly not. You know I'm not."

"Well, you don't believe in all this," he reminded her.

She looked him straight in the eye. "All right, no," she said. "I don't believe in it. I think it's insane. It's not our war. It's South Korea's war."

He gritted his teeth, looked ahead. Although his face was haggard and his eyes red and swollen from lack of sleep, he had never seemed so strong to her as he did now. She wanted desperately for him to turn, to take her in his arms and squeeze away her fear and uncertainty.

"You didn't answer my question, Adrian," he said after a few minutes of silence. "Why are you here in Kojo?"

She buttoned the top button of her coat to keep out the cold breeze blowing over the hill. "I'm here because General Stoddard sent me," she admitted slowly.

"General Stoddard?" he said, surprised. "Why?"

"I don't know why, Gilbert," she said, frustrated. "He keeps saying you know something."

"I do know something, Adrian," he replied seriously. "Something that scares me when I think about it. You keep asking me why I'm fighting—I don't know why. I just know I have to. If somebody doesn't—"

"Captain!" Banner rushed up to them, slid down on his belly. For a second he was startled to see a Korean foxhole occupied by a beautiful woman with bright eyes and long, flowing black hair. But he shook off his surprise and told Bell the news he had heard on the radio. "They've captured some Chinese soldiers up at Unsan," he reported excitedly.

"How many?"

"They didn't say, but it looks like what you were afraid of is happening, Captain," Brenner replied. "I got Colonel Hawkins on the horn—he wants to talk to you."

Bell nodded, looked at Adrian. "Don't move," he commanded her. "I'll be right back."

Ten minutes later, with Chick Baruchi, he was walking confidently with his gun strapped over his shoulder across the line of defense toward her. They stopped in front of her foxhole and Gilbert offered her a hand up.

"General Smith wants my company to move up north," he explained to her as she came up to ground level. "We're pulling out."

"Up north where?"

"The whole Tenth Corps is headed up toward the Manchurian border, to the Yalu River," he answered. "The Eighth Army is moving up the other side of the Taebaek Mountains."

"You're going *now*?"

"Five minutes from now," he answered.

"But we haven't even talked, Gil," she protested.

"I'm sorry, Adrian. We'll talk some other time. Chick," he said to his friend, "get her in that ambulance."

"Gilbert Bell, damn it!" Adrian exclaimed. "You can't just ship me out this way."

"We're all shipping out, Adrian," he said. "I'm not picking on you in particular. We have to move. Take a look at those seven dead men over there, Adrian," he said, pointing to a line of corpses on the ground. "They'll tell you: the war's not over, it's just starting. If we don't hit the Chinese up north, we don't have a chance down south."

"Come on, Adrian," Baruchi said softly, taking her arm.

She jerked it away. "Gilbert, please don't push me away again," she pleaded.

His face was rigid. "We don't have time for this, Adrian," he said. "Go with Chick; will you do that for me? We'll talk later."

"There may not *be* a later."

"Yes there will," he assured her.

As Chick took her arm again and applied a little pressure to it, she said to Bell, "At least tell me where you're going."

"We're going up the road from Hungnam to Yudam-ni," he answered. "A place called the Chosin Reservoir."

11

CAPTAIN GILBERT BELL'S company was sent into Hagaru to provide defense for the engineers to bulldoze an airstrip that could land supplies for the movement north toward Manchuria. It was quiet for days, except for the noise of earth-moving machinery, but all the time he was there, Gilbert couldn't help but feel that they were being watched by a silent and invisible enemy.

As the fourteen-mile road from Hungnam to Yudam-ni in the hills around the Chosin Reservoir was widened and strengthened for the passage of tanks and trucks, Gilbert and his men waited, and listened to sporadic reports on the radio of sightings of Chinese soldiers here and there below the Yalu River.

The Chinese Communists were in the war, no one doubted that now—but their movements throughout

North Korea were so cleverly concealed that no intelligence reports could even estimate how many there were in the country. As a result, the First Marines were pushing north toward Manchuria, blind against the enemy.

By the time Bell and his men reached Yudam-ni, near the reservoir, the raw Korean winter had arrived. The already stinging temperature dropped even lower, the winds picked up, and the snows began to sweep over the landscape.

On November 27, Gilbert lay next to Chick Baruchi, sprawled out on a frozen ridge at Yudam-ni. His arms and legs ached with the damp, frigid air as he shifted his position on the ice.

"How cold do you think it is, Captain?" Baruchi asked him.

"I don't know. Davis was saying twenty below, a while ago. I'd rather not think about it."

"What I'd give for a new pair of gloves," Baruchi said idly.

Bell glanced at Chick's hands, grabbed one and turned it palm up. His glove was torn open, his skin exposed. "Damn, Chick," he said. "Why didn't you get some more gloves?"

"I just didn't, Gilly," he answered. "I didn't think it'd be this cold."

"Here," Bell said, taking off his gloves. "Wear these."

Chick stood his head. "No, sir. I'm not going to let you give me your gloves."

"Put them on, Corporal," he ordered, then looked back out over the ridge again. "I'm not doing it for you. I don't want your fingers to be frozen when you have to shoot that Browning automatic."

"But Captain—"

"Put them on, Corporal," he repeated. "And stop defying orders."

"Yes, sir," Chick answered, replacing the gloves.

The wind swelling in over the reservoir grew bitter. It began to cut into Gilbert's bones as he lay trying to doze and remain alert at the same time. The colder it got, the more unreal everything became—the ice-covered slopes, the frozen water, the pale white moon hanging in a black sky.

His mind wandered; he thought of Lin Su, the Oriental temptress who had captivated his mind like opium. And Adrian McAllister, the beautiful, exciting woman he loved more than anything else in his life. Why, he wondered sleepily, dreamily, did the thought of the first woman make him so impatient and abrupt with the other? Could he ever admit his love for Adrian, or would they always be apart, at odds with each other?

"Captain!" Baruchi was shaking his shoulders violently. "Look at that!"

Gilbert raised up, jerked his carbine ready. He saw them immediately. From the northeast they were moving toward them, thousands of Chinese soldiers, all alike, all pushing obliviously through the wind and snow toward the marine encampment.

"Chick," he said, "better spread the word. We're going to have to dig in."

"Yes, sir."

"Chick—over there. That looks like another division coming down from the northwest."

"There must be more than a hundred thousand of them," Baruchi gasped.

"Captain?" Davis said, coming up. "They've cut off

the road. They're everywhere. We're trapped in here."

"Then let's hold on to this god-forsaken cake of ice for as long as we can," Gilbert instructed him. "Tell Poe and Wilson I want to see them right now."

"Yes, sir."

But before Gilbert could make any plans or take any orders on the phone, the massive Chinese army struck. Organized, fearless, persistent, the attackers marched in columns up the ridges, were shot to pieces, then what was left retreated, regrouped and pushed forward again. As soon as they got within throwing range, they broke out in all directions and began heaving grenades into the lines. Sometimes they yelled incoherently; at other times they screamed out in blood-curdling English, "Marines! Snakes! Kill!" as they flung their bodies desperately into showers of machine gun fire.

Outmanned as they were, the marines could do no more than tighten their perimeter and hold through the night. Then word came from corps command the next morning to hold on another day. Again they dug in and faced the thousands around them on all sides.

Yudam-ni was a caldron of death for the next two days. There was no cover. The only refuges were foxholes lined with stacks of Chinese bodies for protection against enemy mortar fire. The weather made fighting almost impossible. Guns froze, jeeps trying to move over the four thousand-foot Toktong Pass stalled and had to be abandoned. Men passed out from the shock of thirty-degrees-below-zero temperatures.

As they held, the dismal radio reports came in. The Eighth Army had been repelled by nearly two hundred thousand Chinese and had retreated behind the Chongchon River; another Chinese division had hit Hagaru, south of the reservoir. The British task force sent in to help the First Marines had lost a third of their men. Two more Chinese divisions were attacking Koto-ri, south of Hagaru.

"Captain," Davis said wearily on the third day, "they've worn us down. We're broken. It's not so much the Chinese—we could handle them. It's this damn cold! It's killing us. The men can't take it."

Gilbert didn't have to respond. Everyone felt the cold. His body was racked with it. His face was stiff, his eyes dry. And he had lost feeling in the fingers of his left hand.

"Where's General Smith, Captain?" Davis asked. "What's he doing? Where's our air power?"

Gilbert lay still and listened to the mortars and machine gun fire all around him. He was so cold, he had almost lost his sense of direction. "Smith has ordered us to break out, Davis," he broke the news.

Davis looked confused. "You don't mean _retreat!_" he said, shocked.

"No, I don't mean retreat. We're regrouping at the base of the reservoir."

"Then what?"

"Then we're going to try to make it to Hagaru, where the supplies are."

"But what about Yudam-ni, Captain? Are we just leaving it?"

"Leaving what?" Baruchi said, sprawling across the ice. "We're not leaving here, are we? Aren't we going to wait for reinforcements?"

"No, we're leaving," Bell said. "Smith's orders."

Davis frowned. "Captain, I know we've been complaining, and God knows any minute now a million

Chinese are likely to come down on us, but even so, we can't retreat. The marines have never retreated!"

"We're breaking out, Davis. Don't question it, just do it. The whole division's going out together. And we'll be going out fighting."

Davis was angry. "Going out—is that what it is? I call it running."

Bell lost his patience. "All right, Davis, that's enough. Do you think I like pulling out? I didn't crawl all the way up into these frozen mountains just so I could turn around and go back. But I obey orders, just like everybody else. Now shape up!"

"Gilly—" Chick began.

"You too, Corporal. I don't want to hear either one of you say retreat again, do you hear me? Just don't say the word. I don't want another man to hear it."

"Yes, sir."

"We're going to try to break through a hundred thousand Chinese. Think about that, nothing else."

"Captain—"

"Davis," Bell warned, "I'm going to forget what you said. But I swear, if you do anything to destroy our morale, I'll shoot you dead, on the spot, so help me."

"Yes, sir."

"All right, Lieutenant Poe!" he called out. "Sergeant Eagerton! As soon as I get the word on the horn, we're moving out of here!"

From Yudam-ni to Hagaru was fourteen miles, along a twisting mountain road. It took Bell and his men a day and a half to reach Toktong Pass, half the way there.

Retreat or not, he knew that every inch of ground would have to be fought for. As they moved out along the mountain slopes, the Chinese struck sporadically, with hand weapons and mortars, and then they would back up and strike again. They were reorganizing themselves to stop the marines' march to Hungnam on the sea, but still they attacked, day and night.

On the road to Hagaru, beyond the Toktong Pass, the division stopped to rest. Gilbert and his men, positioned along the eastern side of the road, were exhausted after the ordeal at Yudam-ni. They needed sleep badly. At about two in the morning, Davis reported to the captain that a platoon of Chinese with machine guns had been spotted a mile away, easing toward them down the slopes.

Gilbert moved hurriedly down the roadbed, rolled down beside Lieutenant Poe. "David," he said, "I want you to take your platoon up that hill over there—" He stopped. "David?" he said, shaking him. "Lieutenant?"

"He's dead, Captain," said a private nearby. "He froze stiff."

Gilbert touched Poe's face; it was hard and cold, like marble. It made a sick feeling in his stomach. "Don't leave him, Private," he said.

"No, sir."

Gilbert sprang up, hustled back to Davis. "We're going up there ourselves, Davis," he announced.

"Our old platoon?"

"That's right. Let's see if we can get them before they hit the road with those machine guns."

A few minutes later, Gilbert, Davis, Baruchi, and the rest of Gilbert's old platoon marched slowly off the road down the snow-covered slopes and headed in the direction of the advancing Chinese. "They're going for the command jeeps," Gilbert told Chick at the foot of a hill.

"I wish we could see them better," Chick complained. "I've never seen a place this dark."

"I don't see them at all," Davis said, straining.

"Come on, let's get closer," Bell ordered them and they began treading cautiously across the snow. Then abruptly he called out in a low voice, "Get down!"

Each man instantly dropped to the ground. Chick took off his gloves, stuffed them into his pockets. "What is it?" he said anxiously.

"There's another platoon behind us, Chick," he explained. "If we don't do something quick, we're dead. Davis?"

"Sir," he answered promptly.

"Davis, see that hut down there?" he said, pointing at the bottom of a hill.

"I see it, Captain."

"All right. We're going to try to draw them out that way. When we're in range, fire that thing up, let's get a little light on the subject. Maybe if we can see them, we can hit them."

"You got it, Captain," he replied confidently. "One burning native hut, coming up."

After Davis left, they scrambled to their feet again and pressed on across the field. The wind wasn't as strong as it had been in the higher elevations, but the thermometer had slipped down further; it was now thirty below. Some of the men could barely feel their toes and fingers anymore. Gilbert's left hand throbbed with pain, his feet felt thick and awkward as they trudged through the snow toward the hut.

Soon they had slipped out from their sandwich position between the two Chinese groups and were setting up to open fire on both platoons as soon as Davis lit the fire.

At his own discretion Davis struck up a blaze. The hut roared with a *whoosh,* and flames shot up ten feet into the black sky. All at once the enemy was visible, broken up into two clusters, a scant twenty yards from the hut.

Bell's men opened fire all at once and the Chinese collapsed like dominoes into the snow. But then Davis yelled out, "Captain! Behind you!"

By the time Gilbert had wheeled around, Chick Baruchi was ten steps out in front of their flank, his BAR pressed tight against his shoulder. Racing toward him were six Chinese soldiers, rifles extended.

"Shoot, Baruchi!" someone yelled out to him.

But he stood still, his back to Bell and the others, stalwartly facing the onrushing enemy.

"Baruchi! Shoot, damn it! Let 'em have it!"

When the Chinese commenced firing, it became clear he wasn't going to. The enemy passed over Baruchi as they charged, with their hot machine guns blasting in the cold air. He crumbled underneath a wave of fire.

Off to the left Davis, in the heat of anger, burst out from behind the hut. "Chick!" he called out. "Chick!"

By now Gilbert and his men were facing the enemy and shooting. "Davis!" he called out. "Get back!"

But Davis was rushing ahead, paying attention to no one. "You bastards!" he cried out when he saw Baruchi writhing in pain. "Bastards!"

He stopped long enough to lift M-1 up to his shoulder. But before he had time to pull off a round, a cloud of machine gun bullets riddled his body, pro-

pelling him backward for ten feet before he fell dead
in the snow.

Bell jumped up, charged the Chinese with his carbine. Bullets flew all around him, but nothing struck
him as he dived into a rifle squad of Chinese. One
of the enemy crumbled under his bayonet, another
had his jaw shattered by a rifle butt, another took
two rounds in the heart at close range. Then Gilbert
whipped around and shot the three remaining.

"Chick?" he said, getting to his friend.

"My rifle froze," he said, reaching for "Barbara"
in the snow. "I'm sorry, Gilly."

"Where are you hit?"

"It's my legs, Gilly. But it's so cold I don't even feel
them. What about Davis? Is he okay?"

Gilbert shook his head. "He's gone, Chick."

"He was trying to save me," he said.

"I know. Be still. Let me take a look." He examined the wounds in Chick's legs. There were two bullets in each. "Looks like you've got some torn flesh
here, Chick," he said. "Maybe a chipped bone."

"I can walk," he grunted, trying to get up.

"You're not walking anywhere, Chick. You're riding—right out of the war."

Gilbert patted him on the shoulder, unconsciously
picked up the BAR and walked across the snow. The
hut was burning low now, but it was still acting like
a huge candle, lighting the way to Davis. Most of
the other men were gathered around the private's
body. Bell pushed aside two of them, making a path
for himself through the circle.

He looked down at the body someone had covered
with a poncho. "Maybe he's not so cold now," he
said sadly.

"He ought not to be there, Captain," said one of the squad leaders, Corporal Madding. He was a stout, muscular young man who was never without a gripe about something. A good marine, but a chronic complainer.

"None of us ought to be here, Corporal," Gilbert said. "Each one of us ought to be home in a warm bed with a woman."

"That's not what I mean, Captain," he said. "I mean it's Baruchi's fault the guy's dead."

Bell looked at him. "Baruchi didn't ask Davis to go running across an open field after him, Madding," he said calmly, holding his anger down. "That was his own decision."

"Yes, sir," he said respectfully, "I know it was his decision. I'm just saying he wouldn't've done it if Baruchi hadn't froze the way he did."

"His *rifle* froze, Madding," he corrected him. "*He* didn't."

"Is that what he said, Captain?"

"Captain Bell," Doug Simmons spoke up. "We've been expecting this a long time. It finally happened."

"You expected what, Simmons?" he asked angrily.

"I know he's your friend, Captain," Simmons ventured, "but I got to say it anyway: Chick Baruchi's a coward. We all know it. He goes around calling his rifle women's names, he acts like a damn sissy. We don't know how the hell he ever got in the marines to begin with. Do we, fellas?"

The other men rumbled their agreement.

"Look, Simmons," Bell said impatiently. "We just saved a couple of colonels from being wiped out by machine guns."

"We don't want him in our platoon, Captain,"

Madding said. "There's another seventy miles to go
to Hungnam. We can fight the cold and hunger and
the Chinese, but we don't want a coward in our
platoon."

"The man's wounded, Madding," Bell reminded
him. "You don't have to depend on him."

"I don't see how that matters, Captain," Madding
asserted. "We don't want him in our platoon."

"Baruchi is not a coward, Corporal," Gilbert asserted confidently. "Now let's get out of here before
we attract any more Chinese."

Madding held up the others. "Why don't you prove
it, Captain?" he said to Bell. "That's his rifle you got
there, isn't it? Prove it."

"Yeah, Captain," Simmons put in, "let's see if his
BAR really is frozen."

The others mumbled their agreement with the idea.

"Chick doesn't have to prove to me he's not a
coward," Bell told them.

"Well, he's got to prove it to us," Madding claimed.
"We're the ones who have to depend on him, not
you."

"Look, Madding, the man's wounded—"

"Let us see the rifle, Captain," he persisted. "Let's
see once and for all if he was lying. If you don't
then we'll *know* he was lying."

As Madding held out his hand for the rifle, Bell
looked around at the men. Like him, they were exhausted, half-frozen, frustrated. He knew they weren't
going to be talked out of this. He hesitated a minute
or so, then without a word he gave Madding the
weapon.

"I guess now we'll know," Madding said, taking
it gently out of his hands.

"Aim at the fire, Dave," one of the men told him.

"It won't matter," another man said. "It ain't going to shoot anyway."

The corporal turned his body toward the burning hut, slowly raised the rifle to his shoulder. He paused to look back over his shoulder at the others. Satisfied that all eyes were on him, he held his breath and squeezed the trigger.

Every man there flinched as an explosion of bullets blew out of the barrel into the flames. Then silence fell over them as Madding turned around and returned the BAR to Bell. "I guess that proves he was lying, Captain," he said, satisfied. "The man's a coward."

"It doesn't prove a damned thing, Madding, and you know it."

"Captain Bell—" Simmons began.

"All right, let's get something straight here," he interrupted. "You've had your say, all of you; now let me have mine. I've known Chick Baruchi a long time, and I know the man is not a coward."

"But what about his rifle?"

"His rifle froze, Simmons. God, man, it's like a meat freezer out here. You've seen other weapons freeze. You know it happens."

"Yes, sir, it happens. Only you just saw it go off," Simmons pointed out.

"Okay, I saw it go off. But I believe the *man*, not some piece of machinery."

The men stirred uncomfortably. "It could've been warmed by the fire," one of them said. "That could've made it go off."

"Madding," Bell ordered, "the demonstration's over,

okay? Let's get back to the road. Simmons, get us some gloves off those Chinese. They won't need them."

"What about Davis?" Simmons asked.

"Bring him. We're carrying our dead into Hagaru."

"Yes, sir," Simmons responded.

Bell left them, returned to Baruchi. "Let's go, soldier," he said, getting a good grip on both his arms.

"Gilly, it did freeze—I swear to God."

"I know it did, Chick," he assured him. "Forget it." He yanked the corporal up over his shoulder and began walking back through the snow.

"As long as you believe me, Gilly—"

"Save your breath, Corporal," Gilbert said. "We've got a long way to go."

By the time they rejoined the rest of the division, the First Marines were on the move again. The line of ten thousand men, stretched out a full ten miles along the road, inched slowly toward Hagaru; every step of the way the Chinese bit and chewed at the columns, attacking sometimes in a force of a thousand in hand-to-hand combat, sometimes from a distance, with mortars.

At dawn on December 3, the division pulled to a stop for a rest. Gilbert eased Chick down off his back and sat down on the road. Down the slopes and up on the ridges he saw a thousand Chinese soldiers creeping south, parallel to the road. But he was so cold, his back so wrenched with pain, that the sight of them so close didn't even bother him. When they got within range, as always, they would open fire on them.

He drew out two cans of C rations and opened them. "Here," he said, handing one of the cans to Baruchi, "dine in the open."

Chick took the frozen can and tried to plow the beans out with his fingers, but they were too numb; he couldn't manage it. "How much further is it to Hagaru?" he asked, giving up on the ration.

"We'll be there tonight," Bell told him, checking the Chinese on the ridge.

Chick nodded, leaned back against his pack and closed his eyes. Bell watched him a minute, then stood up and looked up and down the columns. Most of the men were sitting or lying down in the middle of the road. He couldn't tell the dead from the wounded or weary in some cases.

"Captain," said a voice behind him.

"Colonel," he responded, saluting Lieutenant Colonel Davis as he came up.

"Gilbert," Davis said, "you've got some good men there. I'm proud of them."

"Thank you, sir."

He shook his head. "Funny, isn't it? The papers back home have been saying American men have gone soft; they say we rely too much on machinery. And here we are, stumbling over these winding mountain roads on foot, in ungodly cold, with a hundred thousand Chinese picking at us the whole way. That's not relying too much on machinery, is it?"

"I suppose there's nothing else we can do, Colonel," Bell said. "The Eighth Army can't help us, the ROK can't get near us, nobody can fly us out—we have to keep moving and hope those B-29s upstairs will keep them off our backs."

"That's the spirit, Captain," Davis said, patting him on the shoulder. "Keep it up."

Minutes later word ran through the columns to load up and march. "Let's go, Chick," Gilbert said to Baruchi.

"I think I can walk, Gilly."

"Will you shut up? I need you for balance." He lifted him up, staggered under the weight, then found his legs again. "How can you be gaining weight when you're not eating anything?" he said. Not waiting for an answer, he stood to see his company fall in, and watched the column push forward.

At noon that day the Chinese hit the south section and Gilbert had to take some men out to clear the way for the rest of the division. For two hours they chased the enemy up and down the ridges, through knee-high snow and over frozen streams, but they never caught up with them.

On the way back to the road, they came across a number of abandoned rifles and ammunition belts strewn out over the snow in an open valley. Gilbert and Private Doug Simmons trudged across the field for a hundred yards, following half-filled footprints over a ridge into a gully.

There, huddled together in a trench, frozen to death, were twenty or thirty Chinese.

Gilbert turned his head, gathered his men, started back toward the division. When he saw the slow procession, his pain eased a bit. "Let's keep moving, you guys," he called out. "If we stop now, we'll wind up like those poor bastards back there."

The afternoon was endless. The closer they got to Hagaru, the colder it got, the more often the Chinese struck. But they kept going.

At seven o'clock that evening, they drew close to the Hagaru perimeter, and the columns stopped. The officers came together and conferred, then Bell returned to his men.

"They tell us the press is at Hagaru," he said to them. "Reporters from all over the world are gathered in that nothing of a place to see if there's anything left of us to march in."

"We got plenty left, Captain," someone called out.

"We've still got sixty-eight miles to go to Hungnam, men. Hagaru's not the end of this march, it's the beginning. They know that. If we drag our butts in there looking like a defeated bunch of soft-bellies, they're going to report it to the world. Do you want that?"

"No!" they replied.

"All right, then, let's show them what a marine's made of. Straighten up." He walked through the ranks. "Simmons, button your coat. Edmundson, suck your belly in. You look soft."

"Yes, sir."

"All right, come on, line up! Get your dead or wounded on your backs and line up. Edwards, keep your eyes front."

The men stood erect, began to form even columns. The whole division began to do the same. Within minutes crisp commands were singing out over the heads of the men, and the marines were falling into order.

"All right," Bell called out. "Throw those shoulders back. We're going in like marines!"

12

WHEN ADRIAN STEPPED off the transport plane onto the rough, icy runway at the Hagaru airstrip, she felt terribly alone. Lieutenant Metz was in an army hospital in Tokyo; she was on her own now. She meandered about the place, conversing casually with fellow reporters and Movietone and television cameramen, but her heart wasn't in it. Like everyone else, she was afraid of what she might see when the marines arrived in Hagaru. If Gilbert wasn't with them, she would be alone for the rest of her life.

Most of the time she found herself staring up the road to Yudam-ni, waiting, thinking about him. Once, as she was trying to force down a couple of dry crackers a marine chaplain had given her, she was approached by Robert Kowalski of the *New York Times*.

"It's safe enough," he said, "if that's what you're worried about. We're surrounded by armed men in foxholes. I wouldn't walk out of town, though."

She smiled weakly. "Oddly enough, I'm not even concerned about that," she said.

He nodded approvingly. "You're a good reporter."

"Not *that* good," she smiled. "I'm afraid I'm not really thinking much about a story, either."

"That could only mean you know one of the marines coming in," he guessed.

She looked at him. Kowalski was very tall, six-feet-five at least, and solidly built, but he had an intellectual air about him that make him almost seem weak.

"Do you know any of them?" she asked, evading his question.

He offered her a Chesterfield cigarette, took one himself when she shook her head. "No," he said, lighting it, "I don't know anybody. I'm just covering the story. To tell you the truth, I'm kind of doubting they make it this far. They're bred to riding and flying, not walking."

"They'll make it," she asserted confidently, though his words disturbed her. She had heard it before— "American Fighting Men Turned to Mush by Modern Conveniences"—and she was getting impatient with the idea. "They're strong enough to do anything they have to do," she added.

"Hey, what's this? I thought you were against the war," he reminded her.

She caught herself. "I am against it," she said. "But these men aren't like the ones we saw back in June, Robert."

"You're not like you were, either," he said admiringly. "Last summer, in Suwon, you were a beautiful, cocky young reporter trying to do a big job. Now you're just as beautiful, but you're also an extraordinarily sensual woman with confidence in herself. I like that. I find it exciting."

She noted the gradual movement of his body toward her, but she kept her ground. "I'm waiting for Captain Gilbert Bell," she declared.

He flicked his cigarette into the snow. "As soon as this is over, Adrian," he said, ignoring her words, "I want to show you New York. I want to take you to the best restaurants in the world. I know this little place in the village—"

"Robert," she said, putting him off. "I'm not interested. "I'm sorry, really. Thank you for asking, but I can't even begin to think about such things, with this war going on."

"You're not fighting the war, Adrian," he told her. "You're just reporting it. Besides, it's not even *our* war. It's South Korea's war."

Adrian disliked hearing her own sentiment thrown back at her. It made her ill-at-ease. It seemed all right to express that view to Gilbert or Mallory, but right then and there, it seemed somehow inappropriate.

They were silent for a minute as they watched six formations of B-26 bombers fly overhead, headed north. Finally Kowalski, shifting his weight back and forth from one foot to the other, said, "It's cold out here, Adrian. Let's go find a heater. A cup of coffee, maybe."

She shook her head.

"Are you sure?"

"I'm sure."

He stuffed his hands into his coat pockets. "Well," he said philosophically, "all I can say is, this Captain Bell's got to be some lucky bastard."

"I hope he's lucky," she said distantly.

"Adrian, come on—one cup of coffee. You're going to freeze standing there."

"No, thank you," she said politely. "I think I'll just wait out here a while."

The waiting was hard. The afternoon wore on, and there was no word of the marines. Then, finally, at seven o'clock, the news spread quickly throughout Hagaru. They were outside the city perimeter. In a few minutes they would be coming in. Immediately everyone came to life—the newspeople, the navy medical men, the pilots of the transports waiting to take out the wounded.

All eyes were turned to the road from Yudam-ni.

Next to Adrian in the crowd was the chaplain who had given her crackers earlier. His eyes were bright, he seemed excited and happy. She, on the other hand, could only feel apprehension and fear. The other reporters and military people were nervously talking to each other, creating a monotonous chatter that irritated her, made her want to scream.

Suddenly a hush fell over them as the chaplain announced, "Here they come!"

At first Adrian saw the headlights of the jeeps approaching the town, then she heard the regular cadence, "Hut two, three, four," and then they began to come in. Thousands of marines, as orderly as a color guard on awards day, marched proudly into Hagaru.

But when they passed by her, she saw how haggard and exhausted they really were. Their faces were puffed up with the cold, hundreds of them were hobbling in on frost-bitten feet. Ears were blue, faces ashen. As man after man passed by, tears blurred her vision, chills gripped her spine to see such strength and courage.

An hour passed. The number of men emptying into Hagaru astonished her. She desperately hoped one of them would be Gilbert Bell. She thought she recognized him several times, but it was always someone else. She began to fear that he was one of the dead men being carried into town in jeeps, trucks, and on other soldiers' backs, but she couldn't bear to look at them to see.

Then she saw him. He was coming in, limping badly, but marching all the same, with Chick Baruchi slumped over his back. She couldn't stop herself; she rushed out to him.

She heard the chaplain call out to her to stop, but she didn't pay any attention. She ran straight to him. "Oh, Gil!" she cried, grabbing his arm. "Gil! I thought you'd never come."

He smiled, with effort, and dropped his arm around her shoulder. "Adrian," he said calmly. "What're you doing here?"

"I'm waiting for you, silly," she said tearfully.

Gilbert looked into her eyes, then pressed on. "Chick's been shot," he said.

"Is he dead?" she asked, looking at him.

"No, he's all right," Bell told her, leaning on her a little as he walked on. "He's been out the last couple of miles."

"Miss," a navy medic said to her.

"No," she said. "It's all right. I'll take care of him."

"Miss—"

"Just leave us alone," she told him. "I'll take care of him. I'll take care of both of them."

"Yes, ma'am," he answered, moving up the lines.

"You're kind of pushy sometimes, you know it?" he said fondly.

She felt his weight begin to press down on her shoulder. "When it's important, I'm pushy," she said.

"Anything for a story, hunh?" he said in a low voice.

She bristled at his comment, but let it pass.

"Come on," she said to him, "let's go over here and sit down."

He nodded, grimaced, and limped over to a jeep. With difficulty he lowered Chick down off his back and eased him against a tire. "This is it for you, son," he said to him. "From here it's Tokyo, and then home." He watched Adrian open a first-aid kit and attend to him. "For the rest of us," he said to himself, "it's another sixty miles." He dropped to his knees.

"Gilbert!" Adrian exclaimed.

"I'm all right," he said, easing down on the ice. "I'm just fine. All I need is about five years of undisturbed sleep."

She knelt down beside him, took his head in her hands. "Then go to sleep," she said softly. "It's all right; everything is all right. Go on to sleep."

He looked up at her and smiled. "I guess you're getting quite a story here," he said drowsily.

She smiled, ran her fingers over his cold forehead. "Go to sleep," she said.

He drifted off quickly. He awoke later, when the navy relief team transferred him to the large tent, but he was so groggy with fatigue he could barely stand up. They had to throw his arms around their necks and drag him there.

Adrian stayed with him that night, doing what she could to attend to the other men in the tent as she listened to gunfire and bombs somewhere in the distance and observed through the crack in the tent thousands more marines pouring into Hagaru. By two o'clock, they had stopped coming.

At some time before dawn she was brought away from a wounded private by the sounds of Gilbert groaning and thrashing about on his cot. She came to him, touched his face with a wet cloth. "Gil, it's all right," she said in a calm voice. "It's all right."

He opened his eyes. "Tell Lin Su," he mumbled.

The sound of the Chinese woman's name cut into her like a knife. "Tell Lin Su what, Gil?" she said haltingly.

But he couldn't respond. He had fallen back to sleep.

At seven the next morning, he awoke to see Adrian kneeling a few feet away beside one of his men. Her hair was tousled and she looked tired. He guessed she had been up all night, tending to the wounded men in the tent.

A few minutes later, she came and stood at the foot of his cot. "Well, good morning," she said.

He raised up. "What time is it?" he asked, looking for his watch.

"Seven o'clock."

"Where's Chick?"

"They took him to another tent, Gilbert."

He swung his feet over the side of the cot. "I have to see him," he said, rubbing his forehead.

"All you have to do is sleep," she told him, but she knew what he was going to do.

Gilbert Bell was strong-willed; when he decided to do something, he did it.

Resigned, she helped him outside to a medical unit and stood back and watched him walk with effort over to where Baruchi was lying down. She almost felt jealous of Chick's wounds; if only someday Gilbert would pay that kind of attention to her. If only, someday, he would admit to her and to himself that he loved her. . . .

"Good morning," Kowalski said, coming up beside her.

"Good morning."

"Is that the lucky bastard?" he asked, gesturing with a nod toward Bell.

"Does he look lucky to you?" she said. "He can barely walk, his left hand is numb, he has a wrenched back—"

"Yes, but he also has you, Adrian," he said. "I'd say that makes him pretty damned lucky."

"Robert," she said, uncomfortable with his attention and flattery.

"I know—Captain Bell. Right. I'll let it go. For the moment. But let me warn you: you're too beautiful a woman for me to let go forever. I'll see you later."

"Thank you for understanding," she said.

"Who understands? I'm just being tolerant, that's all."

She smiled, not knowing what to say.

He walked off a few steps, then turned around. "I will say this, though," he told her. "I was wrong about one thing. The marines are not soft. It took more guts than I'll ever have to break out of there and march almost twenty miles with a hundred thousand Chinese shooting at them."

She was warmed by his admission. "It did take a lot of courage."

"Yeah, a lot of courage. But believe me, there's no way on earth they can go another sixty miles to Hungnam. It's not humanly possible. They can't do it."

"They'll do it," she said quietly.

He shook his head. "Unh-unh. Not even the marines," he said. "I'll see you in Hungnam, Adrian," he said and left her.

A few minutes later, when she saw Gilbert talking to Baruchi, she joined them. They were in an open tent among fifty or so wounded, lying about on cots, sitting on the ground, or standing around waiting to be taken out.

"Chick," she said cheerfully. "You're looking better this morning."

"Gilly said you were here," he said, smiling.

"Oh, this is so nice I could live here," she teased.

"Adrian," Chick said seriously, "will you please tell him not to send me back? I can't leave."

She knelt down beside his cot, looked directly at him.

"Why can't you?" she asked. "You're injured."

"No, I don't mean that," he told her. "I mean I can't leave the others." He paused, then added, "Not while they're thinking what they are."

She frowned. "I don't understand."

"Adrian, the men think I'm a coward," he confessed.

"My rifle froze and they think it was *me* that froze. They think I couldn't pull the trigger. But I did pull it, I swear to God. The rifle was frozen."

"I've told him it doesn't matter," Gilbert said. "But he's hard-headed. He won't listen. Look, Chick," he said to his friend, "you're going home; you don't have to worry about us. Besides, what the guys in the company think you are isn't going to change what you really are—is it?"

"No," he said. "It isn't."

"All right, then. Forget it. *I* know you're not a coward, Adrian here knows it. And who the hell else matters but me and Adrian, after all? Right?"

He nodded. "I still don't want to go," he said.

"Well, I want you to, Corporal," Gilbert told him. "I can't carry you another sixty miles. You're too heavy."

"I keep telling you I can walk."

"Do what he says, Chick," Adrian said, touching his arm. "Please. Go home. We'll see what we can do to end the war while you're gone."

He smiled again, just as two men appeared and lifted up his cot. He lay his head back as they carted him off to the transport plane.

Gilbert struggled to his feet and watched until he saw Baruchi's cot slide quickly into the belly of the C-54. Then he sat down on the cot. "I'm tired," he sighed.

"Why don't you go back to sleep?" she suggested. "I'll wake you up if anything happens."

He looked at her curiously. "You're full of surprises, aren't you?" he said wearily. "I never would've taken you for a Florence Nightingale type, but you were up all night with my men, weren't you?"

"Lie down," she said, pushing on his chest. "They won't mind."

He closed his eyes and sighed. "Yeah," he admitted, "I am tired." He stretched his legs out.

She touched his cheek. It was warm now, the color was back in his skin. But he still looked exhausted. She wondered how they could possibly make it to the sea. Last night she had heard the Chinese were concentrating their forces outside of Hagaru. How could one division of bone-weary marines survive a major enemy offensive?

She ran her fingers over his brow and said softly, "I'll have some hot food ready for you when you wake up."

He opened his eyes. "Adrian?"

"Shh. Go to sleep."

"Who was that tall guy you were talking to?"

"Now why would you want to know that, Gilly?" she teased him. "Don't tell me the captain's jealous."

"I'm not jealous. I just asked who he was."

She smiled warmly. "He's a correspondent for the *New York Times*," she said.

"Well, that correspondent likes you a lot," he said, turning over on his side.

"Professional courtesy," she said indifferently.

"Sure," he said, closing his eyes. "For a woman as good-looking as you, professional courtesy. Right."

13

Two DAYS LATER, Gilbert felt his shoulder being gently shaken. He awoke out of his sleep with a start when he realized that standing at the side of the cot was General Oliver Smith himself. He quickly sat up, attempted a salute, felt an intense wave of pain shoot through his head as soon as he moved.

"Don't get up, Captain," the general told him. Smith was a strong, authoritative man of middle age, with clear, intelligent eyes. "How're you feeling?" he asked.

"I feel fine, General," he said. "I've had a good couple of days' rest."

"They tell me this lady here hasn't slept a wink since they brought you in," he said, but didn't wait for a response. He pulled up the empty cot next to Gilly's and sat on it and leaned forward. "Bell," he said in a sober voice, "they tell me the best driver in the marines is in your company."

"I'd say Private Edwards is one of the best drivers in the world, General. He's a magician with anything on wheels."

"Good. It's going to take a magician to do what I want. What we need here is some more diesel fuel, Captain. Almond wants me to abandon my equipment, but I don't want to do that. We need all the machines we have. But we've had to run some trucks off the road north of here because we don't have enough fuel to run them. And some of those trucks are carrying 150 howitzers."

"Where's the fuel, General?" he asked.

"It's at Chinhung-ni, about ten miles south of Koto-ri."

"I'll get Edwards. We'll be ready to go in ten minutes."

"Whoa, wait! I didn't say you were going, Captain. We need you back here. The Chinese are building up outside of town. We're going to need our command."

"General," Gilbert said, "what you're talking about sounds dangerous."

"It is dangerous, Bell, make no mistake about it."

"Then I can't ask one of my men to do it without me."

Smith stood up. "I need that fuel, Captain," he said.

"We'll have it back here tonight, General Smith," he promised.

Smith noted the determination in Gilbert's eyes. "Okay. Meet me at my jeep in five minutes." He looked at Adrian and tipped his helmet. "Ma'am," he said politely, then left.

Gilbert scooped up his gloves, snapped his carbine over his shoulder, then noticed the sadness in Adrian's face. "I'll see you at Hungnam," he said, starting to go.

But she held his arm back. "Gilbert," she pleaded, "you're too weak to do this. Let Edwards do it, for God's sake. Or General Smith. It's his job, let *him* do it!"

"Adrian—"

"Gilbert, this is suicidal."

He looked at her. Even worn and tired, her thick black hair mussed, she was the most beautiful woman he had ever seen. It seemed odd—she seemed more attractive to him now than she ever had before. "Look," he said, holding her hand. "We'll make it. This whole war's suicidal. This won't be any different."

"I'm never going to see you again, Gilly. I can feel it," she said desperately.

"Hush. I'm not going to die. Think positive. Help me out here."

"I'm trying, Gilbert, but damn it, I have you here for two days and you take off on some crazy plan."

"It's not a crazy plan, Adrian," he corrected her. "It's a necessary mission, and it makes sense. Now try to understand. I've got to do this."

"Gil—"

"Stay here and write your story. I'll see you in Hungnam."

"I don't care about the story," she declared vehemently. "I care about you!"

He hesitated. "I wonder how much you mean that," he said.

"I mean it, I mean it. What do you want me to *say?*"

He kissed her lightly on the lips. "I'll see you on the coast," he told her, then left.

Edwards was standing outside by the jeep when Gilbert reported to Smith. As soon as he saw the captain he hopped inside, behind the wheel. Bell saluted the general, slid into the passenger's seat.

"Good luck, Captain," Smith said to him.

"Thank you, sir." As Edwards cranked up the engine, he glanced back at the medical tent. Adrian was standing oustside, looking at them. For a second he wavered; he actually felt like chucking it all and rushing over to take her in his arms. When he saw her raise her hand to her eye to wipe a tear, he almost spoke out to Smith.

But he caught himself, turned his eyes front. "Let's go, Edwards," he said, and the jeep pulled off.

The image of her standing there stuck in his mind, even as Edwards broke out of Hagaru and headed south toward Koto-ri. There was something about her that was different, somehow. He couldn't tell exactly what it was, but he knew it was there, something that was both puzzling and fascinating.

"Roadblock, Captain," Edwards announced. "Better keep low."

Gilbert got his carbine ready, looked ahead at the platoon of Chinese crouched behind sandbags stacked four feet high on the road. Edwards was picking up speed, instead of slowing down. Through his tired eyes the Chinese seemed to be moving toward them. . . .

The jeep rammed through and over the sandbags with a clunk, sending enemy soldiers right and left. Gilbert wheeled around and aimed his rifle, but it wasn't necessary. They were too disorganized to fire.

"Do you drive like that back in West Virginia?" Gilbert said, taking a deep breath as the jeep sped onward.

Edwards grinned. "No, sir. That kind of driving's dangerous back home."

A few minutes later, Gilbert said, "Look over to your left, Edwards. They're gathering their forces."

"Must be a couple hundred thousand of them," Edwards exclaimed, taking a quick look at the armies advancing over the ridges and valleys toward Hagaru. "What do you figure they're doing?"

"It looks like they're setting up for the march out."

"I hope General Smith knows about them."

"He knows," Gilbert assured him. After a pause, he added hopefully, "Maybe with them headed toward Hagaru, we won't have too much trouble on the road."

"The general said we were going after a diesel truck, is that right?"

"That's right. One diesel truck."

"Well, if they're fighting when we come back, Captain, it's going to be like we're riding on a bomb, with all that diesel fuel in back of us."

"One thing at a time, Edwards."

"Yes, sir, I guess so. One thing at a time."

While Edwards drove, Gilbert kept his rifle between his legs and his arms folded across his chest. In the open jeep, racing over the twisting road, it was unbelievably cold. His face, blown by the icy wind, ached; his left hand was completely numb, his whole body at times shuddered uncontrollably.

And still he thought of Adrian. Beautiful and desirable as she had always been to him, he had never loved her, he told himself. She was far too liberal for him, too concerned with moral issues, too much against things he accepted without question. She had always been opposed to war; he had always believed you fought when your country called—no matter what the issues.

But at Hagaru he had seen a new side of Adrian McAllister. She hadn't expressed her disapproval of the war. In fact, without being asked, she had tended to him and his men—for two nights, without rest. She was warm, compassionate, and loving—not the liberal, aggressive reporter for the Sacramento *Sun*. It was possible that side of her had been there all along and he had simply never allowed himself to see it. Perhaps he hadn't wanted to look that deeply, to be enmeshed in what he might have found. And perhaps they had both changed just a little. . . .

The *Times* reporter . . . Gilbert stirred in his seat as he thought of him. The man had scrutinized her, flirted with her. And yet she had ignored him. She ignored a chance to link herself with major league journalism. It surprised him to think of it. Adrian had ignored Kowalski, her job, her beliefs—for him.

Could she, he wondered, love him? And did he love her? Could he forget the enticing image of Lin Su, warm, naked, reaching up to him?

His mind clicked to attention when he saw the movement of bodies out of the hills toward the road. "Slow down, Edwards," he said, sitting up, looking over the other man's shoulder at the massive army, then up ahead of them.

Edwards pulled the jeep to a halt. "They're on the road ahead, Captain," he said.

"They're over here, too," Gilbert said, looking to the west. Under the setting sun, thousands of Chinese were plodding through the snow, headed toward the road.

"What now, Captain?"

Bell coolly snapped the safety on his rifle. "It's either give up, or die fighting, I guess," he said. "It's for sure there's nowhere to go."

Edwards whipped up his M-1. "Well, I never did like to give up," he declared. "I guess we'd better fight."

They stood up in the jeep and waited with fear in their throats as the Chinese pushed languidly across the snow and down the road. Gilbert began to feel choked, as if the enemy were cutting off his air, squeezing his throat, slowly and painfully.

Then all of a sudden, he heard a familiar sound. "Edwards?" he said tentatively.

"Am I going crazy, or do I hear a marine Corsair?"

Edwards held his breath a moment, then smiled. "I hear two of them, Captain," he said. "Maybe more."

The droning grew louder and louder, then one of the planes appeared out of the clouds, then another, and another.

"This is General Smith's doings," Gilbert said, smiling, shaking his head. "I should've known he wouldn't send us out without at least some air support."

"It's not just 'some,' Captain. Look, there's another formation."

They watched the skies as the eight Corsairs passed over, then circled around and came back, launching white-hot rockets into the enemy, then bearing down on them with strafing guns.

"They're opening the road for us," Gilbert said.

Up ahead the enemy began to break up and withdrew for cover away from the roadbed, as the planes swarmed low and blasted away into their ranks.

Five minutes later the road was clear. "Let's go, Edwards," Gilbert commanded. "Put your foot into it!"

Edwards let out a whoop, stomped the accelerator, and sped down the road, in-between two units of scurrying Chinese, and, finally, out of their range. He leaned back, held the steering wheel with one hand. "Gotta hand it to Smith," he said. "The old man thinks of everything."

"Well, we're not through yet, but I have a feeling those Corsairs are going to be around if we need them, all the way to Chinhung-ni."

"Yes, sir. And that's a real good feeling."

The road to Koto-ri was clear. On the way to Chinhung-ni they had to shoot their way across an army treadway bridge over a twenty-foot gorge. It had been erected after the enemy blew the permanent concrete bridge some time before.

At Chinhung-ni, they were greeted by army supply units and shuffled into the fuel truck. Not even stopping for coffee, they turned back toward Koto-ri.

But when they reached the bridge, Gilbert ordered Edwards to stop the truck. For a minute or so he scanned the area illuminated by the truck's headlights. "There should be some guards on that bridge, Edwards," he said.

"Maybe we got them all coming down," he replied hopefully.

"Unh-unh. That bridge is too important. Something's wrong."

They sat and listened. Out in the darkness there was a thin voice, barking something in Chinese. Then another, across the gorge. Gilbert instantly realized what was happening.

"They're blowing the bridge!" he said. "Step on it!"

Edwards didn't hesitate. He slapped the gearshift into low and eased toward the bridge. Suddenly they were bombarded with gunfire. The windshield shattered, the tank pinged loudly as bullets ricocheted off metal. But they inched ahead, onto the plywood and metal spans—where the truck stalled.

"Let's go, Edwards," Gilbert urged him. "Move it!"

"The gear's slipping, Captain."

"Edwards, damn it!"

"I'm getting it," he grunted.

The truck jerked, gears grinding noisily, and crawled ahead, over the tracks, to the other side. "Now we got it," Edwards announced, shifting into a higher gear.

Gilbert turned, peered back through the rear window just as an explosion lit up the sky; the bridge had been blown into the air. He could hear the shattered bits and chunks of metal clanking down into the gorge as they pulled away in the truck.

The trip back to Hagaru wasn't as difficult as he expected. They had to break through two roadblocks near Pusong-ni and Sangpyong-ni, but resistance was light. It was clear to him that the Chinese were concentrating their forces on Hagaru.

As he sat in the covered cab of the truck, he gradually became aware of a fear that seemed to be slowly taking him in its grip. As he thought about the Chinese at Hagaru, his mind kept racing back to an image of Adrian, tending to his men in the warming tent. It was Adrian's presence in Hagaru that was making him fearful. She was in danger there.

When they neared the perimeter of the village in the dark hours of the morning, he began to get restless. Even at a distance, they could tell the Chinese had mounted a major offensive. The sky was ablaze with mortars, white phosphorous rockets, and artillery fire.

Nearer, they could see fiery trails of tracer bullets spewing forth in the black sky. Then a flare would burst to illuminate a thousand uniformed bodies diving to the white ground, then hopping up again and plunging ahead into waiting marine gunfire.

"Looks like we're getting the best of them, Captain," Edwards declared as they reached the perimeter.

"Keep moving, Edwards. Let's hope there's a seam we can cut through. One touch of a mortar to this fuel and we'll light up the sky for an hour."

Edwards kept the truck rolling and somehow, under the cover of marine tanks and 81mm mortars, they slipped into the main encampment undamaged.

When they reached the command post, Bell was taken to General Smith's tent. The warmth produced by his iron stove enveloped Gilbert like a blanket the second he stepped in. It made him want to drop in his tracks and not move until his bones stopped aching.

But he stood erect, at attention.

"Sir?" he said, saluting Smith.

The general stood up from his table. "Bell! Good man. I knew you could do it. Major," he said to the other officer in the room, "take care of that fuel truck."

"Yes, sir." As the officer left, he patted Gilbert's shoulder. "Good work."

"We've got them on the run, Gilbert," Smith proclaimed confidently. "We may have to push them all the way to the sea, but at least we'll be getting off this plateau."

"General," Gilbert said, "we have a problem. The Chinese have blown a bridge over a gorge, a couple of miles south of Koto-ri. It's twenty feet deep; there's no way we can get our equipment across."

Smith frowned. "You don't mean *our* bridge? The treadway? The one we used to replace the concrete bridge?"

"Yes, sir. They blew it a few seconds after we crossed over it."

Smith considered the information, glanced at the map on the table for a minute. "There's no other way around it, either," he said. "And we don't have any pre-fab bridge material here." He eyed the map again, pointed at a spot. "We'll just have to have some air force boxcars drop us a bridge," he decided. "Right here."

"That sounds good, General. But the timing will have to be perfect."

"Yes, it will," Smith said thoughtfully. "If it gets there too soon, the Chinese will take it. If it's too late, the Chinese will take us. We'll be backed up against that gorge with nowhere to go."

Gilbert stood and watched Smith examine his map again. Outside the tent, the terrible noises of war were shaking the ground he stood on, but the general seemed oblivious to all of it. "Can I help with anything, General?" he asked.

"What?" Smith said, looking up. Then, catching himself, he said to Gilbert, "You did a good job, Captain. Thank you."

"Sir . . ."

"Is there something else?"

"Sir, I was wondering about the civilians here. I was wondering if they all got out all right?"

Smith looked straight at him. "No," he said. "A few of them didn't get out. At least not all transports are accounted for."

"I was wondering about the correspondents; did they make it?"

Smith walked a few steps toward him. "We're missing a C-47, Gilbert," he told him. "Was that lady you were with going out on a C-47?"

"I didn't even ask her," Gilbert said, feeling useless. "I was so concerned with myself, I didn't ask. Damn it!"

"Now hold on, I said it was missing, not down. They may be having radio trouble. We may be having radio trouble. It could be anything. You know you can't tell about these things."

"General, I've got to know if she was on that plane."

"There's no way for you to know that, Captain," he said firmly. "You'll have to wait till we get to Hungnam to find that out. Just like the rest of us."

"General—"

"You may return to your company, Captain Bell," Smith said flatly. "That'll be all."

"Yes, sir," he replied crisply, saluting.

"Captain?" Smith said as he reached the doorway.

"Sir?"

"I'll see what I can find out."

"Thank you, sir."

"And if they get that bridge at Koto-ri to us in time, I'll see if I can get it named after you."

At dawn the next day, the marine Corsairs and navy fighters and bombers opened the way for the division to continue its trek to Koto-ri. It was slow going: the procession stretched even longer than before now, with the addition of Chinese prisoners, South Korean refugees hoping to catch a ride out of the country, and elements of the Seventh Army Division from the east.

But no one complained. The men were almost in a stupor, fatigued by the long hours of fighting, half-frozen by the intense cold. Gilbert refused to ride in a jeep; he walked ahead of his company, holding his rifle ready to repel the persistent enemy at any time.

Once, as the line stopped for a minute, Edwards made his way up to Gilbert. "Captain," he said, then fell silent as the procession cranked up again.

"What is it, Edwards?"

"Captain Bell, what are they going to do about that gorge below Koto-ri?"

"There'll be a bridge there ready for us, Edwards," he answered wearily. "There has to be," he added after a moment. "We can't cross without it."

Tired, hungry, and cold, Gilbert was only hoping. He couldn't know the chain reaction his report had set off. Smith's order for the bridges had launched a hundred skilled men into frantic action. All night long army engineers planned and prepared for the drop. Tractor and amphibious battalions worked feverishly with parachute riggings to provide the machinery to execute the engineers' orders.

They plodded on under an umbrella of air support from marine and navy fighters, each step harder than the last, until suddenly the procession stopped. The South Koreans spread out beyond the road, the marines fell at ease, dropping to the ground or leaning against the vehicles or tent packs. Before long, though, the collective mood of the mass changed rapidly. A message ran through the thousands of men like a fire through dry brush: a bridge was out up ahead—Smith was waiting for an air drop of a new bridge.

All eyes turned upward toward the cloudy sky, but there was no sound of any planes aloft. An hour later, only half were watching.

Gilbert, brought up to the front by a lieutenant, was shown promptly into Smith's tent. He warmed his hands near the stove and talked with the radio man for a while. There was no news from Hagaru about the missing transport plane, the corporal told him. "I figure it's just a mix-up, Captain," he concluded. "The marines are always doing things like that," he added wryly.

"I hope that's all it was, Corporal," he said, thinking of Adrian standing by the tent, crying.

"Was somebody you know on that plane, Captain?"

Bell nodded. "Yeah," he said sadly, then changed his tone. "If you get any word on it, let me know," he said, trying to sound casual.

"Yes, sir. I'll see what I can find out. But I'm sure

if any of those C-47s had been hit, we'd know about it."

"Corporal," General Smith said, entering the tent abruptly. "Find out about those air force boxcars. We don't have time to sit around and wait for them. There's an enemy out there."

"I think they're in the air, General," he answered, "but I can't get through to them."

"Well, keep trying. Every living soul up and down that ten-mile line outside is staring up into the sky, waiting for them." He looked at Gilbert. "Captain, I've got a job for you. I want you to take your company and set up a perimeter defense around this place. When that bridge comes in, the engineers are going to need some cover to put it up."

"Yes, sir."

Smith raised his helmet up and scratched his forehead. "This had better work," he said. "The Chinese are already getting wise to us. They're going to be biting at our flanks before long." He walked over to a table and looked down at the map spread out on it, studied it a moment. "We're sitting right on the drop point, Gilbert," he said. "Three and a half miles from Koto-ri. Those sections should've been here an hour ago." He looked toward the radio again. "Corporal?"

"Nothing yet, General," he responded promptly.

"Well, get something, Corporal."

"Yes, sir."

Smith paced up and down nervously for a minute, then went outside. "It's getting cloudy," he said to Bell, gazing up into the sky. "It's not enough to be cold, it has to be cloudy, too. If they do make it, they won't be able to see. They'll drop those ton-and-a-half spans right on our heads."

Bell said nothing as the two men scanned the columns stretching above them as far as they could see. Miles away, to the north, guns rumbled softly like thunder before a rainstorm.

"The Chinese are already closing in on our flanks," Smith observed. "Something had better happen soon."

"If the Chinese ever concentrate their forces, General, we're dead."

"I know. That's why we have to get across that gorge up ahead. Which we can't do," he growled impatiently, accusingly, "if we don't have a bridge to cross it on!"

"General," a major reported from behind. "The trucks are coming in from Koto-ri."

"Good, it's about time. How many are there?"

"Two."

He nodded. "Okay, two will do it. They'll be dropping eight sections, but we won't need but four. Two trucks can handle that."

Bell stood quiet as the huge trucks pulled in and parked. Like the thousands of others, he found himself searching the skies for a sign of the air force planes. Miles to the north the Chinese guns continued to boom, but where he was, everything was quiet. Marines lay propped up so that they could look for aircraft. South Koreans, knowing no English, thinking of the marines as their saviors, fell to searching the skies, not even knowing what they were looking for. Thousands of men were waiting, forgetting the cold and pain for the moment, concentrating on nothing but the great expanse of cloudy heavens above them.

Finally came the unmistakable sound of big airplane engines. Then the low hum suddenly swelled to a roar as the huge air force C-119s burst out of the clouds into view.

Immediately a cheer rang out through the columns as the boxcars made a circle, returned, and opened their bellies and emptied the massive metal spans and plywood centers into the air. Under great open parachutes, the sections floated to earth and stuck in the frozen ground like giant spears.

On Smith's orders the Brockway trucks broke out across the field toward the bridge sections. If the weather held, Bell was told, the engineers could erect the bridge by nightfall, December 8.

But the next day, the weather was bad. In a swirling snowstorm, there could be no air support, so the engineers could do nothing. Gilbert took his company out along the ridges to set up a defense anyway, but all they could see of the bridge was a stack of bridge spans collecting a blanket of snow.

From his position on a hill, Gilbert had a good view of the division. Miles behind, on the road to Hagaru, he could see the thousands of Korean refugees bottled up at roadblocks, waiting uncomprehendingly for the marines to move them down the road to safety. They were patient, but confused. They knew nothing of the delay up ahead; all they knew was that there was a terror at their backs.

Down in the main encampment, demolition crews were blowing holes in the hard ground with dynamite. Gilbert and his men lay stretched out on the ice and watched as a burial service took place in a powdery snowfall.

"Do they have to do it that way?" Edwards asked him mournfully. "Do they have to bury them all together?"

"We don't have enough time to do it any other way," Gilbert said stoically, but he too was deeply moved by the scene. There seemed to be hundreds of bodies, army infantrymen, marines, and British commandos wrapped up loosely in ponchos, being lowered gradually into the pits. The sheer number of the bodies laid out in their separate niches in the cavernous holes made his grief and sadness almost overwhelming.

The company looked on reverently as the rites were performed by a marine chaplain. They were too far away to hear his words, but they remained respectfully silent until he had finished. Then, without another word on the subject, they turned away to their business.

Gilbert awoke the next morning to the comforting sound of marine corsairs in the clear sky. Already the engineers were at the gorge, feverishly laying the spans into place. Edwards joined him as he stood and watched the quick and agile movements of the workers.

"Looks different in the daylight, doesn't it, Captain?" Edwards said.

Bell nodded. "Yes, it does."

"I guess that bridge is about the most famous bridge in the world right now," he speculated, "what with all those reporters coming to Koto-ri to see it." Bell was silent. He was thinking of Adrian. She hadn't been with those reporters. Where was she? Was she waiting in Hungnam for him? Would he ever see her again?

"Captain?" Edwards said after a minute. "Are you all right?"

"I'm all right, Private," he said, turning away. "I'm just tired, that's all."

Throughout that night, a massive stream of people and machinery inched across the bridge. Gilbert was surprised to see how large the procession had become. Besides marines, there were hundreds of enemy prisoners. And North Korean refugees were everywhere, herding each other to get across the gorge. Reporters walked among the ranks, interviewing the weary marines. Photographers snapped bright flash bulbs in the darkness. Some of the natives had even brought their dogs, cattle, and chickens with them, and the officers at the bridge dutifully looked out after them as they passed.

Meanwhile, at their backs, the sounds of artillery fire rolled ceaselessly through the invisible clouds, reminding them of the enemy's constant presence.

Every single marine knew he had many bloody miles to go yet, before he could reach the sea and safety. But crossing the bridge somehow gave them a lift. Gilbert could see it in the eyes of each hungry, weary soldier who crossed the treadway spans to the other side. The marines had acquitted themselves proudly; now they could go back and start over.

14

THE VIEW of Hungnam from the air on December 18, 1950, was so spectacular a sight that the pilot of the C-47 transport called Adrian up to the cockpit to witness it. "Ever see anything like that, Miss McAllister?" he asked proudly. The pilot, a young man with an easy smile and a pleasant voice, leaned back in his seat so that she could see through the glass.

"Never," she answered, looking down at the port as they passed over the beaches. It was an impressive sight. The area was surrounded by UN defense troops. Swarming about in the sky were various formations of marine and navy fighters, while in the Sea of Japan a hundred ships were arriving, leaving, or loading people and equipment onto their docks.

"It's been going on since Tuesday morning," the

pilot informed her. "They're taking out the whole Tenth Corps. Plus all the Korean refugees. And equipment."

She leaned forward to see better, but when she realized she was pressing against him she backed up. "Excuse me," she said.

The pilot smiled warmly. "My pleasure, Miss McAllister."

"Well, thank you for the view," she said, starting to go.

"Miss McAllister, do you mind if I ask you a question? While I got you here."

"Go ahead."

"Well, we were just wondering how you managed to get an army transport to take you to Hungnam. I mean, no offense, but that must've taken some pull."

"It did take a little pull, Lieutenant," she admitted. "But I was stuck in Tokyo for a week before I could get somebody to bring me over."

"Yes, but we heard it was General Bradley himself that arranged it. Is there anything to that? I mean . . ."

"Could be." She smiled enigmatically.

"General *Bradley*?" he said incredulously.

"Will we be landing soon, Lieutenant Massey?"

He seemed to be very amused. "You can go back and strap in now," he told her. "We'll be landing in about ten minutes."

"Thank you."

"Miss McAllister?" he said as she turned to go. "What kind of man is General Bradley, anyway? You know . . ."

She paused a minute, noting the smirk on his face. "I wouldn't know, Lieutenant," she said. "I've never even met the man." Then, leaving the two pilots frowning in confusion, she returned to her seat in the belly of the plane.

Half an hour later, the reality of at last being in Hungnam was disturbing. The place, which had seemed so orderly from the air, appeared to be totally confused on the ground. The port was jammed with navy men of all ranks conducting the evacuation of what looked to Adrian like hundreds of thousands of people. It was so chaotic, she wondered if she would ever find anyone she knew.

As she meandered through the tents and makeshift hospital facilities, she was disheartened by the sight of battered marines and soldiers lying quietly on cots, patiently waiting for someone to take them out of Chinese-occupied Korea. Hundreds of them had severe frostbite, some had their toes and fingers amputated, many seemed dazed, unable to understand where they were or what was happening to them.

In one facility, the wounded were being operated on by physicians flown in by helicopter from a nearby MASH. She stood inside long enough to hear the agonized groans of several Korean children who were lying on their backs, anticipating surgery on their bodies by the American doctors.

In another hospital tent, a man called out to her. She turned around quickly, but didn't recognize the marine who was holding up his hand to get her attention. She walked over to his cot anyway and stood by it. He had lost his left arm, but to her surprise, he seemed to be in a good mood. "You're Miss McAllister, aren't you?" he asked her. He was a homely young man, with a sharp chin and freckles, but had a warm expression on his face that she found appealing.

"I'm sorry—" she began.

"I'm in Captain Bell's company," he explained quickly. "Private Robert Jefferson. I saw you at Hagaru a couple of weeks ago."

The sound of Gilbert's name made her heart start pounding. She touched his wrist and looked at him. "Is he all right?" she asked, then waited in agony for an answer.

"I don't know," the marine replied. "I got knocked out of the company back at Koto-ri. Captain Bell was all right then."

"Where is he now?"

"There's so much going on around here, I don't know where he is, Miss McAllister. When I saw you, I kinda thought maybe he was with you. That's why I called you over." He smiled at her. "Captain Bell's a mighty good man," he said. "I guess you know he's the one who told General Smith about the bridge at Koto-ri. If he hadn't, none of us would be here today."

"Do you think he could've been hurt?"

"Like I say, Miss McAllister, I don't know. But if you find out, I'd appreciate it if you could tell me. They don't let us know much of anything around here. It's like if you're sick, or have an arm missing or something, you don't count anymore."

"Well, you count with me, Private Jefferson," she told him. "I think you're a brave and courageous man. I think all of you are."

He scratched the shoulder of the missing arm. "I hope they think that back home," he said.

"Of course they will. Why wouldn't they?"

"Well, we did retreat, you know," he reminded her. "We're the first marines ever to retreat. It's going to be hard to face, you know."

She looked at him closely. His kind expression had slipped into a kind of stunned, faraway look. On an impulse, she leaned over and kissed his cheek. "Nobody ever fought better than the First Marines, Private Jefferson," she said. "Nobody could."

Half a mile away, in a tent prison compound, Gilbert Bell stood talking to an army captain, Benjamin Quinn. Bell had profited greatly from the six days in Hungnam. He had regained his color, his eyes were clear and bright, he stood strong and erect again.

"What are they planning to do with these prisoners?" he was asking Quinn. "We can't very well keep them here in Korea."

Quinn, a stocky, dark man with brown eyes, wrote something on a sheet of paper in a clipboard, then looked up at Bell.

"MacArthur says we should take them back to the States," he answered. "But I hear Truman doesn't want them there."

"They never seem to want the same things, do they?" Gilbert commented.

"Hardly ever. Truman's already blaming MacArthur for this fiasco," Quinn said. "He's sayjng MacArthur bungled the whole operation."

"Well, Truman ought to know the war's not over. Nobody's bungled anything yet."

"Well, anyway, I think the prisoners will be going down to Koje-do, that little island down by Pusan.

For the moment, anyway, till they can figure out
something else to do with them."

The two men stood and talked a while longer,
then Gilbert left and walked west a few hundred
yards to a mess tent. He passed down the line, allowing the cook to stack his plate high with pota-
toes, meat, and gravy. He had been eating hot food
for six days now, but he wasn't used to it yet. The
aroma of beef cooking in a pot still actually made
his mouth water.

He sat down at a table near the coffee urn and
began to eat. Once again he had tried in vain to
find out anything about Adrian. The C-47 that had
been reported missing had been accounted for, but
not Adrian. She seemed to have dropped off the face
of the earth.

It had felt strange, somehow, not seeing her at
Hungnam when they hobbled in that morning. He
hadn't realized it until then, but it was Adrian who
had kept him going all that time. His concern over
her had given him something to focus on; it had
seen him through chaos. But when he came out, to
safety, she was nowhere to be found.

After a while he was conscious of a man standing
in front of his table. He looked up to see a tall
middle-aged man in glasses.

"Good afternoon," the man said. "Bob Kowalski,
New York Times. May I join you?"

Gilbert jumped up. "Is Adrian with you?" he asked
impulsively.

Kowalski shrugged. "I thought she'd be with you."

"Then you haven't seen her," Gilbert said, disappointed.

"The last time I saw her was in Hagaru, with you."

Gilbert sat back down. "What do you want, Kowalski?" he said, surprising himself with his own rudeness.

Kowalski wasn't affected by it, however. He eased down across the table from Gilbert, took a stenographic pad out from under his jacket, and a pen from his breast pocket. "They tell me you're the one who alerted Smith about the bridge at Koto-ri," he began.

"Is this an interview, Kowalski?"

"Whatever you want to call it, Captain," he said indifferently. "All I'm trying to do is get a story."

"Your story's back in Koto-ri, Kowalski," he said. "A hundred dead marines lying in a mass grave being overrun at this very minute by Chinese soldiers."

"You're bitter about the marines' retreat," Kowalski prodded him.

Gilbert looked at him. "No, I'm not bitter, Kowalski, just suspicious. Somehow I don't think the *Times* reader really wants to pick up his paper Sunday morning and read about me. What do you really want?"

Kowalski smiled, picked up his pad and stuck it back next to his chest. "You're too clever for me, Captain," he confessed. "I plead guilty."

"Why don't you go do the work you're paid to do, Kowalski?" he said, taking a bit of biscuit.

"I can't work, Captain," he protested. "And I can't sleep or eat, either. All I can do is think about Adrian McAllister."

Gilbert looked up. He could feel his face begin to burn red with jealousy. The sound of her name on this man's lips quickly aroused his anger. "Adrian McAllister is no concern of yours, Kowalski," he warned him.

"Hey, take it easy, Captain," Kowalski said, holding out his palms in a mock defense. "I'm just curious about her, that's all."

"Look, if you know where she is, tell me. Otherwise, I don't want to talk about her, okay?"

"Now wait a minute here," the reporter rebuked him. "Wearing that marine soldier suit doesn't mean you can push people around."

"Pushing you around's not exactly hard to do, Kowalski."

"Look at this. The man loves the woman after all."

Gilbert glared at him, gnashed his teeth. "What are you talking about?" he growled.

"What I'm talking about is love, Captain," he said, amused. "A half a million Chinese try to kill you and you're as cool as a cucumber, but let one little woman stir you up and you're like a tiger."

"That's enough, Kowalski," he cut him off. "Get out of here."

The reporter shook his head. "All you had to do was say so—I would've backed off. But the way you were treating her back at Hagaru, I naturally assumed you didn't really care for the lady. Shows you how wrong reporters can be, doesn't it?"

Gilbert couldn't help but think about what Kowalski was saying. He went back over those days in his mind. It was true, he had let her come to him, let her tend to him—and he had practically ignored her for her trouble. He admitted to himself there was something to it, but he still disliked the way the reporter was acting.

"You've made your point, Kowalski," he said. "Now why don't you get out of here and let me eat in peace?"

"I'm not going anywhere, Captain. You just gave me an angle for a story. The oldest angle in the world: love conquers all!"

"All right, Kowalski," Gilbert said, his irritation growing by the minute, "I've heard enough."

"It's a good angle, Bell," he insisted. "It'd make a fine story."

Gilbert got to his feet. "Look, Kowalski, I don't want to talk about her, okay?"

The reporter stood up. "Okay, fine. I'll go see if I can find the lady herself."

"No you won't. You're going to leave her alone."

"Sure I am," Kowalski said sarcastically.

"I mean it."

"What is she to you, anyway, Bell? If you're one of those unscrupulous marines who take advantage of women—"

"Leave her alone, damn it. I mean it. The woman is mine."

"She's what?"

"You heard me. She's mine. All right, I love her. She belongs to me. Are you satisfied?"

The reporter hesitated, replaced his pen in his pocket and shrugged his shoulders. "I guess so," he sighed. "And," he said, rising, "I guess I hope you find her."

"I'll find her," Gilbert declared. He sat back down, not bothering to watch Kowalski leave the tent. But then something caught his eye—something almost like an image materializing. Standing just inside the tent, with long black hair flowing over the shoulders of her fatigues, looking at him with calm, loving eyes, was Adrian.

Rising to his feet, he almost ran over to her, but suddenly he realized that the other men in the tent had probably heard what he had been saying to the reporter. He couldn't compromise Adrian by any further display of his emotion. He had to control himself.

With great restraint, he walked slowly across the room to the doorway, then discreetly embraced her.

"Adrian," he whispered to her. "God, I'm glad to see you!"

She squeezed him tightly, pressed her face against his shoulder, and cried. Then she drew back and looked at him. "My poor darling," she said tearfully, putting her hands on his face. "You've been through so much."

He touched her hair lightly, but didn't dare hold her close any longer. He wanted her so much, he was afraid he wouldn't be able to hold back. "Where on earth were you, Adrian?" he asked. "You said you'd be here."

"Oh, I had some technical difficulties," she laughed, wiping a tear from her eye. "The damned army wouldn't have me in one of their transports because they were being used for something else."

He kept staring at her. Every time he saw her she was more ravishing than ever. What Kowalski had said was true. He did love her, more than he had loved anyone else in his life.

"Well," she said, breaking away gently, regaining her composure, "I must say, you look terrific."

"So do you."

"I mean 'well,' Gilbert. You look strong, healthy . . ." Her voice trailed off as she looked into his eyes. "Oh, I missed you so much," she cried.

"I missed you, too, Adrian," he said, then pulled her to him. "I've thought about you every minute of every day."

"Gil—" Her words were cut off as his lips drew close to hers. Then they kissed and the tent suddenly seemed close and warm and the war outside seemed so far away. . . .

But then he drew back. "Adrian," he said, "I've got some business to take care of for a while. Where are you staying?"

"I'm staying at the Seventh Division army nurses' quarters. But you don't have to go now, do you?"

"I have to go for a while," he said, glancing at his watch. "I'll be back."

"But I just got here," she protested.

"Adrian," he said seriously. "I really do have to go. Besides, the way I'm feeling now, I don't trust myself to stay here. If I look into those beautiful eyes a minute longer, I won't go back to work."

She nodded, trying to be understanding. But all she wanted to do at this second was to hold him, be close to him. "Will I see you tonight?" she asked boldly.

He kissed her again. "You'll see me before then. I'll be back before dark."

Then he was gone.

She waited for him at the mess tent for almost two hours, evading approaches by practically every single marine who happened to walk into the tent and see her standing or sitting alone. She found most of the men pleasant enough, considering their circumstances, but they made no impression on her. Her mind was always on Gilbert Bell and no one else.

At sunset, she went to visit Private Jefferson, but discovered someone else occupying his cot. He had been "taken off," as the nurse put it—sent back home to the United States, Adrian guessed, to try to pick up his life. She stayed around the medical unit anyway, talking and flirting with the wounded men. They brightened at her attention, and made her promise to come back again the next day.

That night, she made her cot in the nurses' tent and sat on it for a while, but couldn't sleep. By nine o'clock the nurses had put an end to their sixteen-hour day and Adrian was lying fully clothed in the darkness, thinking. Finally, too restless to stay still any longer, she left the quarters and stepped outside into the cold air. Ten minutes later, Gilbert appeared out of the shadows.

"Hi," he said. "Have you got a minute? I have a little surprise for you."

She wanted to remind him that he had told her he would see her again before dark, but she let it go. "What kind of surprise?" she asked.

"Come on. You have to see it to believe it," he said cheerfully, taking her hand. He led her through a maze of temporary quarters next to the harbor to a huge tent guarded by army privates. The soldiers acknowledged Bell and allowed them to pass through.

What Adrian saw inside amazed her—hundreds of North Korean and Chinese prisoners were huddled together in quiet groups to keep warm. Unarmed and out of the war now, they seemed as docile as well-behaved children waiting for a school bus.

"They look pitiful, Gil," she observed.

"So do our men when they're taken," he said. Then his voice brightened. "That's not the surprise, though. Look over there, by the doctor."

Adrian's eyes moved across the room, lit upon an army officer who was speaking and gesturing to the physician. She knew him instantly, even with his back turned. "Lieutenant Metz!" she cried.

He turned in time to see her rushing toward him. "Miss McAllister," he said, surprised at first. But as she reached out and embraced him and he felt her soft bosom pressed against his chest, he colored with embarrassment.

"What are you doing here?" she asked excitedly, backing away and looking at him. "I thought you were in a hospital in Tokyo."

He unconsciously rubbed the scar on his forehead. "A lady doctor there repaired the damage," he said self-consciously. "General MacArthur wanted me here, so she fixed me up pretty fast."

"James is here to meet with the International Red Cross Committee," Gilbert explained.

"We're endeavoring to relocate the prisoners you see here," Metz added.

Adrian smiled at Metz's usual formal tone. "I'm sure you'll manage that very well," she said. "You're always very capable."

"Well, capable, yes, but I must say, I could use a bit of your dash and abandon," he admitted. He looked at Bell. "Miss McAllister here is very clever," he said. "I never could keep up with her."

"Neither could I," Gilbert said, looking at her.

"I'll never forget that business with the general's jeep," he said, and related the story to Gilbert. Then, to Adrian's embarrassment, he told about her using McArthur's phone.

After he ran out of anecdotes, Lieutenant Metz excused himself to return to work and Gilbert and Adrian left the prison compound. They walked around outside for a while, talking, exchanging their Korean experiences, and somehow, wound up drinking coffee inside his tent.

"That's true American coffee," he said proudly as he poured her a cup. "Maxwell House. I had to swap a spicy paperback novel to a navy ensign to get it."

She sipped it. "Mmm," she said approvingly. "That must have been some novel. This is very good."

"Adrian," he said abruptly, "will you stay here tonight?"

She had thought about it for hours, but when she heard him say the words, she felt a slight quiver in her breast and a dryness in her throat. She covered her nervousness by drinking more coffee, but it was clear he was waiting patiently for an answer. She was going to have to respond somehow. Finally she set the cup down on the floor and took a deep, halting breath. "I don't . . . think so," she said, rising.

"Adrian—"

"I'm sorry, Gil. I know we spent the night in Pusan, but one night doesn't mean I'm ready to just hop into bed with you."

"I know that," he said, coming to her, holding her shoulders in his hands. "And I'm not asking you to just hop in bed, either."

"Look, Gil, I appreciate your taking me to see Metz, and paying attention to me this afternoon, but—"

"I wasn't just paying attention, Adrian. Don't you

know I'm obsessed with you? I can't think of anything else."

"You could think of Lin Su that night I held you in my arms in Hagaru," she blurted out. "Are you sure it's not *her* you're obsessed with?"

"What are you talking about?"

"Lin Su, Gil. You kept saying her name in your sleep."

"Lin Su is part of my past, Adrian," he said softly, looking into her eyes. "She has nothing to do with me now. I'll always remember her, but she's gone."

"Is she, Gil?"

"Yes. She is. She's a sweet, lovely memory I'll always cherish. But you are someone I can touch, hold, caress, and someone I can love, Adrian. I've never felt this way about any woman before. Nobody has ever taken hold of my whole being the way you have."

"Gil—" she began, weakening under his words.

"I love you, Adrian," he told her. "I love you."

"Oh, Gil," she cried, embracing him. "I've waited so long to hear that—to believe it."

"You can believe it," he assured her.

"I love you, too," she said, kissing him. "I've loved you since the moment I saw you skimming across San Francisco Bay in that sailboat."

"Oh, God, Adrian," he sighed, holding her as close as he could without squeezing the breath out of her body. "Stay with me. Please, stay with me."

She did stay—that night and the next four. Every evening she would pretend to the nurses that she was asleep, then she would slip out and join Gilbert in his tent until just before dawn each day. She felt no shame or guilt about it; their lovemaking seemed so right and natural, their affection so real.

She found Gilbert an attentive lover. He seemed to delight in every part of her body. He loved to run his fingers lightly over her skin, press them against her gently, then gradually ease himself between her legs until she felt as if she were going to explode with passion. Then, when they had found a release together, he had only to look at her nakedness to become aroused all over again.

She learned a great deal about sex from Gilbert in those four days. She learned how to tease, to arouse, to stimulate a man with the touch of her lips and tongue upon his flesh. And, to her surprise, she discovered that stimulating him in that way always set her own feelings on fire. Being so close to him dazzled her mind and made her body reel with a consuming desire to take him inside her.

She found herself thinking of him during the day as they each went about their work. Adding to the anticipation of their lovemaking each night was the excitement of the massive evacuation going on at Hungnam. As Christmas approached, the pace increased. She discerned from her interviews with navy officers that there were over a hundred ships being used to take out the X corps. The numbers were staggering: over one hundred thousand troops, one hundred thousand Koreans, seventeen thousand vehicles, three hundred fifty thousand tons of equipment. It was one of the greatest, quickest, most efficient exoduses in military history.

On Christmas Eve, 1950, Bell was scheduled to leave. Taking their last moments together, she and

Gilbert stood on the dock watching some of the last LSTs being crammed with North Korean refugees. It was then she decided to make a confession to him.

"Gil," she began tentatively. "Do you remember back in Pusan, I said that General Stoddard had sent me to Korea?"

"General Stoddard again," he said, disgruntled. "I can't get away from him."

She felt his hand leave her waist, but she went on. "I don't feel right about this, Gilbert, but I agreed to do something for him if he could get me back over here to cover the war and be with you. I felt wrong about doing it—and wrong about *not* doing it."

"Not doing what?"

She sidestepped the question. "He says you possess information that could be dangerous to a lot of people."

"He's right," Gilbert said. "I didn't think so at first, but it is dangerous."

"Then will you please tell me what it is?" she insisted, looking at him.

"No," he answered after a pause. "I can't tell you what it is."

"Gilbert, damn it. We can't be any closer than we've been the past few days. If you don't trust me now—"

"It's not a matter of trust, Adrian," he explained. "I'm under *orders* not to say anything about what I saw. So I can't—not even to you."

"But I agreed with him to try to talk you into coming home—"

"Oh, come on, Adrian, that's crazy."

"It's not crazy if what you're keeping secret is so terrible."

"It's not terrible," he said reassuringly. "Look, I'll be all right, nothing's going to happen. But I'm not going home. You know I'm not."

She looked at him closely. "You scare me, Gilbert," she declared. "You scare me so much. You'd let yourself get killed just to obey some stupid order."

"It's not stupid," he replied calmly.

"It's all stupid," she said, tears coming in her eyes. "We make love for four nights and all of a sudden you're going back to fight again. Isn't that stupid?"

"Look, Adrian," he began, "I'm a Marine—I follow orders. That's all there is to it. You tell Stoddard this: I obey orders. I'm not telling a soul what I saw in the Pentagon last summer—not a living soul—as long as I'm under orders to keep it to myself. Tell him if I wouldn't reveal it to the woman I love, I'm not going to reveal it to anybody."

"What about me?"

"You, my darling, can take care of yourself better than anybody I know. I'm going to think about you all the time—but worry about you, I'm not."

"Captain?" a corporal called out. "The convoy's pulling out."

"I'm coming, Corporal."

"Gil. . . ."

He reached out, held her close. "I love you so much, Adrian," he said. "This has been an incredible four days."

"I wish you weren't going," she whispered. "I wish we could just keep on."

He looked at her. "You're serious, aren't you?" he asked.

"Yes, I'm serious," she answered.

"Then let's get married."

She smiled through her tears. "You could win a girl over with talk like that, Captain."

"I mean it. I'll start the paperwork. We'll do it."

"Captain!" the corporal called out impatiently.

"Next time, darling, it'll be legal."

"I don't care if it's legal, Gil. I just want you."

"And you'll have me—license, chaplain, flowers, the whole works."

"You wouldn't be saying that to make me feel better, would you?" she said tearfully.

He shook his head. "Unh-unh. I promise you, the next time you see me, I'll have a bouquet of flowers in my hand, waiting for you."

"I'll hold you to it, then," she said. "A bouquet of flowers."

"Captain Bell, sir?"

He reached out and kissed her, deeply, passionately. Then he pulled away without another word. She felt sad and excited; she was thrilled to have him at last, but disturbed at having to watch helplessly as he went back to war. She watched him stride quickly and confidently across the dock and leap onto the loading plank of a LST and disappear in a mass of faces.

"Quite a soldier you have there," said a voice behind her a few minutes later.

She turned to see Robert Kowalski. "Yes," she agreed. "He is quite a soldier."

"Well, you were right and I was wrong, Adrian," he confessed, lighting a cigarette. "The marines did make a heroic march to the sea. It was an impressive thing to see. But it doesn't change one hard fact: this was probably the worst defeat of American forces in military history."

"I'm just happy they made it."

"But Adrian—all those towns they fought through to get here—Yudam-ni, Hagaru, Koto-ri, Chinhung-ni —they're all overrun by Chinese Communists now. So what have they accomplished?"

"I don't know what they've accomplished, Robert. But I do know when I saw them coming into Hagaru that day, I had chills. I never thought I would be proud of them, but I was. And I'm proud of them being in Korea, too."

"You're changing your tune, Adrian. You don't sound much like a pacifist now."

"I just understand more now, that's all."

"Such as what?" he pressed her, interested. "What could change the mind of a war-hater like you?"

"I haven't changed it," she defended herself, then retracted. "Oh, I don't know, maybe I have."

"It looks like the captain has you confused."

She hesitated. "It's just that he believes in what he's doing, Robert," she said thoughtfully. "And he thinks sometimes you have to fight to preserve what you believe in. And I don't know, maybe he's right."

"Maybe he is. Who knows? But one thing's for certain—that kind of attitude could very possibly get the captain killed. The fact is, Adrian, we've got a whole new war now. The Chinese are a whole different army from the North Koreans. China can supply manpower practically forever. We may not be able to stop them. This may be the first war in our history we won't win. It may be a war nobody can win."

"We will win it," she said, surprising herself with the statement. "We have to."

"Well," he said doubtfully, "I hope we do. But I'm afraid we're on the eve of a rather long war here, Miss McAllister. It may be you won't see your Captain Bell for a long, long time."

15

In her warm, immaculate office in Tokyo, Adrian settled down to read Gilbert's letter for the third time. It was dated a month earlier, February 20, 1951, with places and tactical information unmentioned or deleted for security reasons. She knew that the First Marines were part of the current advance of Eighth Army, now under Lieutenant General Matthew Ridgway, against the latest Chinese offensive around the 38th parallel. She guessed that at the time of Gilbert's letter he would have been somewhere around Seoul, which had been retaken on March 15.

The second paragraph of the letter began by describing the Chinese army: "They're more affected by this cold than we are," he wrote. "It's not like Chosin. They're finding life is harder . . . miles from home. They have inadequate medical facilities. The prisoners we take have trenchfoot and frostbite. Even so, our men are dispirited. Yudam-ni isn't easy to forget. Last month the new commander of the Eighth gave us each an eloquent statement of why we're here in Korea, but it hasn't taken hold yet."

Adrian skipped to the second page: "My darling Adrian, I keep thinking about you. And about that little matter we discussed on the beach at Hungnam. I assure you, I will have that bouquet ready. Lately I've felt that you and I were somehow fated to be together, Adrian. It's strange. I believe now that deep down I have always wanted to marry you. Lin Su, precious as she was, was only a momentary fascination. There has really never been anyone but you. . . ."

She placed the unfolded pages down carefully on the desk and breathed deeply. Gilbert's words made her feel close to him, although she hadn't seen him since Christmas Eve in Hungnam. Taking out a pad, she began thinking what to put in a reply to his letter. He had suggested that after they were married perhaps they could go back to Connecticut, where his family ties were; she would begin her response by saying yes to that proposal. Anywhere he wanted to go, she would be happy to accompany him.

Her thoughts were abruptly broken by a sharp rapping at the door. Not bothering to put away Gilbert's letter, she got up, walked over and eased open the door. Standing outside was Amanda Bell, in a startling condition. Her eyes were red and swollen, her mascara was running. Even in her usual elegant tailored suit, she looked disheveled and out of control of herself.

"Amanda!" she said and offered her hand. "What happened?"

The other woman slapped away her hand. "Don't touch me," she ordered coldly.

"What's wrong? What on earth happened?" she asked as Amanda brushed past her. Getting no answer, she closed the door, came around to face her. "Amanda?" she said, concerned. "Tell me what happened."

Amanda lifted her eyes and glared at Adrian accusingly. "You had to do it, didn't you?" she said. "You had to go chasing after him."

Adrian sighed. "If you mean Gilbert, yes," she said, going around to her seat behind the desk. "I had to do it."

"You're so selfish, Adrian," Amanda cried. "You're so damned selfish. You know how he is. He's just like any other man. Women who look and act like you make them lose control."

Adrian sat down. "Look, Amanda," she said, "I love Gilbert. And he loves me. I don't know why you can't accept that."

"I can't accept it because it's a lie, Adrian. You're a lie."

"Why do you hate me so much? What have I ever done to you?"

"I hate you because you're a lie, Adrian!" she burst out. "You play with his feelings and he gets hurt. He *always* gets hurt."

Adrian saw that she was on the verge of screaming hysterically. She decided to do something to stop it. She picked up Gilbert's letter and handed it to her across desk. "Here! Read it. Maybe this will tell you we're both serious."

Amanda seemed dazed as she stared at the two pages for a full minute. Then she took the letter reverently, as if it were a priceless manuscript, and brought it to her lap. Almost coddling the paper, she raised the letter up and began reading.

Adrian watched her face react to the contents, which she now knew by heart. Amanda read the beginning blankly, showed some interest in the second and third paragraphs. But when she reached a certain line, she cleared her throat and read out loud, "'. . . you and I were somehow fated to be together . . .'" Suddenly, letting the pages fall to her lap, she broke down crying.

"Amanda—"

"Leave me alone!"

"Will you please tell me what's wrong with you? You come in here spitting fire at me, then you break down in tears when I let you read Gilbert's letter. Just how tolerant do you expect me to be, Amanda?"

"I don't expect anything from you," she cried and flung the letter at her. "You did it to him. You did it."

"I did what!" she cried, exasperated.

"You got him all worked up, the poor baby. He always got so careless when he got excited. That's what happened to him."

"Amanda, damn you—"

"He's missing, Adrian!" she cried out. "And you're to blame."

Adrian was stunned. Her heart pounded wildly. "Missing?" she managed to say.

"Read it yourself," she said, taking a notice out of her purse and casting it on the desk. "He's on the official list we got this morning—from General Mac-Arthur's headquarters."

Adrian checked the list. Gilbert's name was so prominent to her it seemed to stand out in a different color ink on the page. "Missing in action," she gasped, suddenly feeling all her energy draining from her body. She leaned back in her chair, dumbfounded. "I was just about to answer his letter," she said. "I was feeling so close to him."

Amanda blew her nose into a Kleenex. She had calmed down; she seemed to be in control now that both of them knew. "We were close, when we were kids," she said. "My big brother was always taking up for me. Whenever any boy started getting fresh, Gilly would start swinging. He had the boys asking him if they could go out with me. I never wanted to go out with them, though. Compared to Gilly they were . . . I don't know."

"Is this all the information you have, Amanda?" Adrian asked. Her state of shock was slowly giving in to one of fear. Missing in action—it could mean she might never see him again.

"That's all," Amanda answered and blew her nose again. "It's cold and heartless, isn't it? Just 'Missing in Action, Captain Gilbert Bell, USMC.' Not much of an epitaph."

"It doesn't say he's dead, Amanda. My God."

"He is dead, Adrian. I know it in my heart. Oh, if you had only obeyed that directive, instead of being so god-damned *independent*!"

"Amanda, listen to me—"

"No!" she responded, tears filling her eyes. "I hate you. I hate everything about you!"

Adrian sat silent, cut deeply by the words, even if she knew they were coming from a jealous, distraught woman. She tried hard to think logically. It seemed to her she should try to get close to Amanda. However different their motives and desires, they both loved the same man, and now suddenly he was gone. Maybe somehow they could help each other deal with it.

"Amanda," she started, then paused. "Why don't we see what we can do to find him, instead of shouting at each other?"

"How could *we* find him? I'm stuck behind a desk all day. While Gilly may be lying in a cold ditch somewhere—"

"Amanda!" she said firmly. "Listen, now. We each have some connections. We can find him. You can use the State Department, I can use General Stoddard and the paper—"

"He's dead, Adrian," she cut her off.

"No, he's *not* dead. He's in some horrible cold prison cell somewhere. And it's up to us to find out where and get him out."

Adrian got up, came around the desk. "Look, Amanda," she said, kneeling beside her chair. "We *can* find him. We can. All we have to do is work together."

Amanda looked at her, considered the idea. Then she got up. "If you think I'm going to do anything with you, Adrian McAllister, you're crazy. I'm not a fool. I know. You're the one who put him there. And if he's dead—"

"He's not dead, damn it!"

"If he is," she went on, "and they ship him back home, I'm going to do everything I can to see to it you don't get within ten feet of his body." With those words she stood up, brought the Kleenex to her nose, and stormed out of the office.

After staring at the door for a few minutes, Adrian went to the window and watched Amanda hail a taxi and get into it. Then she picked up the phone and put in a call to General Stoddard. If he knew more about Gilbert's situation than she did, she wanted him to tell her about it. But Stoddard was out of his office. The masculine voice at the other end of the line promised to track him down for her and phone her back.

She sat and waited, got restless, and began pacing. The longer the phone on her desk continued silent, the more apprehensive she became and the more her imagination began to conjure up terrible things that could have happened to him. To settle herself down, she read his letter again, but hearing his strong, concerned voice behind the words upset her more. Worst of all was the thought of all that mysterious information Gilbert was supposed to know . . . dangerous information. Should she have pressed him harder to get out of Korea, as Stoddard had wanted her to? She knew it wouldn't have done any good if she had, but now she felt guilty even so. If Gilly had been captured, did that information truly make his situation even more dangerous . . . ? Imagining the worst about Gilbert at the same time she was waiting for the phone to ring was too much to cope with. It was rubbing her nerves raw. She had to get hold of herself.

But then without warning the office door swung open and Wayne Hunter stepped in. He paused on the rug, eased the door closed behind him. "Adrian," he said in a calm voice.

"Wayne," she said, rubbing her forehead. "If you don't mind, I'm waiting for a call."

He ambled closer to her desk, looked at her over by the window. "That's a coincidence," he said.

"That's what I've been doing," he said. "Waiting for a call. Only you know what? Nobody's calling."

"Wayne, please, I'm not feeling well . . ."

"Nobody has called," he persisted. "In other words, Adrian, thanks to you and Ed Mallory, I can't get a job. You two must have really spread the word, because nobody will even interview me."

"Wayne, can't we talk about this later?"

He hesitated a minute, scrutinizing her. "You're more attractive than ever, Adrian," he commented. "All that chasing around Korea agrees with you." He strode deliberately across the rug, around the desk.

She felt hemmed in as he came nearer, but she stood her ground. "Wayne," she said, "if there's any way I can help you—"

"The only way you can help me right now, Adrian," he said, drawing close to her, "is to forget Gilly Bell for one minute and pay some attention to me for a change."

"Wayne—" She started to move, but he held out one arm to stop her.

"Unh-unh," he said, shaking his head. "You're not getting away that easily."

She felt his arm around her waist before she realized what he was doing. Worried, almost dazed by her thoughts of Gilbert, she was off her guard. All of a sudden she was being pulled swiftly against his body.

"Just calm down," he cautioned her as she began to struggle against him. "All I want is a response, Adrian. For one time in my life I want somebody to respond."

"Wayne—"

"Just one kiss, damn it. Is that so much to ask?"

"I don't want to kiss you."

He held her tight. "Don't reject me, Adrian," he warned her. "I can't stand it anymore. I've been watching you for months now. Don't turn me away. I mean it!"

"Not now, Wayne, for God's sake!"

But he was overpowering her. She was being crushed against his chest, his hand was on her thigh, his fingers were curling up the material of her skirt. She managed to move backward, but only as far as the window. She felt the edge of the wood frame dig into her back as he slid his hand under her skirt and dug his hard nails into her leg.

"I've wanted you for so long," he panted, hugging her. When she forced his hand off her leg, he brought it up to her chest and squeezed her right breast tightly.

"No, Wayne—"

"I love you as much as he does," he said, pressing his face against her. "More."

"Get your hands off me, damn you!"

"Forget him, Adrian," he moaned. He pushed her harder against the window, began working his hand inside her blouse.

"Wayne, stop it! If Gilbert finds out about this—"

"He'll what, Adrian?" he said relenting a little, looking her straight in the eyes. "What can the poor bastard do now?"

"He can break your arm," she said sharply, shoving his hand away from her breast.

"That'd be hard to do, all the way from a prison cell, wouldn't it?" he said, trying to get closer.

His words made her shiver all over. How did Wayne Hunter know Gilbert was in a prison? Even

Amanda didn't know that. Suddenly her irritation with this man she had known for years gave way to harsh, cold fear. She realized more than ever how little she really knew him. What was he up to? Who was the man he was always with? Whatever the answers, she knew she couldn't trust him.

"Wayne, please, let me go," she begged him.

"Not this time, my love," he said. "I've been turned away for the last time."

"I swear, Wayne, if you don't let me go this instant—"

He answered her threat by plunging his hand into her blouse, inside her bra, onto the naked flesh of her breast. "Just give in, Adrian," he pleaded. "Just let go and give in."

She closed her eyes, then nodded. But as soon as she felt him loosen his grip on her, she shoved him back and slammed her knee up into his groin. He yelped and dropped to his knees. "Damn!"

She straightened her blouse and caught her breath. "How do you know he is in prison?" she asked. "Tell me!"

Wayne groaned in pain as he raised himself up. "I'm not going to forget this, Adrian," he threatened her. "Believe me. I won't forget."

"I'm sorry, but what did you think I would do? Roll over and play dead?"

"I don't know what I thought," he said, grimacing. "But whatever it was, I guess I was wrong, wasn't I? I swear to God, if Gilly Bell's dead, you'll take his tombstone to bed with you."

She crossed her arms over her chest as a chill ran through her body like a current of electricity. "Is he dead?" she managed to ask.

"How should I know?" he growled. He held his fingers on the lower part of his stomach as he eased toward the door. "Ask his sister."

"Please, Wayne, if you know anything at all about him . . ."

"Forget it, Adrian," he said coolly. "After what you just did, I wouldn't give you the time of day."

"All right, I'm sorry I kicked you. I'm sorry I rejected you. "What do you want me to say?"

He stared at her coldly. "Just say your prayers for Captain Bell," he told her. "He's going to need them. Wherever he is."

Outside the office building Elliott Stoner was sitting on a bench by the moat, smoking a cigarette. He ground it out with his heel as Wayne came up, then touched a wet finger to the ashes to make sure they were cold and neatly flicked the butt into a trash container by the bench.

"All right," Wayne said as he stood up. "I've had enough. If the party wants me full time, I'm theirs."

"It's not *theirs*, Wayne," Elliott reminded him. "We're all in it together. It's *us* and *ours*, not them and theirs."

"Okay, whatever. What do you want me to do?"

"We want you to do what you do best: write. You'll freelance articles for various magazines and papers around the country. We'll set it up."

"With the catch being, I write what you tell me," Wayne added.

"You will write what is consistent with the party's views," Stoner corrected him. "Not what I or anyone else will tell you."

"Fine," Wayne replied, thinking about Adrian. "But

there's something I want you to follow up on, Elliott," he said, looking at him. "I'm convinced now
that Captain Gilbert Bell knows something important. Whatever it is, he's had Adrian and General
Stoddard and half the consulate watching his every
move since last summer."

"Then we'll find out what it is," Elliott said calmly.
"We have very subtle, very effective ways of extract-
ing information from prisoners."

"Where is he now?"

"He's a prisoner, that's all I know. But I'll find
out. Peking will be happy to know about him. They'll
probably move him into China, where they can put
their best people on him."

"Do it," Wayne said vindictively. "I want to know
what's so precious about Gilbert Bell."

At that moment, it was near midnight in Stoddard's
office in the Pentagon, where the general sat watching
Harry Truman march anxiously back and forth across
the beige carpet. The president had designated Stoddard's office for the meeting because the White House
was undergoing renovation. "Besides," Truman had
said, "this thing ought to be laid in your lap, Lucius,
not mine."

But after a half hour of talk, Truman had sprung
to the offensive. He stopped his pacing, unbuttoned
his double-breasted suit and looked at Stoddard. "Now
let me get this straight, General," he said in his familiar let's-get-down-to-business voice. "Do you mean
that this Captain Gilbert Beck—"

"Bell, Mr. President."

"Bell, Beck, whatever the hell his name is," he
said with irritation. "This marine captain is now *at*

this moment in the hands of the Chinese, knowing what he knows?"

"Yes, sir. That's what intelligence is saying."

"Then tell me, just what do you think is going to happen when they start brainwashing him?"

"We don't know that they'll do that, Mr. President. They may not pay much attention to him. He's no more than a captain, a new one at that—"

Truman held up his hand. "Let's cut the crap, Lucius, okay?" he said seriously. "I'm not even going to mention these secert meetings you people are having over here. I'll save that till later. What I want to know right now, from you personally, is this: what will happen if they find out what he knows?"

"We don't know, Mr. President. Maybe nothing."

Truman frowned, took off his glasses, rubbed them on his white shirt. "I don't like maybes, General," he said, putting his glasses back on. "We're in desperate times here. We're in a cold war with Russia, we're in a hot war with the Chinese in Korea. Any little thing could touch off another world war. And with the atomic power we have at our disposal now, Lucius, I don't know if any of us would survive another world war."

"Yes, sir," Stoddard agreed.

Truman walked over to the window, gazed out over the lights of the city across the Potomac. "Did you know," he said thoughtfully, "when the Atomic Energy Commission set off those explosions in Nevada last month, people in San Francisco saw the flashes. That's over four hundred miles away. Think about that, Lucius. That kind of power could destroy us all."

"We're not going to use nuclear weapons in Korea, Mr. President."

"We're not if I can help it, General, but damned if I can always help it. As it is, I'm having the devil of a time getting the Senate to approve the use of ground forces to defend Western Europe. What are they going to do if I have to plunge us into a nuclear world war? We'll be burned to a crisp before they take a roll call."

"What do you want to do, Mr. President?" Stoddard asked helplessly. "You know I have no idea where Captain Bell is."

"No, we don't know that," Truman said, starting to pace again. "So we can't do anything about that. But we can do something about our other threat—General MacArthur."

Stoddard watched him take a few more steps, then tap the floor with his cane and look straight at him. He listened attentively as the president gestured toward him with his open hand.

"MacArthur is saying we ought to go into China, Lucius," he said to Stoddard. "He's saying we should invade mainland China."

Stoddard winced at the fear in Truman's voice. But he understood what the president meant. "Everybody knows you don't want that, Mr. President," he said. "Why don't you just let him say it? You're commander in chief of the armed forces. Every country knows your word is the one that counts."

"Yes, but it won't count a dime's worth if the Chinese brainwash Captain Bell," the president pointed out. "MacArthur alone they may dismiss, but if they find out what Bell knows, too, then it's all over, Lucius. They'll pull the trigger as sure as we're talking in this room."

Stoddard stirred uncomfortably, anticipating what Truman was going to say. "But there's nothing we can do about Bell now," he said. "All we can do is try to find him."

"All right, do that, General. Find him. "I'll leave that to you. In the meantime, though, there is something I can do about MacArthur."

"Sir?"

"I can fire him, General. I can cut off his authority. Discredit him. If the Chinese and Russians think I support MacArthur, and he makes a public fuss about invading China, we're in a war. But if I say publicly I don't agree with him . . ."

"That's pretty radical, Mr. President."

"You're damn right it's radical. We need something radical here. We need a quick change. MacArthur hasn't exactly brought home the laurels, has he? Why the hell don't we give somebody else a chance at it? Like Matt Ridgway, for instance."

"Sir—"

"I've made up my mind, General," he declared. "Unless you can deliver Captain Gilbert Bell to me within a month's time, I'll can MacArthur."

"I can't do it that quickly, sir. I have to locate him first."

"Then MacArthur's out." Truman started for the door, then turned. "I'd keep this under my hat, if I were you, Lucius," he cautioned. "Who knows? MacArthur may shape up yet. If he doesn't—if he pushes his plan to invade China—then by God, I'll just have to rap him on the knuckles and send him home."

16

GILBERT BELL hadn't seen another American since his capture two months before. At a prison somewhere in North Korea, he had been slung into a ward with more than a hundred South Koreans. Then one day he was singled out and whisked away by helicopters over the Manchurian border to another camp. There he was deposited into a small and windowless room without a word of explanation and left to eat and sleep with no more company than the single thirty-watt light bulb hanging from a cord from the ceiling.

The rations at the new prison were spare but adequate at first, and the room was heated with a coal oil stove. But a week after he got there, the conditions gradually began to worsen. The only food he got now was rice, and it was unclean and its taste was disgusting to him. Then one morning he awoke shivering and discovered the stove was gone. He complained loudly through the peephole in the metal door, but he got no response from the guard.

After a while, the lack of food, the constant damp and frigid air in the cell, and the awful unending silence of the long days and nights began to break him down. By the time the big metal door clanked open with an echo in the hall and a Chinese officer stepped into his cell, he was desperate to talk to someone—anyone.

"Captain Bell," the Chinese said to him in perfect English, "I am Lieutenant Rhu. Would you come this way, please?"

"Where are we going?" Gilbert asked.

"This way, please," Rhu said, turning his back.

Between the guard and Rhu, Gilbert walked, half-staggered at times, down a long concrete hall, into a large, comfortably furnished sitting room. Gilbert couldn't help but stare at the American-looking decor of the room. It was warm, homey, comfortable—like nothing he ever expected to see in a Chinese prison.

"Please," Rhu said. "Sit down."

Hesitantly, Gilbert took a seat on the sofa, while Rhu stood by the fireplace, with his hands behind his back. He was a hard, compact little man with dark eyes that seemed to look straight through you. But his voice was warm and friendly, and, Gilbert decided, well-trained.

"You'll be very unhappy to hear that California lost in the Rose Bowl," Rhu informed him. "Michigan beat them, fourteen to six. A pity, for a Californian like you."

"I'm not a Californian," Gilbert said, looking around the room.

"Yes, that's technically correct; you're not. But you've adopted California as your home, haven't you?"

"What if I have?" he said suspiciously.

"Your family is from the northeast, aren't they? Your father was Colonel Samuel Bell, your mother's name was Brenda. You have a sister Amanda who works in the consulate in Tokyo."

"All right, you did your homework," Gilbert conceded. "I'm impressed."

"You're very strong to have been existing on minimum rations, Captain," Rhu said. "You're not ready to talk to us yet, are you?"

"No, Lieutenant, I'm not. And what's more, I never will be."

"Fine," Rhu said, undaunted. "We have time. We have been here since 2000 B.C. We will be here a while longer." He said something in Chinese to the guard, who came to escort Bell from the room. But just as he reached the door, Rhu spoke again. "You know Joe Louis lost his fight with Ezzard Charles."

"I don't keep up with boxing, Lieutenant," Gilbert said.

"Joe Louis is a tired old man. He shouldn't be in the ring. You know he's fighting to pay his government a million dollars in taxes. You did know that, didn't you, Captain?"

"Can I go now?" Gilbert asked wearily.

"Joe Louis is a black man, isn't he, Gilbert? Your government is using a black man to show its strength to the rest of the world. At the expense of a human being. A poor black man with a great talent."

"Let's go," Gilbert said impatiently to the guard. Then, sarcastically, "I want to make it back to my cell in time for supper."

"Go ahead," Rhu said, smiling. "We'll talk again."

They did talk again, hundreds of times over the course of the next several months, but Rhu had no success with him. Although it took Gilbert a while to understand exactly what was happening to him, he did eventually realize how the Chinese were conducting their interrogations. The process was simple: they broke down your physical defenses, then proceeded to try to break down your mental ones.

They were always calm, soft-spoken, even monotonous in their conversations with him. In their friendly, concerned voices they told him that he was presumed dead by his family, that he should consider staying in China because he was branded a traitor back home, that America was a big clumsy society where the poor naturally suffer and the rich naturally abuse the middle class.

It was difficult for him. At times during the long cold winter months he wasn't sure what was real and what wasn't. Rhu had an immense store of facts. He would mix a harangue about John Masefield's poems, Rodgers and Hammerstein's musical, *All About Eve*, or Al Rosen's thirty-seven home runs last year with "factual" statements that his "girl," Adrian McAllister, was currently sleeping with a Japanese soldier in Tokyo.

Once he was jerked out of a restless sleep and taken to a projection room and shown a series of slides on the cracked concrete wall. One of the pictures was Douglas MacArthur shining Joseph Stalin's boots, another was of Dwight Eisenhower's house being patrolled by soldiers wearing Mao Tse-tung insignia.

"And this man," Rhu said as a shot of General Stoddard flashed on the wall, "is an American general who supplies us with relevant information about the United Nations' governments. He has worked with us since before the Second World War."

"This is all lies, Rhu," he groaned wearily. "Why do you bother showing me this junk?"

"And this," Rhu said in the same voice, "is Lin Su. And this is a picture of one thousand North Korean captives shot to death by the American forces in Unsan. . . ."

Gilbert's mind seemed suddenly to play tricks on him. Had he seen a picture of Lin Su? He waited as the series of photographs played on, another two hours, then three and four. Whenever he would doze off, he would be shaken out of his sleep by invisible arms in the dark and straightened up in his seat. After six hours he saw it again: a portrait of Lin Su, smiling at the camera. Then more lies, more trick photographs.

The slide show went on for months. At any time of the day or night he could be ripped out of his sleep and made to watch eight or ten hours of propaganda, mixed with realistic pictures, or the portrait of Lin Su. After a while, he began to feel that he was losing the distinction between the real and the unreal. He had seen MacArthur shining Stalin's boots so often, it didn't seem absurd anymore. It began to look like the truth.

At clear moments, during the night in his cold cell, he deciphered their method. The North Koreans were bloodthirsty; he had seen them slice the throat of a captive rather than worry about transporting him. The Chinese, on the other hand, were far more sophisticated. They were using their prisoners as weapons. Some were treated royally and sent back, hoping they would convince others not to fight such a humane enemy. Others they twisted psychologically; they made them believe that America was a heartless, bigoted, disgraceful country that should be destroyed from within. A few they just broke down and discarded.

At other times, though, when Bell was numb with cold and his insides burned with the absence of food, his mind wandered and none of that seemed important. He felt lost, as if he were wandering in a frozen black forest, with no guideposts, no benchmarks, no roads. And, worst of all, no place to go. At those times he concentrated on the picture of Lin Su and tried to blot out the rest. But he always wondered if he could hold onto reality much longer.

One morning he heard the door clank and Rhu entered. As he had for almost as long as he could remember, Gilbert asked what day it was. Although Rhu never told him, he kept asking, trying to fight their repetition with his own. But this day was different. Rhu responded.

"It's a lovely summer morning, Captain Bell; August, nineteen fifty-two."

Gilbert knew it was summer from the heat in the cell, but he couldn't believe the year. "You mean fifty-one," he said.

"You've lost count, Captain," Rhu said. "It's fifty-two. Seventeen months, six days you've been our guest."

Gilbert didn't have the energy to stand. "I'll never be able to pay my bill," he joked.

Rhu squatted down beside the cot. "Always defiant, aren't you?" he said angrily, slipping for a moment out of his monotone. Then he reverted to it. "Is that what's kept you going all these months? Natural defiance?"

"Just stubbornness, Rhu."

"Tell me something, Captain. In all these months, you've never asked about the girl. Why is that? Are you playing games with us?"

"What girl is that, Lieutenant?" he said weakly.

"That's not just a photograph, you know," Rhu said. "It's just as real as all the other scenes we've been showing you. Lin Su is very real. A warm, loving woman who can make any man feel like an immortal god. She possesses secrets of lovemaking only the ancient cultures know."

"Why don't you go home, Rhu? If you have a home."

"All right," he said, rising. "I only came to tell you of a report our intelligence received this morning. Your girl, Adrian McAllister, hung herself a week ago in her apartment in Tokyo."

Gilbert was unfazed. "You're lying, as always, Rhu. Adrian is probably back home in San Francisco."

"Her home is Sacramento, Captain Bell. Are you losing your grip?"

"I meant Sacramento," he said, rubbing his forehead.

"Whatever you say, Captain. And whatever you want to believe."

He turned to go, but paused at the door. "Oh," he said, facing Gilbert, "there's one other thing. Lin Su is a resident of this prison, you know."

"Sure," he sighed. "I'll bet she is. Just like Mac-Arthur and Eisenhower. Only the best at the Manchurian Arms."

"We've arranged for you to see her tonight, Captain," he said. "At the knock on the door, step up and look through the hole. She'll be there."

"I'll look forward to seeing her," he said sarcastically as he lay back on the cot and closed his eyes.

He had no awareness of the rest of the day, or how long into the night he slept. But at some time during the dark hours, he was awakened by the crisp knock of a wooden object against the metal door. At first he ignored it. Then, on the wild chance Rhu was telling him the truth, he stood up and stumbled over to the door and peered through the hole. But there was nothing but blackness. He languished at the door, his forehead pressed against the hole. Every bone in his body ached, his mind was swarming with images and pictures and the dull sounds of monotone sentences. He closed his eyes and tried to focus on one thing, but his head was reeling; he couldn't control his thinking.

Then he heard a voice in the darkness beyond the door. He held his breath and listened. A minute later, it was there again: a low, soft, feminine voice.

"Hello!" he called out through the hole. "Hello! Who is it? Who are you?"

Silence. He waited, beat his fist against the metal door, but his blows were too weak to make a noise. He leaned back against the door and panted. Then he heard it again.

"Gilly?" it said.

He turned his face to the hole again. "Hello! Who are you?" he yelled.

"Gilly?"

"Lin Su? Lin Su—oh, God. Is that you?"

"Gilly," she said in a firm, clear voice.

"I can't see you, Lin. Where are you?" He listened again, but there was nothing. "Damn it," he cried. "I heard it. I know I did." He pounded on the door again. "Lin Su! For God's sake, answer me!"

But there was nothing more to hear. The voice was gone.

Every day for the next two weeks Rhu brought him out of his cell to witness the slide show again. And every day he allowed the portrait of Lin Su to stay up on the wall a little longer. Then Rhu began to show more pictures of her—snapshots, close-ups, candid photos of her and her family—and Gilbert unconsciously began to pay more attention to the other scenes. In spite of his strong will, he felt himself slipping, beginning to accept as truth what months before had seemed ludicrous.

When the weather turned warm again, the food set down on the concrete floor once a day took a turn for the better. One day he was actually given bread, then vegetables, then meat. He suspected the change was all a part of their plan, but he had been hungry so long, he didn't care. He dug into the food with his fingers and enjoyed it while he could.

He was busy eating one of those meals in the middle of the day when suddenly, out of nowhere, Lin Su's face appeared in the peephole in the door. Flinging the tin plate aside, he rushed over to the door.

"Lin!"

"Shh," she whispered. "Not so loud, Gilly. I'm not supposed to be here."

"Lin, I can't believe it! What are you doing here?"

"I've been trying to sneak in more food for you."

"Well, yes—"

"I've got to go," she told him and disappeared out of sight down the hall.

His heart beat rapidly as he turned around and looked around at the rough, gray walls. He closed his eyes and tried to calm down. He wondered if what he had seen was actually real. Maybe they were succeeding at last. Maybe he was getting ready to tell them what he knew.

But Lin Su was flesh and blood. She came the next day and the one after, always in a hurry, always afraid, he thought, that Lieutenant Rhu would find out what she was doing. She became a preoccupation to Gilbert, then an obsession. Every second of the day was merely something to be endured, something to get through in order to see her again. He thought of her day and night. Now, when he saw her delicate, pretty face through the opening in the door, he felt his passions surge again. He was gaining physical strength through the food she was giving him and psychological strength through the desire he was feeling for her.

Finally, after months of seeing her through a six-inch square hole in metal, the door to his cell creaked open and she walked in. His knees grew weak when he saw her. She was dressed in a plain Chinese uniform, but it was like covering porcelain with burlap; her beauty had no trouble beaming through her clothes. She was one of the loveliest women he had ever seen. Large, dark, friendly eyes, a perfect oval face, skin naturally vibrant and flawlessly smooth, hair so black and thick, it was all he could do to keep from reaching out and touching it.

But he didn't know how she would react. "You're more beautiful than ever," he said to her.

"Gilly, Lieutenant Rhu is dead," she announced sadly. "He committed suicide last night."

"Lin," he said, ignoring her words, "will you please tell me what you're doing here? What all this cloak and dagger business is about?"

"I've had to see you without Rhu knowing about it," she said simply. "Come, sit down," she invited him. They sat on his cot and she took his hand in hers. "You've had such a terrible time," she said, touching his face. "I'm so sorry."

"Lin," he said impatiently.

"All right, Gilly," she replied, "I'll tell you. I work here. It's the only way I can keep my parents alive."

"Then you're not doing this of your own free will," he said hopefully.

"Oh, no, Gilly," she said quickly. "How could you think that? I love you. I will always love you. Nothing will ever change that. Not our different lives, not this war. Nothing will change it."

He placed his hand on her hair. "How can something as lovely as you exist inside this cold, damp place?" he said sadly. "You should be out in the sunshine, in a flower garden somewhere."

"Shh," she whispered, placing her fingers on his lips. "Not now. I will be back tomorrow night."

"You can stay a while longer."

"No," she said, getting to her feet. "This is my job now. I have to be careful. They say Rhu committed suicide, but I saw his body. They killed him. They had forced a hose down his throat."

She was gone before he could protest again. He waited nervously until the following night, expecting her to slip inside his cell again, but that didn't happen. He was taken to the sitting room, where Lin Su was standing in front of the fireplace, almost in the same posture Rhu had adopted before.

He walked uncertainly to the couch and sat down. "What is all this, Lin?" he asked. "Is this all some scheme to drive me crazy?"

She looked at him sadly for a moment. She seemed almost ready to burst into tears and rush over and embrace him, but she held fast. "I told you it was my job, Gilly," she answered. "I've been selected to replace Rhu."

"But don't they know about us?" he said, confused, not certain what to make of this unexpected role in which he now found Lin Su.

"Yes, they know about us. They think I can use that."

"God, Chinese Communists are relentless. They never give up. If one thing doesn't work, they try another."

"Will you help me, Gilly?" she asked him.

"Help you what? What can I do?"

She came over to him, knelt beside the sofa and looked up into his eyes. Suddenly her stiffness and formality were gone. She was the warm, loving woman he had known in San Francisco. "You could help me fool them. Will you do that, Gilly? My family's lives are depending on it."

"Fool them how?" he asked.

"Just go along with me—please," she pleaded. "Oh, Gilly, I love you so much." She reached out and kissed him softly, lightly, on the lips, with feeling.

He moved toward her as he felt his desire stir, but she put him off. "Not now," she said, standing, straightening her uniform jacket. "They'd kill me if they saw this."

"Lin, you're tearing me up. I don't understand this. What's going on? What are you doing?"

She cleared her throat, called for the guard, and ten minutes later he was back in his cell.

He spent the next two days thinking about her, reliving the touch of her lips on his. Always before he had spent his time thinking, figuring out the reason for everything that was done to him. It had always managed to keep him balanced on that fine line between reality and unreality. But now his brain was clouded with emotion. He didn't know what Lin Su had meant about fooling the Communists, and he didn't care. All he wanted was to touch and feel her, to kiss her again, to make love to her.

Early one evening he was taken out of his cell and led down to the sitting room again. It was empty, so he took the opportunity to jostle the coals in the fireplace with a poker. It felt good to be doing something. For almost two years he had had nothing to do except hold his plate once a day. He stirred the embers vigorously enough to create a flame and turned his back to the warmth.

When he saw Lin Su enter the room, he almost dropped the poker. She was stunning; she was wearing a bright blue silk dress zipped high at the neck. The smooth material clung closely to her luscious form. She had thin but shapely legs, rounded hips, a diminutive waist, and small but sensuously upturned breasts. As she took a step toward him and her left leg slid into the open through a high slit in the dress, he could barely keep from running over to her.

"We'll be alone for a while, Gilly," she said, walking gracefully toward him.

He eased the poker back against the fireplace stones, waited, then felt her warm, soft body slip next to him. He wrapped his arms around her, then looked down at her exquisite face.

"What's the matter?" he asked her, wiping a tear off her cheek.

"Nothing," she said and pressed her face against his chest.

He shook his head. "I can smell your perfume and feel your skin, but I still don't know if this is real, Lin," he confessed. "I'm not sure I can tell anymore."

She took his hand and placed it gently on her breast. "It's real, Gilly," she said. "It's all real."

He kissed her and she responded tantalizingly, touching his tongue with hers, uttering little sounds of pleasure as he reached around her waist and brought her close to him and pressed her against his hardness.

"My God," he gasped, "it's been so long!"

"Make love to me, Gilly," she said, clutching at him. "Now, please. Make love to me."

He reached up to her neck and pinched the zipper and slid it down her back. The dress parted and he slipped the silk off her arms and let it drop to the floor. He was surprised for a second to see that she was naked underneath the dress, but his mind was too dazed by the throes of passion to wonder about it. All he wanted to do was hold her small, firm breasts in his hands, then take her nipples in his mouth. . . .

She enticed him down to the rug in front of the fire and pulled him on top of her and quickly into her. After a few moments she began to heave up and down beneath him, grinding her body in rhythm with his. Gilbert felt that she was concentrating her whole body and mind into giving him pleasure. She brought his desire up, satisfied it, then raised it to an even greater urgency the next time. She was an exciting, exhilarating woman who was able to manipulate and control his emotions more skillfully than he would have ever thought possible.

At some time past midnight, they lay wrapped together under a blanket in front of the dying fire. Lin clung closely to him and squeezed him each time he moved to change positions.

"Gilly?" she said, pressing tightly against him.

"What? Am I hurting you?" he asked.

"No, you're not hurting me. I just wondered if you would do me a favor."

He laughed. "Are you kidding? After what you just did for me?"

"I'm not kidding, Gilly; I'm serious."

"All right then. Sure. Name it. Anything I can do from my little room, I will do."

"Gilly," she began, changing the tone of her voice, "I do care for you, and I've missed you terribly." She sat up. "But I have to tell you: I did this to save my family. Please try to understand that."

"You did what, Lin?" he said. "I don't understand."

"I did this," she answered, meaning the sex. "I was supposed to get you to tell me what you know. What you learned from this General Stoddard."

He was startled. "Damn it, Lin Su! What are you talking about? I thought we cared for each other."

"I do care, Gilly. That's why I'm telling you this."

"For the first time since I got to this place, could

I have the truth?" he asked angrily. "Will you just tell me what the hell it is you do in here?"

"I do . . . what I just did, Gilly."

"Oh, no—"

"I do it to keep my parents safe, Gilly. And to keep myself out of a cell like the one you're in. I'm sorry, but that's the way it is."

"You sleep with prisoners?" he said, stunned.

"Yes. I sleep with them. I make love with them. It's ugly, but I do what I have to, just like you do." She looked at him. "But, Gilly, I do care for you. I swear I do. More than any man I've ever known. With you it was beautiful."

He got up, pulled on his pants. Watching her lift the blanket modestly over her breasts, he shook his head. "Would you like to hear what I know, Lin?" he asked her. "I can tell you in two minutes. All of this trouble for two minutes of information."

"No," she replied firmly. "I don't want to know. Whatever it is, I don't want to be the one to get it out of you. Just keep it to yourself."

"I'll tell you anyway."

"No, Gilly. Don't tell me anything. Listen to me: I deceived you. They sent me here from Peking to find out what you know. I don't know what it is, and I don't care."

"I'm going to tell you anyway."

"No!"

"I want to. I want to trust you, Lin. I want to believe you wouldn't tell them."

"No, Gilly."

"I want to show you I believe in you, Lin Su."

"No, Gilly, don't. They're listening!"

No sooner had she said the words than the door

to the sitting room banged open, a guard burst in and stood aside, at attention. Then, emerging out of the dim light of the hall into the room was the compact, hard figure of Lieutenant Rhu.

Gilbert looked at her in amazement. "You even lied about him," he said. "Why?"

"Gilly, please do one thing for me. If I mean anything to you, do this: don't believe anything you see or hear."

"All right, Lin Su," Rhu broke in. "That is enough."

"It's the only way to survive it, Gilly," she persisted. "Don't believe *anything*."

Rhu said something in Chinese to the guard and the man marched briskly over to Lin Su. Without a word the guard reached down and clasped onto her arm and jerked it.

"Leave her alone," Gilbert yelled at him. But the guard pulled her up to her feet. "Damn it, leave her alone!" Gilbert demanded and swung at the man's face. His fist struck hard jawbone, and the guard crumpled down to the floor. Gilbert wrapped the blanket around Lin Su's shoulders and pulled her next to him.

Lieutenant Rhu shook his head, laughed. "You Americans are very amusing," he declared. "The woman betrays you and you take her to your bosom. It doesn't make any sense."

"It makes sense, Rhu. It's just something a man like you will never be able to understand. Lin Su is a friend. I care for her. I'm not going to turn on her because she's doing what she has to."

"Well, you're right, Captain," Rhu agreed, "I don't understand. But I do understand this: the woman betrayed us, too. And friend or not, she will be treated accordingly. That is *our* way. Lin Su will spend the rest of her life in this prison."

"No, please, don't!" she pleaded.

"Your parents will be provided for," he told her coldly. "They are loyal members of the People's Republic of China."

"You're a heartless bastard, Rhu," Gilbert told him.

"Yes, I am heartless. But efficient. As for you, Captain, I'm afraid your holiday is over. Tomorrow morning you will be back on rice again. And since we won't be coming for you for a while, you may as well take the opportunity to reflect on what you've done here. Your little secret, whatever it is, will cost this exquisite creature her youth and beauty. It's very sad, isn't it?"

Gilbert said nothing. He drew Lin Su close to him. "We'll get out of here someday," he told her. "Just hang on."

"Gilly," she said tearfully. "Will you forgive me?"

He kissed her, then brought her to his chest. "Never mind," he comforted her. "Forget it. There's nothing to forgive."

3

17

FOR ADRIAN MCALLISTER, the Korean War changed the moment she learned that Gilbert Bell was missing in action. For the rest of America, it changed a few weeks later, when President Truman removed Douglas MacArthur from his command and replaced him with General Matthew Ridgway.

The war was with the Chinese now, and the Chinese were a surprisingly determined and sophisticated people. They were capable of bluntly charging seven hundred thousand troops at the UN forces while hiding behind the human shields of South Korean women and children; they could deviously agree to the armistice negotiations in Kaesong in order to initiate clever propaganda attacks against the UN ambassadors who were there bargaining in good faith.

Against such a foe there was now no Patton or

MacArthur to rouse the American spirit. Instead of clear-cut, understandable, dramatic offensives like the Normandy invasion in World War II, or the Inchon Landing in Korea in 1950, there were now "limited objective" offensives all over Korea, aimed at battering down the constantly moving enemy.

The newspapers, Adrian's included, faithfully reported the developments in Korea, but the Sun's public, for one, became weary of such meaningless operations as "Thunderball," "Ripper," and "Strangle." It had become so confusing, they had almost lost their grip on it. The general feeling was expressed in a cartoon appearing in Chicago *Sun-Times* syndicate in 1952. A grizzled sergeant, holding a cup of soup in his hand, was telling the new, fresh-faced, freezing troops: "Don't ask me what it's all about, lads! . . . All I know is nobody can win it, lose it, or stop it . . ."

And when the *Sun's* readers lost their grip on the war, they also lost interest in it. Adrian was brought home; there was no urgent need for a war correspondent now. "All our readers want is for the thing to be over," Mallory had explained to her. "The only reason they read the stories every day now is to see if somehow the war ended while they were asleep last night."

The "police action" in Korea had become The Unpopular War. For the first time in American history a major conflict was being waged through a complicated maze of propaganda, prisoner brainwashing, and limited military offensives against the enemy. Standing ready in the background was always the nuclear bomb, but the fear of unleashing its power was greater than the fear of a continued war. The first explosion of the hydrogen bomb in November, 1952, was so frightening it wasn't reported officially for over a year.

Finally the Korean War became a political football and Americans turned to an old-style military hero to end the conflict once and for all. "I say," a reader wrote to the *Sun*, "if a five-star general can't end this war, we ought never to have gotten into it to begin with." America agreed with him: General Dwight David Eisenhower was elected president of the United States in November, 1952.

All of this time Adrian did her work, and did it well. She made occasional trips to Korea, interviewed Bob Hope after one of his Christmas shows, spent three days with a MASH unit in Uijongbu and wrote an account, in the form of a diary, of the production of Edward R. Murrow's *See It Now* film interviews with American soldiers in Korea. That piece won her a Sacramento Press Club award two weeks after it was published in the *Sun*.

With all her first-hand exposure to conditions among the UN forces in Korea, Adrian's attitude toward the war had changed, too. But unlike many Americans, including her parents, Adrian was beginning to understand why it was being fought, and more important to her, why it should be fought.

"Operation Little Switch, they're calling it," Mr. McAllister said to her one day, disgustedly popping the latest issue of the *Sun* with the back of his hand. "I can see why. We get six hundred prisoners, they get six thousand."

Adrian continued to rock gently back and forth in the swing, saying nothing. It was a warm, bright Saturday afternoon and she had nothing particular to do. She preferred to let her father go ahead and express his irritation at the war, as he always did, and offer nothing in reply. She had argued many hours with him before, and it had never accomplished anything.

"Adrian," he said, "why didn't you mention the prisoner swap in your column?"

"Ed Mallory asked me not to mention it," she answered. "He says the readers are tired of the war. Just like you are."

He lowered the paper, looked at her. "You won't ever get it out of your system, will you?" he said.

"Not it, Daddy," she corrected. "Him. I won't ever get him out of my system."

"Look, Adrian, honey," he said, folding the paper, "don't you think it's time you forgot about him? He wasn't in the list of Americans released at Panmunjom. We may as well face it—he may not have made it."

"He's still alive," she asserted defiantly. "I know that."

"Well, even if he is, honey, it's just not healthy to keep thinking about him. If you're not working, you're sitting out here in the swing, thinking about him."

"I like to think about him," she said.

"Well, it's unhealthy," he proclaimed, and opened his paper to the sports section. A few minutes later he mumbled something about the Yankees being on top again, then passed on into silence.

It was strange, she thought, how everyone seemed to have shut out the war, how they could glance over casualty lists and shake their heads and then turn to the baseball scores. To her the war was a real thing—real, living people with breakable arms and legs and perishable skulls fighting impenetrable steel machines and clever, illusive enemies. To her father, it was nothing more than an irritation in his newspaper.

"Adrian!" her mother called from the screen door. Then she came out on the porch, wiping her hands on her apron. "Adrian," she said, "Melissa Townsend is on the phone. She's giving a Coke party for Amanda Bell, some kind of homecoming."

"Tell her I'm working," she said. "I can't make it."

"I'll tell her nothing of the sort. I think it's very sweet of her to invite you, considering how terribly you and Amanda get along."

"Tell her I'll call her back, mother."

Alice McAllister shook her head. "So you're just going to sit out here all day? All you do is work and sit, Adrian."

"I know, mother."

"Well," her mother said after a pause, "you be sure and call her."

"I will."

Adrian closed her eyes when she heard the screen door slam again. How far away Korea seemed now, as she sat on a porch swing in Sacramento. All the suffering, the cold, the love. . . .

"Adrian?" her father broke into her thoughts. "Cathy's wanting to see this *House of Wax* picture, this three-dimension thing. What do you think?"

"I think she should," she answered.

"Well, now, they tell me it's a pretty scary picture. And if that three-dimension is anthing like what they say . . ."

"Cathy's a big girl now, daddy. Let her go."

"Now that's a cavalier attitude if I ever heard one," he reprimanded her. "How do you know if a picture like that is suitable?"

"Daddy, it won't hurt her. I once saw a man's head —oh, never mind."

He looked at her sternly. "I told you not to talk about things like that, youny lady. Nobody wants to hear you talk about things like that."

"No," she said, almost about to cry. "I guess they don't."

"Well," he announced, standing up, looking at his watch, "I think I'll go watch that ball game. Are you coming?"

Adrian shook her head and watched him disappear inside the house, then leaned back in the swing and closed her eyes and let the soft, warm breeze blow gently in her hair. After a while, she decided to go inside, but then something in the street caught her eye.

An official-looking two-door sedan slowed down, moaned into a lower gear, and turned the corner. As it ground slowly forward, she could make out the "USMC" on the left door, and the dress uniforms of the noncom driver and of the officer in the passenger seat.

Her heart almost stopped beating when she realized that the car was coming to a slow halt in front of the house. She closed her eyes, took a deep breath, and tried to prepare herself. At last, she thought; they've come to tell me Gilbert is dead. It's finally happening. When she opened them again, she recognized the distingiushed-looking man walking toward the porch. It would be just like him, she decided, to be so thoughtful as to tell her in person.

"Adrian," the officer greeted her. He removed his hat as she drew near to the edge of the porch.

"General Stoddard," she said. "How are you?"

"I'm just fine, Adrian. Do you think I could talk to you a minute or two?"

She nodded. "Is the porch all right?"

"Fine," he answered, then came up on the porch and took a seat in the swing.

Adrian was a little surprised that Stoddard seemed a good deal older than he had a year ago. But he still looked fit and ready for military action. "Is this about Gilbert?" she asked him as soon as he was settled.

He nodded. "Yes, it is. We found him, Adrian."

"Is he dead?" she asked quietly.

"Oh, no, he's not dead. We know that for a fact. He's in a prison in Manchuria. I found out about it during the switch at Panmunjon."

Adrian was relieved and hopeful. "When they finally sign the armistice, they will let him go, won't they?"

He shook his head. "I'm afraid they won't, Adrian," he said. "Not out of China."

"But you can't just leave him there," she said accusingly.

"I don't intend to leave him there. We're getting him out three days from now. I'm on my way to Tokyo now. I wanted you to know about the operation before it happened—just in case it goes badly."

She was thoughtful a minute. "Why is Gilbert so special, General? Why are you doing this?"

"I'm doing it to prevent another war, Adrian—a nuclear war. The Chinese are about ready to agree to an armistice, and when they do, Washington will publicly declare the war is over. But that's not the way it works anymore. The fighting may stop, but we'll always be at war with Communism—Chinese, Soviet, or whatever. That's why we can't slip up and give them an excuse or a reason to push the button on us."

"You didn't answer my question, General," she gently rebuked him.

"I can't answer it right now, Adrian," he said apologetically. "You know yourself how crucial this brainwashing of prisoners has become. As of this month we've had thirty-eight separate 'confessions' by released American prisoners that we used inhumane germ warfare on the North Koreans. The world believes them; it's looking at us with critical eyes right now. One slip and the Chinese will come down on us and rally a great part of the rest of the world on their side."

"So you're going to get him out yourself?"

He nodded. "Myself and three others, all crack marines. One of them you know—Sergeant DeWitt Baruchi."

"Chick? I'd lost track of him."

"Baruchi was transferred into intelligence after Chosin. In fact, he's the one who located Captain Bell."

"I'm glad. He always felt guilty about leaving Gilbert in Korea."

"Adrian," he said seriously. "I'm going to have to ask you to keep this mission secret. You can imagine what the Chinese could do with this—our invading Manchuria to rescue a prisoner."

"It sounds very risky, General."

"It's more risky than you can imagine. President

Eisenhower has approved of the mission, but he can't sanction it officially because of the possible political results. So if we're caught, we're on our own."

"Well, I guess we'll just have to be careful then, won't we?"

He looked at her with surprise. "Now wait a minute here," he cautioned her. "*You're* not going, Adrian."

"Oh but I am going, General."

"Adrian," he said in a lower, confidential voice, "what I'm talking about is a commando raid."

"I know what you're talking about, General Stoddard," she assured him. "I've been around the military long enough to know."

"In Manchuria," he added.

"Right. Manchuria. When are we leaving?"

"You're not leaving at all," he said sternly. "This is one time you're not going to manipulate me, Adrian. This mission is far too dangerous. . ."

"For a woman, General?" she said when he trailed off. "You're beginning to sound like Lieutenant Metz. Tell me, what do I have to do to prove myself? I was at Seoul when it was evacuated, I was at the Pusan perimeter, at Inchon, at Hagaru, Hungnam, the Punchbowl—"

"I know you've been in the war since the beginning, Adrian. I don't mean to belittle that. All I'm saying is, you aren't trained for this kind of mission."

She paused a minute. "I can still help," she said.

"No, it's out of the question."

"Adrian?" her father called out, then stepped out on the porch. When he saw Stoddard, his face expressed great. surprise. "Good afternoon," he said, walking over. "I didn't know we had company."

Stoddard stood up, offered his hand.

"This is General Stoddard," Adrian said. Then to Stoddard, "This is my father."

"General Stoddard?" McAllister said, puzzled. "What can we do for you, General?"

"The general is here to tell me about Gilbert," Adrian explained. "They've found him. He's in a prison."

"Oh. Well, it's good to know where he is," he said to Stoddard. "It's not knowing things that wears us down. Adrian's been worried about Captain Bell for a long time now."

"General Stoddard's going to get him out," Adrian said boldly. Then, ignoring Stoddard's censuring stare, she added, "He'll be back home in a few days."

"What Adrian means," Stoddard said quickly, trying to cover up, "is that we hope to negotiate his release soon."

"Good," McAllister declared. "I'm glad to see the war is finally winding down. It's gone on far too long. I understand the talks at Panmunjon will be coming to a head in the next month or so."

"He wants me to go with him," Adrian said.

McAllister frowned suspiciously. "Go with you where, General Stoddard?" he asked. "Not to Panmunjom, surely. She's been all over Korea—isn't it time she was allowed to do her work in safety?"

"It's not Panmunjon, daddy," she said, then looked at Stoddard, waited for him to finish her statement.

He gave her a hard glance, then looked pleasantly at McAllister. "The place is confidential at the moment," he said. "We can't reveal it to anyone."

"Yes, but why Adrian?"

"Because I *love* Gilbert, daddy."

McAllister shook his head. "I don't like it. It's time

Adrian stayed home for a while. She has no business running off to a place like that, especially now that the war's ending."

"I agree with you," Stoddard put in.

"I'm glad to hear it. Just between you and me, General, Adrian has her way a bit too often for her own good. If I had had a choice in the matter, I never would have let her go off to Korea in the first place. I don't think it's done her much good."

McAllister stayed a while longer, commenting again on the inordinate length of the war, then left them alone on the porch.

"Damn, Adrian. You just about blew it," Stoddard said irritably. "If you had told him where Gilbert is, or what we're planning . . ."

"He would have told everyone in his law firm?" she suggested.

"Yes. That's right. He would have. Well, thank God you didn't tell him," he sighed, putting on his hat. "I would've lost faith in your integrity, and the rest of us would've lost a lot more."

"If you wait right here, General," she said, "I'll be ready in thirty minutes."

"Oh, no—"

"General, if you let me go with you, and we succeed, I'll write a story on this mission that will win the Pulitzer Prize. It'll equal any Chinese propaganda ever written, I promise you. Except this story will be the truth."

He considered the idea. "What if we fail?"

"Then we fail. No story. Anyway, we'll probably be dead, anyway, won't we?"

"Probably," he conceded.

"Well?"

"Adrian, if we do fail, and word gets out that we crossed the border into Manchuria, the president will have to look the other way and claim the mission was unauthorized."

"We won't fail, General," she told him. "Remember how we got to MacArthur's phone in Suwon? You and I work well together."

He smiled, in spite of himself. "That was fun," he admitted. "But this is a great deal more dangerous."

"Then we'll be a great deal more clever."

He laughed. "You've got an answer for everything, haven't you?"

"Everything that matters," she answered. "And Gilbert Bell matters. I'd go anywhere or do anything in the world to help him."

He looked at her. He couldn't help but envy Bell, having such a beautiful, intelligent, vibrant woman so much in love with him. She had actually gotten prettier, he decided, in the past three years. She had blossomed into a woman during the war. He had had trouble keeping up with her energy and resourcefulness in Suwon three years before. Now, he knew he had no chance against her.

"Adrian," he said in a fatherly voice, "I admire your loyalty, but don't you think this is a bit too much to ask? You're taking advantage of me because I like you."

"I have to go, General. I just have to."

"And if I don't let you, you're going to tell your father all about it," he guessed.

"I'll tell him everything I know. And what I don't I'll put in the paper."

He laughed. "I don't believe for a minute you would do that," he said. "But then with you, I can never tell. I can see I'm not going to have any choice in this. Okay, go. Pack something. We'll see what happens."

She smiled warmly, leaned over and kissed him on the cheek. "You're nothing but an old teddy bear, General," she teased him. "How'd you ever get to be a marine?"

"Not by ordering women around, I can tell you."

"Give me thirty minutes," she said, going.

"What about your parents? You'll have to tell them," he called out after her.

"Unh-unh," she answered back. "That's a job for the Marine Corps. You tell them."

18

T HREE DAYS later Adrian was in a transport plane squeezing a parachute ripcord with her trembling fingers. Sitting across from her were two marine noncoms and General Stoddard. Next to her was Chick Baruchi, and a private first class named Mark Hollister. Everyone else appeared to her to be calm and unafraid, but she was so nervous it was all she could do to remain seated.

It was pitch black outside. In the belly of the plane only the wire-protected red bulb was burning, casting an eerie, bloody glow over everyone. She took a deep breath, tried to keep her nervousness out of her voice.

"Where are we, General?" she managed to ask.

"We're still over the Yellow Sea."

She imagined how the black water below them must look. If the plane went down, either the sea would suck them under, or the North Koreans or Chinese would pick them up. She wondered which would be worse. But she shook off the idea and looked over at Baruchi. "What am I supposed to do with this?" she asked, showing him the snap at the end of her cord.

"We showed you, Adrian," he answered. "You clamp it on the bar."

She looked up at the rod running along the fuselage, over her head. "I know you showed me," she said. "I guess I just don't believe it."

"It opens your chute for you," he explained. "Once you're out, all you have to worry about is pulling the lines to guide yourself down."

"Great," she said, tapping the snap on her knee. "I thought I'd have a lot to worry about."

"General?" the pilot called out. "We're over land. We're approaching Sinuiju."

"Just tell us when, Major," Stoddard said calmly.

Adrian could feel her heart pounding in her chest as she tried to recall the details of the plan Stoddard had outlined. The prison was in Manchuria, across the Yalu River from North Korea. They would be dropping down with a raft to go up the Yalu at Antung . . .

"General? Two minutes," the pilot announced.

"All right," Stoddard said. "Hook up!"

One of the three commandos stepped up to the door and jerked it open, just as she snapped onto the rod. The roar of the propellers blasted in with a rush of air and sent a chill through her body. As the line filed forward, toward the noisy opening, she noted that there was nothing but a frightening darkness on the other side.

"Adrian?" Stoddard said. "Are you all right?"

"Yes, I'm all right," she answered. "I can't tell you how much I've always wanted to jump out of an airplane into total darkness."

"You can still back out," he reminded her in a sober voice. "Why don't you stay here?"

"No, I'm going," she said, though not very confidently. The truth was, she was scared half to death.

"Now, General!" the pilot called out. And suddenly, without a word, the men in front of her peeled off into the black hole and disappeared, leaving their ripcords dangling on the bar.

She neared the edge, felt the great rush of air gushing powerfully at her legs. "General?" she yelled back at Stoddard. "If I get lost down there, for God's sake, find me!"

He nodded and waved at her, she held her breath and leaped out of the plane into the air. When the wind swept her body up, she thought her parachute hadn't opened, but then, quickly, she felt herself gliding down into the darkness with a pleasant pulling sensation coming from above. Soon she could see the ground beneath her, pale and ghostly in the moonlight, and off to the right, three of the other chutes floating down easily through the air toward a range of dark hills.

The feeling of euphoria passed quickly. The closer she got to earth, the more frightened she became. She thought something must be wrong, she was going much too fast; but there was nothing she could do but hang on and hope. All of a sudden, she was rapidly approaching the ground, at an angle. She yanked on the left line, but the ground came up too quickly, crushed into her shoulder, and tumbled her over onto her leg.

When she stopped rolling, she undid her chute and wadded it up as she had been instructed, but then had to sit down. Her ankle was throbbing with pain.

Twenty minutes later, Stoddard and the others had joined her. "What happened?" he asked her. "Are you hurt?"

"I just twisted my ankle," she said.

"Damn!" he reproached himself. "I was crazy to let you come along, Adrian. How did you talk me into this?"

"I'll be all right, General," she said. "It's nothing, really. Just help me get up."

He raised her up. "Do you think it's broken?" he asked.

"No," she answered, pretending not to feel the pain when she set her weight down on the ankle. "It'll be all right. I can walk on it."

"I can carry you," Baruchi offered.

"No thank you, Chick," she insisted. "I'll carry myself."

"All right," Stoddard said. "Sanders, have you got the raft?"

"Packed on my back, General. And Hollister has the motor."

"Then let's go."

In silent, secret pain Adrian trekked with the marines over the cool ground, hanging close to the coastline, proceeding north toward Sinuiju. At the

Yalu River, below that town, Stoddard ordered Sanders to remain on the North Korean bank. "You too,
Adrian," he said.

She shook her head. "Unh-unh."

"Adrian, we're going into Manchuria, for God's
sake."

"Then let's go. We're wasting time."

The raft inflated and the motor attached, they proceeded slowly up the river. Just below the bridge at
Antung on the Manchurian side, Mullins shut off the
motor and they paddled quietly beneath what looked
to Adrian like a legion of guards conversing with
each other in low, serious voices. Slowly the raft eased
up against the currents, beneath the spans.

Half an hour later, they put in at the shore. As
soon as Adrian's foot touched ground, an intense pain
knifed through her leg, but she said nothing. They
proceeded over ground for about a mile, they lay
prostrate on a hill. She was happy to lie down on
her stomach and take the weight off her foot.

"That's it down there, General," Baruchi said. He
handed Stoddard a pair of infra-red binoculars.

"Good," Stoddard said, looking through the lens.
"It looks practically empty."

"Just like our reports say," Chick observed. "They
only kept a few prisoners after the switch. Gilly's
one of them."

Adrian strained to look at Chick in the dim moonlight. He was older, more mature than the day she
and Gilbert had sent him out of Hagaru, but there
was still an innocence about him. She could understand how the men might think he was a coward, or
why he would switch from combat to intelligence.
He seemed so gentle, so incapable of using the ma-

chine gun he was now carrying. And yet Gilbert had told her Chick was a good soldier, a man to whom he would entrust his life. She knew if it came to it, she would, too.

"How many guards do they have, General?" Hollister asked.

Stoddard rolled the focus on the glasses. "I can't tell. Except for the flood lights, the whole compound looks empty."

"There are supposed to be six guards," Chick said.

Stoddard lowered the binoculars. "Why don't we go down and see for ourselves? How's your foot, Adrian?"

"I'd forgotten about it," she lied.

"I don't suppose you'd consider staying here . . ."

"No, I wouldn't, General," she said impatiently. "I'm going in there, too."

"Okay, let's move out, then."

There was enough moonlight to see by, when the clouds weren't in the way, so they had little trouble moving across the level ground to an eight-foot wire fence surrounding the camp. Panting, Adrian stared through the mesh wire at the massive concrete structure beyond. It was three stories high, fifty yards wide, and, except for the top floors, windowless. She swallowed, cleared her throat, swallowed again. Was it possible? she wondered. Could Gilbert have been lying in that hard, forbidding place for two years? If he had been, what would be left of him now? What would they find inside the walls? A mindless vegetable? A skeleton?

Hollister was busy slicing through the mesh wire with the huge cutting pliers he had brought in his pack. The others held their rifles ready, looking cautiously around the area. Adrian could see only two stationary flood lamps on the building. Their beams crossed and lit up a spot on the bare yard twenty feet from the fence. But she saw no other sign of life.

Suddenly a uniformed soldier appeared in the yard, carrying a rifle out in front of his waist. He hesitated a minute, then walked straight through the light beams, toward the fence, his eyes darting from side to side as he neared the wire. Quickly they rolled away from the cut wire, froze, and watched him closely as he approached. Adrian lay close to the ground, ready to spring up and run at any instant.

Spotting the cut wire, the guard walked carefully over, kneeled down and lifted up the severed strip. Immediately he yelled back toward the building. A few seconds later an answer in Chinese came back from a lookout post and then the two flood lamps poured down their beams on the guard's back.

Just as the guard was about to call out again, Hollister sprang up, leaped forward, and plunged his fixed bayonet through the fence, into the chest of the guard. As he was struggling to pull the blade back through, a rifle flashed and cracked beyond the fence and struck the wire over his head—once, twice.

Adrian knew this was a moment of truth. They had to choose one way or the other now—they could go on in, or back off. But Stoddard, Baruchi, and Hollister didn't even pause to consider it. They dived one by one through the opening and rolled onto the yard.

When she got through, she raced across the yard under their cover, dodging the endless spray of bullets coming from behind the floodlights. For the moment she forgot about the pain in her ankle as she rushed across the hard ground toward the corner of the building. Just as she reached it and slid out of the illumination, she heard a rattling of fire behind her.

She braved a look, saw Baruchi standing in the center of the yard, firing his automatic rifle into the lights. Glass shattered, bulbs exploded, smoke billowed, a man yelped in pain, and suddenly the whole place was shrouded in darkness.

Adrian stood with her back pressed hard against the rough, cool concrete and struggled for breath. Somewhere up high she could hear quick, sharp voices exchanging words at a distance of twenty yards. She could hear too, inside the building, a rumbling of people. She hoped they were prisoners and not guards.

"Adrian." Stoddard's hand touched her shoulder.

"Is Chick all right?" she whispered.

"He went inside."

"Well, it's probably better in there than it is out here," she said shakily.

"There's his signal. Let's go!" Abruptly, he yanked her toward him and ran holding her hand along the edge of the building wall. When they reached the door, Chick kicked it open with his foot and they ducked inside.

"Where's Hollister?" Stoddard asked him.

"He's inside."

"Bell's supposed to be on the first floor," Stoddard said. "Adrian, you stay with me. Sergeant, take the north wing. And watch out for Hollister."

"Yes, sir."

As they started to go, two guards appeared at the door, but Baruchi was too quick for them. He wheeled and chopped them down before they could squeeze a trigger.

Then she and Stoddard plunged into silence as they entered one of the long halls and began moving slowly and carefully down its length. All along the corridor were closed cells, every one of them empty.

"General," Adrian whispered, "there's nobody here."

"Just keep moving."

Their steps on the slick floor echoed against the damp concrete walls as they made their way down the hall. Adrian checked the view hole in each cell for prisoners, but there were none. She began to be afraid that Chick had been wrong about the prison. But then she told herself, if Gilbert trusted Chick Baruchi, so should she. Anyway, she could feel that Gilbert was there, somewhere.

They turned a corner, kept walking. Adrian expressed her amazement at the presence of a room at the end of the hall, a well-furnished sitting room with a fireplace, but they didn't stop to examine it. All along the way, she checked each cell, until finally she saw something.

"General!" she exclaimed excitedly. "Look!"

Stoddard glanced up and down the corridor, stepped quickly over to the door and peered into the cell. A single light bulb, suspended by a cord from the ceiling, was burning, casting a sickly pale color over the dreary room. "Somebody's been here recently," he said. "The food in that plate's not spoiled."

Adrian looked in again. "General," she said breathlessly. "That's a captain's helmet on the bed!"

"Take it easy, Adrian."

"It's Gilbert's, I know it is."

"It could be anybody's, Adrian," he cautioned her. "Don't get your hopes up."

"But somebody is here," she insisted.

"Yes, somebody is. But where? Damn, I'm getting too old to be doing this kind of thing," he said, leading her on down the hall.

Two cell doors down, they discovered through the view hole in the door a prisoner curled up on the cot in the shadows. "It's a woman," Adrian told him.

Stoddard lowered his rifle and looked in, but since the prisoner's back was turned toward him, he couldn't tell what sex the prisoner was. "Let's get him out of there, Adrian. Or her—whoever it is."

"Why don't you try a key?" said a voice behind them. "No—now don't raise your weapon, General," the voice cautioned as Stoddard made a move. "Just lean it against the wall."

Adrian turned and looked at the man holding an automatic pistol on them. He was a Chinese officer, small, compact, with hard eyes and a rigid face.

"Please, go on in," he said, reaching over and unlocking the metal door. "Be our guest."

The moment she entered the cell, Adrian felt sick. The dense air in the room was cold, damp, and stagnant. It was a strain to breathe in such a putrid atmosphere. But she ignored the conditions for the moment and rushed over to the person on the cot and turned her over.

"Lin Su!" she said, almost in tears. She recognized her but the woman was far different from the beautiful Chinese girl she had seen in San Francisco five years ago. Her skin was washed out, her eyes glazed, her hair coarse and dull.

"The woman is a traitor, General Stoddard," Lieutenant Rhu announced. "She turned against her country."

"She's dying," Adrian said accusingly.

"I assure you she is dying of a natural disease," Rhu declared. "We haven't had the luxury of physicians here since the prisoner exchange."

Adrian bristled with anger, but that was overcome by her pity for the woman lying so coldly in front of her. She touched her forehead with her fingers, found it hot. "Lin Su," she asked gently, in a low voice, "where is Gilbert?"

"Captain Bell is dead," Rhu coldly answered. "He died of typhus over a year ago. Typhus spread over Manchuria by your government, General Stoddard."

"That's a lie. The United States has used no germ warfare in China."

"Lin?" Adrian said. "Is Gilbert alive? Is he?"

"The woman hasn't spoken a word for weeks, Miss McAllister. I assume that is who you are. Adrian McAllister, Captain Bell's—I believe you were his lover, weren't you?"

"You can't just let her die, man," Stoddard charged him. "She's a human being, for God's sake!"

"Then why don't you stay and comfort her?" Rhu said, backing up. "I have to take care of a few very foolish American marines." He eased out of the cell, slammed the door, and locked it.

Seconds later a terrifying thought struck Adrian like a hard slap in the face: she and Stoddard might never see another living person again. If Baruchi and Hollister were caught or killed, she might wither away and die, as Lin Su was dying, in a terrible, ghastly prison cell thousands of miles from home. The thought of it made her shudder.

"General—" she began, but tears stifled her words.

He reached over and brought her to his chest and held her close. "It's not over yet, Adrian," he said. "Baruchi and Hollister are out there. We still have a chance."

"Oh, General, I'm so sorry. Maybe if I hadn't insisted on coming—"

"Hush. None of this is your fault."

"But to die in this horrible place. And for nothing!"

"Shh. Listen."

They held their breath for a few moments and listened to the sounds of machine gun fire somewhere in the building. Then from outside there was a noise, an explosion, and all of a sudden the light bulb in the cell went out, and they found themselves in total darkness.

Adrian waited a while for her eyes to adjust to the dark, but before long she realized she wasn't going to be able to see anything. The blackness was absolute. It was disorienting; there was no form, no shape, no top, bottom, or sides to anything in the room. Nothing but darkness.

The sounds around them now seemed greatly magnified. Each shot, each yell or order in the prison building grew louder and louder until she heard in the hall beyond the door an ear-shattering eruption of shots and the pounding of bullets against the walls.

Then there was silence, followed by the loud clicking sound of boots upon the corridor floor, growing closer and closer until suddenly the lock on the door was being rattled and shaken and the big metal door swung open with a clank.

Adrian flinched as a flashlight beam struck her eyes. She turned her face away in fear and held tightly onto Stoddard—until she heard a familiar voice behind the glare of the flashlight. "General?" it said. "Are you two all right?"

"Baruchi! Thank God!"

"General, you've got to get out of here. Hollister has three guards pinned down in the north wing. I can give you cover."

"We can't leave her," Adrian said.

Baruchi flashed his beam on Lin Su's face. The pale, sickly expression told everyone at once that she was too near death to be moved. "I'll take care of her," Chick said.

"But Gilbert—"

"Gilbert's not here, Adrian," Chick told her. "We've checked every cell."

"Oh, Chick—"

"We have to go—now!"

Before anyone could respond, a guard appeared at the door and opened fire into the room. In the loud, frightening confusion Adrian felt something brush her leg, then Stoddard yelled out in pain and dropped at her feet.

Chick wheeled around quickly, squeezed his trigger, and quickly blew the guard out of the doorway back into the hall. Then he flashed the light around to check the damage.

The flesh of Stoddard's left leg had been ripped open. Adrian was unhurt. The Chinese woman on the cot had caught a single stray bullet in the exact center of her throat.

"Okay, let's go, General," Baruchi said, lifting Stoddard up. "Adrian, you're going to have to help him out of here. I'll stay back and give you cover."

She felt the heft of Stoddard's body on her shoulder. "We'll all go together, Chick," she said.

"Just get me my rifle, Sergeant," Stoddard groaned. "We'll make it."

"You won't make it without cover, General. And that's what Hollister and I are going to give you."

"No you're not."

"I'm sorry, General," Baruchi told him. "I don't want to be disrespectful, but you're wounded. You're going to need some cover."

"Chick," Adrian pleaded with him. "You can't stay here. It's suicide."

"Adrian," he said, "I have to do this. This is why I came on this mission. I have to prove to myself I can do it."

"Chick, for God's sake!"

"No, I mean it, Adrian. I've been called a coward so many times I'm just not sure anymore. I have to see."

"You've proved it to me, Chick. Now let's go— together."

"No," he said firmly. "You help the general, I'll cover for you."

"Sergeant Baruchi—"

"General, I mean it. Don't give me an order I'll have to disobey."

Stoddard paused, then relented. "All right, but protect yourself, Sergeant. We'll wait for you outside the fence."

By the time they made it down the halls to the light outside, Adrian was aching under the weight of the general's arm around her shoulder. The open expanse of yard between them and the fence seemed twice as spacious and deep as before. But she took a deep breath and prepared herself to make a run for it.

An exchange of fire off to the left set Baruchi off. "That's Hollister!" he cried. "Go!"

Those fifty yards were the longest of her life. Under the cover of darkness all she had to cope with was the ever-increasing weight of a man dragging her body down, but then a flashlight beam shot out of the darkness and hit them and the ground started kicking up with bullets, and she had to move faster or be killed.

Close to the fence Stoddard's feet gave way and he collapsed, bringing Adrian down with him. "General," she begged him, "get up, please."

He grunted, stood up. "I'm all right," he told her. "I can make it."

Then Adrian felt something very strange happen to her. Just as they reached the cut wire, she was aware, all of a sudden, of a sharp pain in her forehead that moved like a bolt of hot lightning through her brain, down into her back. The hard stoney ground seemed to rear up and jar her brain violently. On her back, she groaned and unconsciously raised her hand to her forehead. When she drew it back, it was washed with blood.

"Be still, Adrian," Stoddard was saying, laying something softly upon her head. "You've been hit. Take it easy."

A wave of nausea took hold of her for a second, then more pain, this time in her eyes, and then darkness. Sometime later, she heard someone running toward them.

"Where's Baruchi?" Stoddard asked.

"He's holding them off, General."

The voices were distant, small, almost childlike to her dazed mind. She tried to get up, but then realized she didn't possess enough strength to raise her own body off the ground.

"We'll wait for him," Stoddard was saying.

"We can't, General. It's too late. He said to go on."

"We'll wait a little longer," the general declared. "We're not leaving him unless we have to."

"You're losing blood, General. Both of you. You'll die if we don't get back to the raft soon."

Their words trailed off after that. The rest of it was like a dream. Somehow they made it back to the raft and down the Yalu River into the Yellow Sea. She recalled later that someone, Hollister, she believed, strapped her into a harness and then stood back, watching her being whisked up into the air and pulled into a helicopter.

Next she remembered lying on a bed in a hospital ship somewhere at sea, and General Stoddard, in a clean, fresh uniform, limping into her room on crutches.

"Did Chick make it, General?" she managed to ask him as he drew near.

"He held them off long enough for us to escape," Stoddard said. "Bravest damned thing I ever saw a man do."

"What about Gilbert?"

He shook his head helplessly. "I don't know about Gilbert, Adrian," he said sadly. "I'm sorry. I don't know what happened to either one of them."

19

ADRIAN OPENED HER EYES, adjusted the Band-Aid on her forehead, and counted the squares in the Cellotex ceiling of her bedroom for the twentieth time. On the radio a disc jockey switched abruptly from Eddie Fisher's "I'm Walking Behind You" to a quick news summary. Armistice talks had been resumed, Syngman Rhee was disappointed in the Americans, Edmund Hillary and Tenzing Norkay were scaling Mt. Everest . . .

She reached over and flipped the dial to another station, listened to Les Paul and Mary Ford, the Ames Brothers, then clicked the radio off. She had been in bed two days now, long enough to go over the mission in Manchuria a thousand times in her mind. The Chinese interrogation officer had said Gilbert was dead, Chick had said he was nowhere to be found . . .

yet she clung to the belief that he was still alive,
somewhere. She couldn't bear the thought of spending
the rest of her life without him; she had to believe he
was alive.

"Well," her mother said, entering the room without
knocking. "You're looking much better, Adrian." She
sat down on the edge of the bed and smiled. "Doesn't
it feel good to be home, in your own bed?" she asked,
straightening the pillow Adrian was propped up
against.

"I guess so," she said, not very enthusiastically.

Mrs. McAllister patted her leg through the white
cotton spread. "You look just fine, Adrian. When I saw
you in the hospital Friday, Lord knows, you scared me
half to death."

"I know, mother. I'm sorry."

"Well," her mother sighed, "it's not as if your father
and I didn't tell you not to go. We certainly did. But
you never want to listen to us. You just seem to be
attracted to that awful place, for some reason. I wish
you could stay away from it."

"Mother, the war is still going on over there! Doesn't
anybody care?"

"Of course we care, Adrian. But your father and I
care a lot more about you than we do about any war."

"Well, maybe you shouldn't care that much about
me," Adrian snapped. "Maybe you should care more
about other people."

"Adrian!"

"Let's forget it, mother, okay?" she asked. She knew
she would never be able to penetrate her mother's
shell of tradition, or whatever it was. She needn't
bother trying.

"Listen." Mrs. McAllister's tone suddenly became

cheerful. "You have a very handsome visitor outside:
Wayne Hunter."

"Oh, God."

"Now, Adrian. He's come all the way up from Los
Angeles. The least you can do is see him. Besides, he's
a very successful man now, you know. That column of
his is in seventy-five newspapers now. He just told me."

"Mother, I don't want to see Wayne Hunter, all
right? I don't like him, and I don't want to see him."

"I don't understand. I'll admit there is that business
about his parents," she conceded thoughtfully. "We
don't really know if they ever did marry. But in spite
of that the Hunters are a fine family, Adrian. They go
back to the first families of Virginia, you know."

"I know—"

"And Wayne is so successful now. . . ."

"I don't care how successful he is, mother. I don't
want to see him."

"Well," Mrs. McAllister said, patting her leg again.
"I can't very well turn him away after he's come so far,
can I? Why don't you just lie there and be pretty? I'll
send him right up."

Adrian shook her head in defeat, and waited.

Wayne looked better than usual, dressed in an
expensive blue summer suit. But as always, just seeing
him made her feel uncomfortable. Without a word he
slid a chair next to the bed and sat down in it, making
her even more ill-at-ease.

"Your mother tells me you're all right now," he said,
unbuttoning his coat.

"I'll be fine," she replied. "It was just a concussion.
I'll be out of bed tomorrow."

"She also said she didn't even know how it happened," he prompted her. "She said you wouldn't tell her."

"No. I wouldn't," she said enigmatically.

Hunter nodded, looked about the room for a minute, then stared at her. "You're lovelier than ever, Adrian," he said.

"Thank you."

"I've never met anyone as beautiful as you are. I don't think there is anyone as beautiful as you."

"Wayne," she said impatiently. "Considering how you acted with me the last time we saw each other, I don't think you ought to say things like that."

"No, you're right," he confessed. "I behaved badly back in Tokyo. But I've changed, Adrian. I'm successful now. My column is being picked up by more papers every day. I feel better about things."

"I'm glad, Wayne. Really."

"I feel better about you, too, Adrian," he told her. "I feel for the first time I can come to you as an equal, not someone everybody has rejected."

She stirred uncomfortably at that confession. The last thing she wanted to do now was cope with Wayne Hunter.

"Wayne," she said, putting him off, "I'm not feeling very well."

But he ignored her words. "I don't pretend it wasn't wrong to force myself on you that time—"

"Wayne," she interrupted, "you don't have to go into this now."

"I want to go into it, Adrian," he insisted. "I want to show you I've changed. I have something to offer now. I swear I'll be kind and considerate to you. I'll give you everything you want. You can work, you can have your freedom. Anything. Just say yes. Just say you'll marry me."

She was stunned; she sat and looked at him in silence, then blurted out, "No!"

"You don't mean that."

"I do mean it," she said, softening her tone. "I can't marry you."

"Why can't you?"

"Wayne, you know I love Gilbert."

"Gilbert! You haven't even seen the man in two years, Adrian. How do you know you still love him?"

"I just know it. I'll always love him."

He stood up, went to the window, turned around to face her. "Just what in hell do you want, Adrian? I'm successful, I have money. I've got everything a woman could want. What do you want?"

"I don't want all that, Wayne," she answered. "I just want Gilbert."

"Gilbert. It's always Gilbert," he said angrily. "For years that's all I've ever heard from you. Gilbert, Gilly. Well, let me tell you, it's too late now, Adrian. Your precious Gilly is dead."

"No he's not."

He came closer. "You're so stubborn. You're clinging to a dream, Adrian. Wake up."

"It's not a dream," she insisted. "Someday I'll see him again, and then all *this* will seem like a dream."

"Pay attention, Adrian," he said sharply. "Gilbert's dead, do you understand? He's dead. And running off to some prison isn't going to change that one bit."

The words hit her like a blow to the face. "How did you know about that?" she asked. "Nobody knows about it."

He turned away. "I just know, that's all," he mumbled.

"Wayne—how did you know about that! Tell me!"

He faced her. "Will you forget about Gilbert Bell for once in your life?" he demanded. "Just once. Forget him. He's gone. The man is dead, Adrian. Dead!"

"No," she said steadfastly. "He's not!"

"He is! Forget about him. I know what I'm talking about, damn it."

Adrian was in tears. "You don't," she insisted. "You don't know anything about it!"

"What do you want, Adrian? Proof? Is that what you want?"

"Yes! I want proof!"

"Well, here," he snarled, reaching into his pocket. "Here's your proof, damn it." He flung two shiny objects attached to a chain across the room onto the bed.

Adrian's heart sank when she recognized what they were: metal marine identification tags. For a few seconds all she could do was stare at them lying there facedown on the spread. The room was silent, except for the sound of her own uneven breathing; she heard the bed creak as she leaned over and picked them up.

"Adrian," Hunter said, taking a step forward.

She could see in his eyes that he regretted throwing the tags, but the damage was done now. She had to look. With her fingers trembling, she turned over one of the tags and read Gilbert's name, rank, and serial number inscribed in the metal. "Oh no," she cried, bringing the tags up to her breast. "Oh God, no."

She cried softly for a while, clutching the tags against her bosom, trying to deny what she had seen by saying no over and over. But the tags were real; she held them in her own hands. She looked up at Hunter. "Where did you get them?" she said tearfully.

"I shouldn't've shown them to you," he said, avoiding her gaze.

"Wayne, where did you get them? Tell me!"

"What difference does it make where I got them? They prove one thing; he's dead."

"Oh no," she said as the truth dawned on her. "You're in with them, aren't you? That's why you were always changing my reports. And that's how you got your column, isn't it? That man you were always with in Tokyo—he's a Communist, isn't he?"

He stared at her a minute, gritting his teeth angrily. "All right, he's a Communist. So what?"

Her mind was racing, fitting everything about him into place. "I don't believe it," she said, shaking her head. "I can't believe you would do this."

"Why shouldn't I do it?" he defended himself. "They didn't turn me down, the way everybody else has all my life. The army, the navy, you—"

"Wayne! The communists *kill* people. Don't you understand that? You're not a murderer. How could you work with anyone who could take people and torture them—"

"I don't do any of that, Adrian," he broke in. "I just give them information, that's all."

"But there are the people who took Gilbert and put him in a cold, wet prison cell and tortured him, the people who killed him, damn it!" she screamed, throwing the tags at him. Then she buried her head in a pillow and burst into tears.

Hunter calmly picked the tags up off the floor and replaced them in his pocket. Turning and gazing out the window, he listened to Adrian cry. After a while, he walked slowly across the room and stopped near the bed. "Adrian, I've always hated Gilbert," he admitted. "He's always had everything, everybody always liked him. He was everything I couldn't be. Every time somebody turns you away, there's always some lucky bastard like Gilbert there to show you what you're missing. I just got tired of it, Adrian. I got tired of everybody being acceptable but me."

"Chick Baruchi was that way too, Wayne," she said through her tears. "Everybody rejected him, too. They thought he was a coward."

"You see what I mean?" he said.

"But he did something about it, Wayne. He saved lives with his courage. He didn't have to die and he didn't want to die, but he was *willing* to. But all you're willing to do is feel sorry for yourself."

"I want you, Adrian," he said. "I'm not going to be turned down. Not now. Not after all this."

She stared at him silently, not believing what he was saying.

"One way or another, Adrian," he said, "I'm going to have you."

"I think you'd better leave," she said, squeezing her fingers together tightly, trying to hold in her anger.

"I'm not leaving till I make you understand something. I don't care about Gilbert Bell, okay? I don't even care about the Communist party. All I care about is you."

Adrian tried to shut out his words, but she couldn't. Suddenly he seemed to be shouting at her. And the room seemed very close, the air thick. She felt as if she were losing control of herself.

"When Mallory gave you the job as war correspondent," he went on, "I hated myself. I thought you were better than me. That's when I agreed to go along with them."

"Oh God, Wayne. Don't make me feel guilty, too—"

"Just be quiet and listen to me," he said coldly. "I thought you were better than me, so all I could do was grovel at your feet. But that's all changed. I have a place now, Adrian. I have influence. I don't have to grovel. I can ask you outright to marry me."

"Wayne, please!"

"You will do it, Adrian," he said. "I'll see to it."

She looked at him. "Do you think I could stand living with the man who worked for the people who put Gilbert in prison?"

"I did more than that, Adrian," he said. "I told them about him and Stoddard. On my word they interrogated him."

"Dear God, Wayne. How could you?"

"I only did it for you, Adrian. Everything for you."

"You're insane."

"No, I'm not insane. I'm in love. With you. And for the first time in my life, I'm going to get exactly what I want. You will marry me, Adrian."

"I'll never marry you. I'll die first."

He buttoned his coat, cleared his throat. "I know about your little venture into Manchuria, Adrian," he said. "It was you, wasn't it? That's where you got that head wound, isn't it?"

"I don't know what you're talking about."

"I'm talking about Manchuria, my love. China. An unauthorized invasion of China by four military personnel and one civilian reporter. Imagine how the negotiations in Panmunjom would go if that were made public."

"Wayne, four million people are dead because of this war!"

"I don't care. I'm not talking about four million people. I'm talking about you and me, Adrian. All I'm concerned about is getting what I want. And what I want is you."

"I did not go into China," she said stiffly.

"Deny it all you want. I have enough information to convince anyone in the world. All I have to do is put it in my column and they know."

Suddenly the prospect seemed disturbingly real to her. Wayne had the means of doing exactly what he was threatening to do. All he had to do was write it up and hand it to someone.

He waited a few minutes, then asked. "What will it be, Adrian? I'll give you the choice. Either you marry me, or I'll release the story to the press."

"You can't be that spiteful," she said. "You just can't."

"Oh, but I can, my love," he said, a taunting smile on his face.

Adrian took a deep breath and tried to calm down. "If you don't care," she said shakily, "what that would do to me, at least think about General Stoddard. He's a good man—all he was doing was trying to save Gilbert."

"Gilbert again," Hunter said, disgusted. "You even have an army general chasing after him."

"Don't hurt him, Wayne, please. He's an important man in the Pentagon. Don't embarrass him."

"It's ironic, isn't it?" he observed. "After being turned down by all the military services, I get a chance to turn them down. I can turn their faces down in the mud where they belong." He paused a minute, came next to the bed with a pleading look on his face. It changed to impatience, though, when he noted Adrian shrinking back from him. "I'll let the whole business go, Adrian," he told her. "All you have to do is say the word. Just say you'll marry me and it's forgotten."

She swallowed, but the tightness in her throat remained. He was forcing her to decide. "I can't do it, Wayne," she said flatly.

"Why can't you?" he said angrily. "Am I that repulsive to you?"

"I just can't."

"Adrian," he said, reaching out, touching her leg. "Let me make love to you. Once. Right now. Then you can decide."

"No!" she said loudly.

"Just once," he repeated, digging his nails into her leg. "I promise you it'll be worth your while. I've waited so long for a chance to show you how much I love you. Don't turn me away."

"Stop! I'm not going to prostitute myself, Wayne."

"Not even to save your friend Stoddard?" he asked, moving his hand up to her thigh.

"No!" she told him and struggled to pry his hand loose.

"Adrian, for God's sake—I'm on fire. Just this once."

"Get away from me!"

But Hunter was on the verge of losing control of his emotions. His eyes were dilated and flaring with desire for her. His hand moved involuntarily over the curves of her body and up to a soft warm breast, loose under her thin nylon nightgown.

Adrian considered the possibility of doing what he asked, of closing her eyes and letting him have his way with her. All she had to do to save General Stoddard great embarrassment and maybe even prosecution was to close her eyes and let Wayne Hunter pour his lust into her. . . .

"No!" she screamed when his cold fingers closed on her flesh. With all the strength she could muster she swung at him. As her palm struck solidly against his cheek, he recoiled, silently backed away from the bed.

Instantly the door flew open. "Adrian?" her mother cried, bursting into the room. "What is it? What's wrong?"

"It's nothing, Mrs. McAllister," Hunter said, buttoning the top button on his coat. He was in control again now. "It was just a professional argument."

Mrs. McAllister shot him an accusing glance, then looked questioningly at her daughter. "Adrian," she said, concerned. "You're crying."

Adrian yanked the covers up to her chin, curled down into the bed, and said nothing.

"She'll be all right," Hunter said to Mrs. McAllister. "She's a little angry because she lost the argument. You know how she is when she doesn't get her way."

"Well, you two shouldn't carry on like that over just work," she said, relieved. "You should've heard how awful it's been sounding downstairs."

He apologized to her, walked toward the door, turned and looked at Adrian once again. "Is that your final word?" he asked her. "You're willing to let me write the column?"

Adrian closed her eyes, lay silent under the covers. "Then I suppose I'd better get started on it, hadn't I?" he said, storming out of the room, leaving the door open behind him.

20

ON JULY 1, 1953, Wayne Hunter's syndicated column *On the Right Side* appeared as usual in
seventy-eight newspapers in forty-one states.
But this particular day it ignited a fire that seared
the editorial pages of every major paper in the country, from the Los Angeles *Times* to the Kansas City
Star to the Boston *Globe*. The column was read and
discussed on radio shows across the nation. Hunter
and his story even became the subject of a special
See It Now episode on CBS television.

The July 1 column was a powerful piece of journalism. His title for the piece was "U. S. Marines
Invade China." In it Hunter described (inaccurately,
but convincingly) the daring but aborted commando
raid in Manchuria conducted by General Lucius T.
Stoddard, three hand-picked marines, and a female

correspondent from the Sacramento *Sun.* He depicted the raid as a direct and willful invasion of Chinese territory, a violation of all the principles Americans were supposed to stand for.

To support his contention, Hunter suggested that this was only another example of the abhorrent treatment the United States gave to the People's Republic of China. He listed these "facts": (1) In May, 1952, two American pilots admitted dropping infected insects across the 38th parallel. He quoted one of them: "The capitalistic Wall Street warmongers in their . . . ruthless greed, have caused this horrible crime of biological warfare in order to get more money for themselves. . . . I was forced to be a tool of these warmongers, made to drop germ bombs and do this awful crime against the people of Korea and the Chinese volunteers."

(2) The Chinese had received from American prisoners thirty-eight "admissions" that the Americans had tortured and otherwise mistreated Chinese prisoners of war.

(3) After the North Korean prisoner revolt at Kojedo in May, 1952, the commandant of the camp, Brigadier General Francis Dodd, issued this statement: "I do admit that there have been instances of bloodshed where many prisoners of war have been killed and wounded by U. N. forces." He signed an agreement promising the U. N. would "stop torturing and mistreating prisoners to make them say they are anti-Communist."

The effect of combining the year-old prisoner controversy surrounding those two unfounded statements by American officers with Stoddard's apparently unauthorized invasion of China set the news media into action and produced a blistering reaction throughout the nation.

America clamored to know: was Brigadier General Stoddard doing exactly what their hero MacArthur was fired for wanting to do? Was Eisenhower engineering a war with China behind the backs of the American people? Was this marine invasion going to end with someone starting a hydrogen war that would ultimately obliterate all of mankind?

Fear was clutching at the throats of all Americans, and they wanted answers, so they turned to the military and demanded that it account for itself.

On July 8, 1953, Secretary of Defense Charles Wilson directed the Joint Chiefs of Staff to conduct an informal hearing to investigate Hunter's accusations. A week later an out-of-the-way place was chosen for the hearing—a courthouse in Hagerstown, Maryland —and witnesses were subpoenaed in response to an "official and informal Department of Defense inquiry."

The administration tried to keep the hearing a secret, but word inevitably leaked out. By the time Wayne Hunter arrived in Hagerstown on Monday, July 17, in a U.S. Army sedan, the grounds in front of the courthouse were jammed with people—newspaper reporters and photographers, television cameramen and correspondents, magazine writers, and hundreds of irritated, restless spectators screaming for answers.

They all converged on Hunter as he stepped out of the car door held open by an army corporal. Questions flew at him wildly in the hot, humid air.

"Hunter—are you saying the military is planning a war with China?" a reporter yelled out.

"Is Stoddard a traitor, Wayne?" another bellowed. "Are you saying Stoddard should be court-martialled?"

A woman stuck a microphone at him. "Mr. Hunter, is it true you're in *love* with Adrian McAllister? Is this some sort of vendetta—"

"Excuse us, folks," the corporal broke in. "No more questions, please. We have to get inside."

"What about that, Hunter!" a man hollered. "Answer the woman."

"Just keep moving, Mr. Hunter," the corporal said, pushing through the crowd.

Wayne felt another soldier behind him, touching his back as they inched across the sidewalk toward the courthouse steps. All around him, as far as he could see, were people, mashed together, squeezing toward him. All the way up the walk he kept hearing questions, accusations, even threats. His column had awakened the long pent-up frustration of the American people, and that scared him. Now he had to follow through with his story; if he backed away, these people would tear him apart.

"This way, Mr. Hunter," an army lieutenant said, opening the door for him. "Corporal, stand by that door."

"Yes, sir."

They slipped inside, the door abruptly shut out the noise, and Hunter sighed in relief not to hear any more questions. He looked at the lieutenant. "I'm expecting a call," he said worriedly. "From a Mr. Stoner. Elliott Stoner. Has he called yet?"

The lieutenant shook his head. "We've had no calls from a Mr. Stoner," he answered.

Wayne was puzzled. "But I left word for him," he said. "He must've called."

"No, sir. No one by that name has called."

"He *has* to have called, damn it."

"I'm sorry, sir," the lieutenant said politely. "I'll check again to make sure. If you'll stay here . . ."

"Thank you."

At that moment the massive crowd, growing larger by the minute, reacted to the arrival of another official military vehicle, this one a USMC Ford two-door sedan. Crammed together on the courthouse lawn, unable to move, all the crowd could do was turn its collective face toward the pretty and stylishly dressed young woman getting out of the car.

A reporter got to her quickly. "Miss Bell, can you tell us why you're being summoned to the hearing?"

"It was my brother they were trying to rescue," she reminded him.

"Yes, but what good will *your* presence do?" the reporter persisted. "Were you involved in the scheme?"

"No! I wasn't involved in any scheme to rescue my brother. I didn't know a thing about it."

"Miss Bell . . ." A television reporter pushed a microphone in her face. "We understand you and General Stoddard and Miss McAllister have a history of being on opopsite sides of the fence. Are you on the opposite side today?"

"I've been asked to come, that's all I know," she said, trying to put them off. "Now if you'll excuse me—"

"Just one more question, Miss Bell—"

"Please, excuse me."

"Let the lady pass, please," her marine escort announced.

Minutes later, attention shifted to a third car.

"There she is!" a reporter exclaimed excitedly. "There's Adrian."

As soon as the marine sedan stopped, it was engulfed by people. Adrian sat in the back seat and trembled to witness the sea of faces staring inquisitively at her through the glass of the window. She waited quietly next to her father until the driver cut his way around the rear of the car and managed to pry the door open for them.

No one could have looked prettier than she did this day. Her dark hair was thick and fluffy about her face, her eyes bright and beautiful, if a little shadowed, her face smooth and clear. And yet she felt unsure of herself. The hundreds of faces out there were overwhelming. To have lost Gilbert, to have been threatened by Wayne, and now, to be responsible for General Stoddard being dishonored—it was too much.

She had phoned Stoddard to warn him of Wayne's intentions, of course, but the general had regretfully concluded that there was nothing he could do. After all, this was America, and freedom of the press still meant something. But they had truth on their side, even if concern for national security meant that they couldn't draw on *all* of the truth in their own defense. Wayne was too unbalanced to stand up to the inevitable heavy questioning, Stoddard had assured her, and his ties with the Communist party would be his undoing. Adrian had taken comfort from his words, but as she looked about at the crowd she felt more guilty and hopeless than ever.

"I'm right behind you, honey," her father comforted her as she stepped out.

Adrian was immediately barraged with questions.

It was dizzying. She wanted to dive back into the car to escape the loud, incoherent battery of voices shouting accusingly at her.

But then one reporter assumed a stance of dominance. He drew close to her, spoke loudly and directly to her. After a minute or so, the others began to listen and let him take the lead. "Miss McAllister," he said, staring at her with hard, cold eyes. "What's Captain Bell to you? Were you two lovers?"

"Please—"

"Well, were you? Some members of the Department of Defense say you were. They say you were lovers in Korea. Is that true? Were you lovers in Korea?"

Mr. McAllister spoke out. "She doesn't have to answer your questions. She'll be doing that inside."

"Then you were lovers," the reporter persisted.

Adrian winced. She had no idea people of her own profession could be so cruel. They all seemed to be ready to crucify her. Why were they so angry? She tried to follow the marine corporal, but he wasn't having much luck pushing through. She felt trapped, closed in, stifled.

"Well, Miss McAllister. *Were* you?" the reporter demanded.

"She doesn't have to answer that," her father said.

"Were you lovers, Miss McAllister?" he said again.

"Yes!" she blurted out. "We were lovers. Now will you please just let it be?" She pushed ahead, but the mass of bodies wouldn't move for her. Instead, some of them slid in behind her, cutting her off from her father. He called out to her, but she couldn't move to get to him. Again she withstood a wave of questions stimulated by her answer, but she closed her mind to them. She stood somewhere on a cement sidewalk, twenty feet from her car, separated from her father and the marine driver. There must have been two thousand people around her, but she had never felt so alone in her life.

Then she saw Robert Kowalski.

She noticed his tall frame moving through the crowd toward her before she recognized who it was. But when he broke through and grabbed her hand, she almost cried with relief.

"All right, fellows," Kowalski announced calmly but firmly to the others. "Let's let the lady get through."

"Wait a minute," an assertive reporter put in. "I've got a few more questions."

"Why don't you back off, McIntire?" Kowalski told him. "Leave her alone."

But the reporter ignored him. "What about the general, Miss McAllister?" he asked her. "Were you lovers with him, too?"

The crowd suddenly began to quiet, then a hush fell over everyone. "What?" Adrian said, not sure she had heard him correctly.

"I asked you a simple question, miss. Were you and General Stoddard lovers?"

"No! Of course we weren't."

"Are you sure about that?"

"You're out of line, McIntire," Robert warned him. "Back off and let us through."

But the reporter tenaciously hung in. "You and Stoddard did spend the night together in his tent in Suwon, in June, 1950, didn't you?" he asked.

"No!" she said, startled at his implications. "We did no such thing."

"What about Tokyo, later that year? Just before the Inchon landing?"

"That's enough, McIntire," Kowalski threatened. "Let her be."

But McIntire wasn't going to let up. "Didn't the general get you permission to go to Inchon?" he asked. "And to Wonsan? And Hagaru?"

"Yes, he did. But—"

"Well, obviously the general took very good care of his lady," the reporter said. "No wonder you could send in such sizzling reports from the front."

"Damn it, McIntire," Kowalski fumed. "Get the hell out of the way."

"Answer me this, lady!" he called out. "Who *else* did you sleep with?"

Kowalski's fist bolted out of nowhere to crash into McIntire's waiting nose. A look of surprise flashed across his face a second after it hit; then when he discovered he was bleeding, he blindly swung out in Kowalski's direction, striking a television cameraman in the back of the head.

A large-scale fight could have developed, but two other reporters grabbed McIntire and held him back while the crowd reluctantly parted in front of Adrian, allowing her to pass on to the courthouse. At the steps, she squeezed Kowalski's hand. "Thank you," she said. "You were a god-send."

"McIntire's jealous of your war stuff," he explained. "He was just venting his frustration."

"Well, thank you for socking him. He deserved it."

He smiled. "And to think you used to be a dyed-in-the-wool pacifist," he said. "What do you know."

"Well, I do know this much, as a result of following this war," she said. "Sometimes people *do* have to fight."

He glanced at his aching knuckles. "Maybe you're right," he conceded. "Maybe sometimes they do."

"Adrian!" her father said, breaking through to the steps. "Are you all right?"

"I'm fine, daddy," she answered. "Thanks to Robert."

"It was entirely my pleasure, ma'am," Kowalski said.

The crowd began to stir again as General Stoddard's car pulled up out on the street. Kowalski hesitated, smiled at her and kissed her hand. "Good luck in there," he said, then faded back into the crowd.

"Who was that?" Mr. McAllister said.

"Someone I met in Korea," she answered, following the marine's lead up the steps. They made it to the doors and ducked inside the courthouse. The first face she saw inside was Wayne Hunter's.

Usually, in such close quarters he would look directly into her eyes, but today his glance fell to the floor. He nodded, unsure what to say.

"Wayne," she acknowledged him as she started to pass by.

But he grabbed her arm. "Adrian," he said, "I didn't mean for it to go this far. I swear. It's gotten out of hand."

She didn't respond.

"Adrian—" he began as she started away. But he knew she wasn't going to answer him.

The courtroom was large and airy, with high ceilings and banks of tall windows, but even with the overhead fans whirling at full speed, the place was hot. Adrian unbuttoned her jacket as she sat in the spectators' seats with her father. The sun spilling in from the western side of the courthouse cast a strange orange glow on the mahogany furniture of the room. The light reminded her of the sunset at Inchon, which seemed so far away now—a lifetime ago.

She looked around the room. The judge's platform was set up with five upholstered chairs for the Joint Chiefs of Staff; to the left, at what was usually the defendant's table, was General Stoddard, alone with two marine majors. He sat erect, poised, displaying no emotion in his face except for one warm and friendly smile he gave her.

Wayne Hunter had reached the table to the right and was now sitting down, alone. He looked apprehensive, Adrian thought. He glanced all around the courtroom before he would sit down, then did so shakily and began nervously tapping the tabletop with his finger nails.

"Thank God they didn't let the reporters in," Mr. McAllister whispered to his daughter. "We'd never hear the end of this if a bunch of reporters got hold of it."

She nodded politely, glanced over to her right at Amanda, then turned her eyes to the front as the military men filed in, wearing the handsome, fully decorated uniforms of their respective services: General J. Lawton Collins of the army, Admiral William Fechteler of the navy, General Lemuel Shepherd of the marines, and General Nathan Twining of the air force. They sat down and Omar Bradley, the Chief of the Staff, rose and spoke.

"Ladies and gentlemen, officers of the army, navy, air force, and marines, we're gathered here for this hearing for one purpose alone: to hear all sides of the controversial matter described by Mr. Wayne Hunter in his syndicated column, *On the Right Side.* Now let me say at the beginning, this is not a trial, and it's not a court-martial. It is a hearing. That means every person involved will be given a voice, if he wants one. The other chiefs and I are here to listen, not to judge." Bradley paused a minute, then continued: "The Joint Chiefs and I have agreed to allow Captain Arnold Rosetti of the United States Army's legal staff to preside over the hearing today. Captain Rosetti—"

A short, dark Italian man in his early forties stepped forward, nodded in Bradley's direction. He wore a serious expression, had a businesslike air about him as he announced that Wayne Hunter of Lynmark Syndications, Incorporated, would be the first person allowed to speak in the hearing. He stood by with his arms crossed as Hunter was led to the witness chair and sworn in.

"Now, Mr. Hunter," he said in a crisp New York accent, "you may begin."

"I don't know where to begin," Hunter said haltingly.

"Since this is an irregular hearing, Mr. Hunter," Rosetti told him, "you may begin anywhere you like."

Wayne glanced at Adrian, shifted in his chair, then looked at his watch. "I said a great deal in the column, Captain," he said. "I'm not sure what else you want."

"I don't want anything, Mr. Hunter," Rosetti said seriously. "I would be just as happy to listen to General Stoddard's rebuttal, if that's what *you* want."

"No, wait."

"Is there more than you reported in your column?"

He stared at Adrian, hesitated, then said rigidly, "Oh yes, there's more. There's a great deal more. Only I warn you, it won't make the military look that good."

"We'll take our chances, Mr. Hunter," Bradley interjected.

"Go ahead, Mr. Hunter," Rosetti prodded him.

"Well," he began nervously, "everybody says Captain Gilbert Bell was such a great hero. And General Stoddard is such a loyal American." He paused, took a deep breath, then shook his head.

"We're waiting, Mr. Hunter."

He stole another look at Adrian. "I warned you," he said under his breath, then looked at Rosetti. "Well, I say both of them are traitors," he declared. "Bell and Stoddard."

Hunter watched the people in the room mumble and shift in their seats. He knew he had gone too far to back out now. But he wondered where Elliott Stoner could be. Stoner was supposed to be at his table, advising him, helping him. He felt alone, and desperate. But this was his big chance to get them all back, to make them all pay for turning him down, making him feel inept and useless. If he didn't follow through with it, he would end up looking like a fool again."

"That's a strong accusation, Mr. Hunter," Rosetti told him.

"General Stoddard and Captain Bell—Lieutenant Bell, he was then—collaborated with the enemy, beginning with a meeting in the Pentagon on June twenty-seventh, 1950. Captain Bell was then in close contact with a high-ranking Chinese Communist in

Peking, a Miss Lin Su. In fact, they were once lovers."

The audience stirred noisily again, and Wayne noted the look of horror on Adrian's face. It spurred him on. "Miss Lin Su was in that Chinese prison General Stoddard raided. In fact, that was one of his purposes for taking such a chance, of going on that secret mission."

"What do you mean?"

"I mean they killed her, Captain. Because she knew too much."

"Wayne!" Adrian stood up, shouted. "How can you lie like that? It's not true. A Chinese guard killed her."

"Miss McAllister," Rosetti said sternly.

"But he's lying!"

"Please, sit down, Miss McAllister!"

She eased down, stunned by the boldness of Wayne's lies. She could sense that he was desperate, almost to the point of losing control. He kept checking the time and glancing hopefully at the doors. He was tapping loudly on the arm of his chair.

"What about Captain Bell himself?" Rosetti asked.

"Bell died in prison last March," Wayne stated coolly.

"Now how would you know that?"

"I know because I talked to a Private Donnelson who was among the prisoners swapped in Panmunjom in April."

"Donnelson never even saw Bell," Stoddard spoke up. "I talked to him myself."

"General, please," Rosetti cautioned him.

"I'm sorry."

"Go on, Mr. Hunter."

Hunter wiped the perspiration off his forehead with his handkerchief, and continued. "Private Donnelson told me Bell confessed to him that he was a traitor. He and Lin Su and Stoddard were all in a conspiracy with the enemy. Those three and one more: Adrian McAllister."

Stoddard forgot himself and sprang up. "Now see here," he said. "Donnelson is dead. You can't corroborate that story."

"Yes, sir, I can corroborate it," Wayne answered him. "Donnelson gave me something that day we talked. Bell gave it to him the day he confessed. Just before Bell died." He reached inside his pocket and drew out the identification tags and handed them to Rosetti. "Those are Captain Bell's dog tags," he said.

"No!" Adrian burst out. "He showed me those *weeks* ago! He's lying."

"Why don't we let him continue, Miss McAllister," Bradley said to her. "We'll hear your side soon enough."

"But he's lying, General," she said weakly.

Captain Rosetti handed Bradley the tags. "They're genuine," he observed. "I don't know how else he could've gotten them."

The Chiefs of Staff examined the dog tags, pronounced them authentic. Rosetti went on. "Then you're saying General Stoddard's raid was a secret mission designed to free Gilbert Bell and murder this Lin Su who could incriminate them?"

"That's correct. And they accomplished half of it: they killed Lin Su."

Rosetti rubbed his chin, looked at Hunter thoughtfully. "I'm afraid I don't see where Adrian McAllister fits into all this. What would a war correspondent for the Sacramento *Sun* have to do with a conspiracy?"

"Adrian McAllister wrote articles for the *Sun* which were deliberately slanted to be unAmerican."

"Wayne! *You* did that, not me."

"Miss McAllister—"

"If you'll look in that briefcase under the table," Hunter told him, "you'll find those articles. Read them yourself."

Rosetti did as Hunter suggested, and he and the Joint Chiefs of Staff took out the news articles and read them over quickly. Adrian's heart sank as she saw each of them nodding as he read.

"Stoddard's job was to make sure Adrian moved all over Korea," Hunter said. "He used his influence to combat the State Department. Amanda Bell will tell you that."

Rosetti looked over at Amanda, then turned back to Hunter, and asked him to continue. Adrian sat dumbfounded by what followed. Wayne took facts about her and Gilbert and Stoddard and twisted them around and made them seem ugly and incriminating. With the Chiefs of Staff listening attentively, Wayne boldly distorted one thing after another. He described Stoddard's visit to her in August, 1950, accused the general of revealing secret information about Operation Chromite to Adrian so that she could pass it along to the enemy.

And, he contended, she was aided always by Stoddard's influence. Rosetti allowed Amanda Bell to describe the general's defiance of State Department directives concerning the "immoral conduct" of Adrian McAllister.

"But Gilbert wasn't a traitor," Adrian insisted. "Wayne is wrong about that. He wasn't."

But Rosetti paid no attention to her personal opinions. He stuck to the "facts" as Wayne Hunter was presenting them. By the end of the afternoon, Stoddard's—and her—doom seemed to be sealed. "It looks bad, honey," Mr. McAllister told her. "If I didn't know you better, I'd believe him myself."

Adrian didn't have to be told; she could see it in everyone's eyes. The "facts" were overwhelming: the unauthorized raid, Gilbert's connection with the Communist Lin Su and Lin Su's murder during the raid, her getting Stoddard to cut red tape for her to go into Korea, her anti-American articles, Stoddard's visits with her in Tokyo, and the clinching evidence, the dog tags. They were physical, tangible proof of Gilbert Bell's treachery. They made all the rest of the testimony come together. How, she wondered, could Stoddard sit there and look so unruffled? He had been angry with Wayne's lies, to be sure, but there was an underlying confidence that she was far from feeling herself.

At six o'clock, after four hours of testimony and discussion, Bradley called a recess, with the hearing to be resumed at ten the next morning. Wayne Hunter, drenched with sweat, more shaky than ever after his testimony, hurried out into the hall and slipped into a phone booth.

His hands trembled so much when he picked up the receiver that he dropped the dime, but he finally got through to his office on Wilshire Boulevard in Los Angeles. The receptionist, a Miss Donner, answered the phone.

"Edna," he told her, "let me speak to Elliott. Hurry."

"I'm sorry, Mr. Hunter, Mr. Stoner isn't here."

"Well, where is he? I need him back here."

"I'm afraid he's gone, Mr. Hunter."

"What do you mean, gone? Gone where?"

"Just gone. His office is empty, his desk has been cleaned out. He just up and left."

He hung up, called Stoner's apartment house in Westwood. After an exasperating runaround with a superintendent and a maintenance man, he got the manager. "I'm looking for Mr. Stoner," he explained. "Apartment six-A. He doesn't answer his phone."

"No wonder he don't answer it," a gruff voice responded. "He ain't there to answer it."

"Do you have any idea where he is?" Wayne asked. "I have to speak to him. It's important."

"Sorry. Stoner left this morning. Moved out, lock, stock, and barrel. No forwarding address, nothing. And I'm going to be stuck with a month's back rent and mail I don't know what to do with."

Hunter hung up the phone. He could feel his heart pounding as he rubbed his sweaty hands together, then wiped them on his suit coat. He had been avoiding it, but what he was afraid to face really was true. Stoner had deserted him. The party stood behind you, all right—to a point. Then it disappeared. He was left to face the hearings by himself.

He opened the door of the booth and stepped out into the hall, where Adrian McAllister was waiting for him. He thought about walking past her, but for some reason, he couldn't make himself do it.

"You lie very well, Wayne," she said to him. "I

never realized how accomplished a person could be at lying. You're a master. You've distorted everything. It's so close to the truth, it's frightening. You scare me, Wayne."

"I warned you, Adrian."

"I don't think I really understand till now just what it is we've been fighting in Korea, Wayne. Not till you sat there and lied and twisted the truth around the facts and made a mockery of everything a decent person like Gilbert Bell or Lucius Stoddard believes in. We're not fighting some foreign power. We're fighting a terrible way of looking at life. The way you're looking at it."

"Men like Stoddard deserve it, Adrian," he said. "It's people like Stoddard who have always thought I was nothing. They deserve being knocked down."

"You're not trying to knock them down, Wayne. You're trying to destroy them. Can't you see what you're doing?"

"You can still stop it, Adrian," he told her. "Right now. All you have to do is marry me. I'll go back in there and change it all. I swear."

She considered the proposal again for a minute, then shook her head. "I don't believe all this lying and distorting and brainwashing has to be fought that way, Wayne."

"Then Stoddard's going down the drain, Adrian. And you're going right along with him."

"No we're not," she declared.

He laughed. "The Joint Chiefs are ready to hang him, Adrian," he pointed out. "Even Rosetti's ready to hang him."

"No," she said. "We haven't lost thirty thousand

American men in that awful place for nothing. We'll stand up to these lies, head-on, and the truth will come out. I know it will."

"You talk like I'm the enemy, Adrian. I'm not. All I've ever wanted is you."

"But you are the enemy, Wayne. That's what's so insidious about it. They've played on your weakness and without your even realizing it, you have become the enemy."

"Adrian," he said as she started to go. "One more chance. Please. Do it. Accept me, and it'll all work out."

"No," she said firmly. "I won't do that. I can't do it."

21

A T TEN O'CLOCK the next morning, as the partici-
pants in the hearing took their places about the
courtroom there was a sudden scuffle, and everyone quickly sprang to his feet as a tall balding white-
haired man entered the room from the judge's chambers.

"That's the president!" McAllister whispered to
Adrian. "What's he doing here?"

Adrian answered with a shrug, but her low spirits
were immediately lifted by Eisenhower's presence.
She watched him walk over and shake Bradley's hand
and smile and say something to him. She was surprised at how much warmer he seemed in real life
than on television. He elicited a feeling of trust and
well-being that was soothing to her, even at the moment. And he seemed to have the same effect on

others in the room besides her: they were all standing in quiet respect and surprise at seeing the president at the hearing.

After Bradley introduced him, and Adrian and the others took their seats, Eisenhower stood in front of them and spoke. "Last night," he began, "I read the transcript of yesterday's hearing and I was so moved by it, I asked General Bradley if I could attend the session this morning." He looked over at the chairman of the Joint Chiefs and nodded. "He has graciously allowed me to do that. But I also asked him if he would allow another audience in this courtroom today. Captain Rosetti," he said in a kindly voice, "would you open the doors and let the public in, please?"

"Yes, sir."

When Rosetti swung open the doors, the collected bodies gathered outside instantly poured in. At first the flooding through the gates was chaotic, but as soon as the newcomers realized Eisenhower was present, their mood changed.

They eased in calmly, quietly taking seats or standing in the aisle. There was no disorder, even though the crowd now spilled all the way out of the packed courtroom into the hall, even to the sidewalks outside.

Eisenhower formally greeted the crowd, and made a short speech explaining why he had broken tradition and allowed them in. This was no time for secrecy, he told them. The American people still felt duped by the Truman-MacArthur decision, they still felt unclear about who the enemy was. "Not knowing the truth can sometimes cause great wrongs," he said, "as was the case, I believe, with a young man in this courtroom yesterday afternoon. If he had known the truth, maybe we wouldn't be here today.

"But we are here. And I want to take this opportunity to announce to you and to the world that I not only knew of Brigadier General Stoddard's raid on the prison, I approved of it and unofficially authorized it."

The crowd buzzed excitedly with the announcement, then calmed down again. "Now," the president continued, "if you will give General Stoddard your attention, he'll explain to you the reason we felt we had to violate Chinese territory."

Again the people in the courtroom reacted noisily, but as soon as Stoddard got to his feet, they became quiet again. For a moment Adrian could hear nothing but the fans over her head, stirring about the hot air in the room. Then Stoddard cleared his throat and began to speak.

"The reason we went into China to get Captain Gilbert Bell out is simple. Captain Bell possessed information which we believed could ignite the fuse to a world war, and we wanted him out before the Chinese Communists brainwashed him into revealing that information. A few hours ago the president authorized me to reveal to the American public what that information was."

Adrian took a deep breath, waited anxiously along with the other reporters and writers and politicians in the room.

"Back in June, 1950," Stoddard continued, "just after the invasion of South Korea, I brought Lieutenant Bell to Washington to question him about his connection with an American-born Chinese woman, Lin Su, who was then an active Communist in Peking. As it turned out, he knew nothing of her political views, but while he was in the Pentagon he stumbled onto a meeting of several high-ranking military men, including General Bradley and President Eisenhower. What Lieutenant Bell inadvertently overheard and saw in that meeting were the military plans for a full-scale invasion of China."

An eerie quiet fell over the courtroom. Everyone was stunned, dazed into silence by Stoddard's statement.

"We made many such plans in 1950," he explained. "It was common practice. But this one turned out to be extremely dangerous because of China's entrance into the Korean War, and because of Truman's fear of a war with China. In the hands of a young, dedicated soldier like Captain Bell, who had no inkling of the number of invasions we plan, *just in case*—knowledge of such a plan could be devastating. I made it my business to keep track of Lieutenant Bell thereafter, wherever he went in Korea. And I used Miss Adrian McAllister to help me keep track of him."

Stoddard paused a minute to let the information sink in, and then went on. "Then, when Captain Bell was captured by the Chinese, the situation became very tense. A world war was possible at any time. If the Chinese knew of invasion plans by the great generals Bradley and Eisenhower, they would either have an excuse for a war, or the most powerful piece of propaganda in the world. We couldn't take that chance. We had to get him out."

"So," Rosetti said to him, "you had to plan a secret raid on the prison where Captain Bell was being held."

"Yes. Unfortunately, the woman Lin Su, who was being held prisoner there herself by that time, was killed by a guard during our escape."

"What about your frequent visits to Miss McAllister and your overriding the consulate in Tokyo?" Rosetti asked.

"All that was necessary to maintain a watch on Captain Bell's state of mind. And it was done with the permission of the president and the secretary of state."

"Then Captain Bell was not a traitor."

"He's hardly a traitor, Captain," Stoddard asserted. "He was a hero at Seoul and he probably saved the marine retreat out of Yudam-ni by discovering the bridge out at Koto-ri. And he possessed dangerous top secret information, but underwent two years of brainwashing by the Chinese Communists and never once cracked. Hardly a traitor."

Rosetti looked over at Hunter, who seemed to shrink as hundreds of eyes focussed on him. "There's one thing I don't understand," Rosetti said, going over to the exhibit table. "These dog tags," he said, picking up the chain.

"I told you," Hunter said, squirming in his seat, "Private Donnelson gave me those tags."

"When he told you that Bell had confessed to being a traitor . . ."

"Yes, that's right. Bell told him that just before he died. It was a deathbed confession, Captain Rosetti. It had to be the truth. A dying man doesn't lie."

"It never happened, Mr. Hunter," Stoddard said. "Donnelson never even saw Bell."

"Then how did I get those tags?" Wayne asked, his voice quivering.

"You got them from a man named Elliott Stoner," Stoddard replied. "A man we've been watching since I noticed him three years ago in Tokyo, a man who is a member in good standing of the Chinese Communist party."

"No! That's not true. Donnelson gave me those tags."

"You may as well admit it, Wayne," Stoddard told him. "Admit he took you in, took advantage of you, made you lie and accuse—"

"No, damn it. You can't prove it. Whatever you say, I have the tags. Gilbert Bell confessed, just before he died. All right. Maybe you and Adrian aren't traitors; fine. But *he* was. Gilbert Bell was. I swear it. He admitted it with his dying breath!"

"Did he?" Stoddard asked. He hesitated a moment, then nodded to an army corporal standing near the door of the judge's chambers. As the corporal disappeared behind the door, Stoddard cleared his throat. "We have an unexpected visitor this morning," he declared. "I hope all of you will give a rousing welcome to one of the great heroes of the Korean War—Captain Gilbert Bell!"

Adrian couldn't believe his words at first. For one second she hated Stoddard for playing such a cruel joke on her; but then the door to the judge's chambers opened and she saw him, and her heart felt as if it were going to explode with joy.

All of a sudden the courtroom was filled with applause, then cheers. The building seemed to shake with the resounding roar of the crowd as they rose to their feet and clapped their hands until they were red and stinging.

Adrian couldn't hold herself back. She burst for-

ward, rushed past Stoddard and the other officers and
flung her arms around Bell.

"Oh, Gilbert, Gilbert!" she cried, tears streaming
down her face.

"Adrian," he said. "God, I'm glad to see you."

Only then did she realize he was pale, thin, weak-
looking—and on crutches.

"Oh, Lord, Gilbert, let me help you," she said. "Lean
on me."

He placed his arm around her neck. "You're better
looking than I remembered," he observed as they
started to walk forward. "I didn't think that was possible."

She looked at him and laughed and cried at the
same time. "I don't know what to say. I love you so
much, I've missed you so much—"

"You don't have to say anything." He smiled lov-
ingly. "Just help me walk over there."

As they moved slowly forward, the crowd continued to cheer and applaud him. When he looked
around at them, amazed at what was happening, she
said through the noise, "They love you."

He looked straight into her eyes and kissed her—
to new, louder cheers.

"Give her a good one, Captain!" someone yelled.

"Marry them, Mr. President!" another called out.

"Don't let him get away again, Adrian!" a thin feminine voice shrilled above the rest. The people laughed
joyously in response to the plea.

Gilbert looked at Adrian. "I've got something for
you," he said reaching inside his coat pocket. After
some difficulty, he drew out and unwrapped a handkerchief containing a handful of small dried flowers.
Presenting them to her, he said, "I got these in Unsan

a while back. They're a bit wilted, but they still count as a bouquet, don't they?"

She nodded, speechless, full of love for him.

"I said I'd bring you one," he reminded her.

She impulsively hugged and kissed him, still dazed, still wondering if what was happening to her was real. Amanda suddenly walked over to them, wiping the tears from her eyes.

"Mandy," he said, kissing her lightly. "How're you doing?"

"Gilly," she said soberly, "I'm so sorry. I realize now all my fighting with Adrian over you could've gotten you killed. I was being so selfish."

"Never mind that," he told her. "Forget it. I'm back."

"Adrian . . ." She broke off, unable to find the words.

"It's all right, Amanda," she replied. "I understand."

Stoddard was trying to get everyone's attention. "Captain Bell," he was saying, "was picked up last night by an army helicopter near Unsan. He had spent almost three months secluded in the mountains between Sinuiju and Unsan in North Korea."

"I spent them with Sergeant Chick Baruchi," Gilbert said as the crowd came to order. "Chick was responsible for getting me out of prison," he added in a voice that was noticeably weaker than it had once been. "He saved my life. He held off the Communists until General Stoddard's commandos escaped, then he found me in an upper-story cell more dead than alive. He broke us out, single-handedly killing every guard in the compound, and all the time he was carrying me on his back."

He paused a minute to catch his breath. "Then,

though I'll never know how he did it, he took care
of me, the whole time we spent in the mountains. I
don't know where he kept coming up with the food
to keep us going. I was almost dead, we couldn't
move, and we were trapped in North Korea, miles
away from any friendly forces—but somehow he always came up with enough for us to eat. Or enough
for *me* to eat. Sometimes he went without. But he
never complained.

"Yesterday," Bell went on, struggling with the
words, "when the army helicopter came down for us,
Chick performed his last act of courage. He drew
the fire of a Communist rifle squad in order to give
me enough time to be taken aboard. Sergeant Baruchi was killed before the helicopter left the ground."

Adrian was so touched by Chick's bravery and his
love for Gilbert, she nearly broke down into tears.
As she tried to regain her poise by looking around
the courtroom, her eyes fell on Wayne Hunter, who
was sitting with his face buried in his hands. When
he looked up, their eyes met, and she could see
through her own tears the expression of crushing sor-
row, guilt, and embarrassment in his face. She felt
sorry for him. . . .

Gilbert shifted his weight onto his crutches and
moved closer to Eisenhower. "Mr. President," he said,
"if you don't mind, I would like to say something
else before this hearing is over—something that I've
been wanting to say ever since I walked in here
today."

"Go ahead, Captain," Eisenhower replied. "I know
every man and woman here and the rest of the American people as well would like to hear what you
have to say about your experience."

"Thank you, Mr. President," he said and turned around to face the audience. "I'm not much of a speech-maker, but what I wanted to say was, I think because of what I've been through I realize something I never realized before. I've always just sort of accepted fighting. I never thought much about war; I just figured it was our duty to fight when there was one, and I would always do my duty. But Sergeant Baruchi made me understand it's more than duty. He showed me *why* we're out there now, fighting in a strange land against people we sometimes can't even recognize as enemies. Most of the short time Chick was alive, he lived a lie. Not because he wanted to, but because other people made him. Everybody always thought because he was gentle, he was a coward. That hurt him. He had to end his life before anyone would believe different. But Chick Baruchi was willing to die for what he believed in— what was real and true to him.

"It's the same thing I learned in prison. We're not fighting a lot of bodies in Korea—nameless, faceless bodies. We're fighting for what's real and true. Communism feeds on lies and distortions and half-truths. It plays on our weaknesses, not our strengths. Communism is a lie and the only way to destroy it is with the truth. That's the only thing that kept me going in prison. Someone there told me the only way to survive was not to believe anything, because in prison everything was confused and twisted around. But she was wrong. The only way I could survive was to find a truth, something I believed in, and hang onto it for dear life." He looked at Adrian and felt the bond between them. The people didn't have to know it was love he clung to all those months—love for her.

Gilbert paused, swallowed, and looked around him. Hundreds of attentive, concerned faces stared transfixed at him. "One last thing," he said. "What General Stoddard and President Eisenhower have told you about the invasion plans I saw in the Pentagon is still very dangerous information. They are taking a terrible chance by bringing it out into the open, especially now, when it looks like there may be a breakthrough in the armistice talks at Panmunjom. But . . . somehow, I think it will be all right. I think the American people can conquer anything or anybody in the world that threatens our way of life —as long as we recognize and know and believe in the truth."

Adrian broke into tears again, came to him and hugged him tightly. "You're really something, you know it?" she said, sniffing. "I love you."

He took her hand and squeezed it. "I'm tired, Adrian," he sighed wearily. "Could we go home now?"

They waited a moment, though, to watch the mad exodus of reporters from the courtroom to the phones, to call in their stories. Adrian's mind automatically began conjuring up a headline for the situation, but then she pushed the possibilities out of her mind.

"Gilly?" Amanda said tentatively, a few feet away.

"Come here, Amanda." He beckoned her, extended a welcoming arm. She came to him and he put aside the other crutch and draped his left arm around her.

Adrian looked across the room in time to see a smile on the president's face as he was turning to go. Somehow it made her feel even closer to Gilbert. She held his hand tightly.

"Adrian?" he said. "You know you're letting these other reporters scoop you."

"I know I am," she said, touching the little bouquet to his cheek. "Let 'em scoop."

"Don't tell me you're not going to file a story?"

She smiled. "Oh, I'll file a story," she assured him. "Don't worry about that. But not right now. All I want to do right now is be with you. The Sacramento *Sun* can wait."

Epilogue

NINE DAYS after the hearing in Hagerstown, Maryland, on July 27, 1953, Lieutenant General William Harrison and Lieutenant General Nam Il met in Panmunjom, North Korea, and signed eighteen copies of an official armistice agreement between the United Nations and the Communists. The Korean War was over. It had ended in a stalemate.

Six days later Gilbert Bell received a promotion to the rank of major, United States Marine Corps.

On August 17, 1953, Sergeant DeWitt "Chick" Baruchi was posthumously awarded the Medal of Honor.

Don't miss
these other exciting
titles in
The Freedom Fighters *Series*